"Wh-where are you goin'?" I asked.

She slipped the shawl over her shoulders and drew the hood to hide her curls. "I gotta go. Cover for me?"

Heather, come on. You can tell me what you're up to. You tell me every-thing 'cause you're almost my sister. I didn't say that.

"They'll notice you're gone."

"They're drunk on honey wine, and Mama has baby brain. It's all she thinks about." She giggled. Her face was soft, but her voice needy. "Do this for me, Ivy."

"Will you tell me what's going on?"

"So many questions. Now, I've gotta go, so please? I'll tell you about it later."

I should've pressed harder. Instead, I sighed in tacit agreement. "What do you want me to tell them? If Marsh notices —"

"*If* that man realizes I slipped out, say I'm checking the horses."

"Heather, with the animals gettin' killed, I'm worried."

"All the more reason for someone to check the horses, don't you think?"

"No!" I winced at the loudness of my voice, and Heather went to the doorway to make sure our parents were still occupied while I trailed be-hind her, whispering, "Let Marsh do it, or my daddy, if you're so worried." She glared over her shoulder, and I realized she wasn't concerned about the horses at all. "It's night, and isn't safe."

Her lips perked in a coy smile. "Sometimes you gotta face danger to find what you're looking for."

That was where we differed. Heather wasn't afraid. I was terrified.

I closed my eyes with a sigh. She gave me a swift kiss, and then disap-peared out the back door without a sound.

I should've tried harder to keep her.

THE MAY QUEEN MURDERS

THE MAY QUEEN MURDERS

SARAH JUDE

Houghton Mifflin Harcourt
Boston   New York

www.hmhco.com

The text was set in Minion Pro and Aegean.
Hand-lettering by Chris Rushing

Library of Congress Cataloging-in-Publication Data is available.

ISBN: 978-0-544-64041-2 hardcover
ISBN: 978-0-544-93725-3 paperback

Manufactured in the United States of America
DOC 10 9 8 7 6 5 4 3 2 1
4500648316

To my sister, Ericka, my tether,
who just *knows*

So you must wake and call me early, call me early, mother dear,
To-morrow 'ill be the happiest time of all the glad New-year:
To-morrow 'ill be of all the year the maddest merriest day,
For I'm to be Queen o' the May, mother, I'm to be Queen o' the May.

— Alfred, Lord Tennyson
"The May Queen"

PROLOGUE

Now

Kerosene slopped from the rusty pail and splashed against the abandoned stable. Fumes burned my eyes but didn't blur my father's silhouette as he faced the building, bucket in hand. It would burn and, with it, the body inside.

"Go to hell!"

Papa's shoulders twisted as he wheeled back, shouting, sweeping the pail around. More kerosene rained against the wood while bile scorched my throat. I was too tired to get sick on the hay, my body wasted from screaming. I wiped my hand over my mouth and something snagged my lip. My fingernail was missing, a ragged root jutting from the bloody bed. Bitten off and swallowed by someone who wanted me dead.

This ain't real.

Yet I smelled the kerosene and felt the spring air and the dust in my nose, my feet firm on the ground. No matter how my mind ached to fly away, it tethered to a stark truth. This was real.

"Ivy, stay back," Papa warned, and then looked to Mama, close by with an antique lantern shedding dim light. The night sky swelled with clouds like spiders' egg sacs ready to burst, but the storm would miss Rowan's Glen. The hay, the ground, the stable were kindling-dry, and every movement kicked up brown clouds. Mama pulled me until we were safely away. The clink of her silver bracelets racked together as she eased her arm around my shoulder.

"Don't worry." Mama's still-thick Mexican accent lilted her voice, but her expression was stoic except for a pinch around her eyes. That blankness scared me.

"This must be done," she whispered.

I wadded my fingers into my long skirt. The blue patchwork was smeared with blood and dirt. Last summer, my cousin Heather and I sewed peasant skirts together. They flared when I spun, round and round, always with Heather.

The last time I saw Heather, she was wearing a skirt with red ruffles.

Papa trailed kerosene on the ground and retreated from the stable before tossing the pail inside. I couldn't see into the shadows. The body lying on the stone floor might yet have a pulse. A shiver tugged at my neck, my chest rising and falling with shallow breaths. One clear thought pierced my mind's muddle, and it sickened me.

I *wanted* that body to burn.

"Timothy." Mama fished a book of matches from a pocket in her apron and gave them to Papa. He took the matches and stretched one hand to hold mine. He was strong. My throat ached when I swallowed, from being choked in an attempt to silence me. Now I said nothing as Papa struck the match.

The fire didn't whoosh to life. First, the match hit the ground and breathed. Then a blue worm of flames emerged from the earth and devoured one blot of fuel before moving to the next. Upon reaching the stable, the worm bloated into a dragon that blazed yellow and orange. The wood planks hammered by my great-great-grandfather when he was young crackled, bone-dry from drought. Fire twisted through the stable while coils of smoke erupted from the windows. The pulse of the body inside *thump-thump*ed in my head. Frantic. Dying.

"Mama?" I whimpered.

"It's only fair," she said.

Papa didn't speak. Rage had made him do the unspeakable. *For me,* even though I'd survived. But also for those who hadn't. Fire was cleansing. Fire was vengeance. The flames burned red, as red as the ruffles of Heather's skirt. As red as Heather's hair.

CHAPTER ONE

Now, Ivy girl, you gotta know there's bad out in them woods, and the worst kind of bad Rowan's Glen has ever known is Birch Markle. Things weren't ever right with the Markle boy. There was no real reason for the things he done, but sometimes, well, evil's like that.

Then

Yet another LOST DOG sign marked the animal clinic's window. This one stung. Mrs. Knightley had brought her beagle Jones in for a heartworm test only last week. I'd given him one of Aunt Rue's dog biscuits, and Jones's tail had wagged with glee. Now he was one more missing face. The curled papers blanketing the glass rustled against the April wind. Some had been there since January, when the dogs began disappearing. Papa wouldn't take them down.

"There's gotta be hope, Ivy."

Glass shattered in an exam room, and I slid out from behind the counter. My sketch of Whimsy, my Morgan mare, would wait.

Heather swept up remains from a broken jar and cotton balls. More glass crunched under her red Converse high-tops.

She pushed a tendril of hair from her forehead. "Uncle Timothy needs to buy some Plexiglas jars. I'd break a lot less."

"Plexiglas is p-poison," I replied.

Heather snorted. Papa's diatribes on warfare against pesticides and plastics were common. Most Rowan's Glen residents long ago decided that if we couldn't raise, craft, or repurpose it, then we wouldn't use it. Over time, the buildings converted from no electricity to solar energy. Our clothing was handmade, came secondhand from kin or the town thrift store if splurging.

Glen kind looked different from the rollers in the trailer park and the townies. We were hillfolk, with our boys in trousers and suspenders and girls clad in long skirts. Once a Missouri Ozarks outpost for Scottish travelers searching for permanency, Rowan's Glen kept life simple and the outside world at bay.

It was my home.

The forever horizon of fields was dotted with horse pastures and goats. Comfort came in knowing your neighbors and them knowing not only you, but generations of your kin. It was a good place—even with the screams that sometimes came from the forest, the screams that had been there my whole life and longer.

"Rook's almost as bad as Uncle Timothy," Heather remarked. "Last week in ecology, he claimed polluted water gives men tits."

The mention of Rook Meriweather fevered my cheeks. "You're t-terrible."

She drew a circle with her shoe in the broken glass, her smile taunting. "Don't say you ain't enjoying the subject. And what a subject Rook makes! I've seen your sketchbook."

"Shouldn't you clean up your mess?" I tried to smooth the bristle in my voice, but Heather only laughed.

"I'm kidding with you, Ivy. You know that, right?"

She took my hand and squeezed. Of course I knew.

The day had wound down, which meant stocking the delivery of Mama's homeopathic flea powder would wait. There wouldn't be enough time to take Whimsy on a trail ride. Since the dogs began going missing, wandering the fields after dusk was frowned upon. Even before then, we had stayed away from the woods. There were stories.

I returned to the waiting room and glanced toward the clock.

"What's wrong?" Heather asked.

"The clock stopped."

The clock's hands had halted at 4:44. It was a wood box with a pendulum, older than anyone in the Glen. Normally, the metal rapped the wood in a perpetual hollow note. Now it was mute.

"Fix it tomorrow." Heather picked a section of my hair to braid.

"I have to fix the clock now," I said. "Bad luck."

Heather tsked. "You're too superstitious. Mamie got you good."

A draft plucked my neck. "You remember how when Gramps died, Mamie stopped all the clocks in the house? She stopped death from coming for more of us."

"Huh. So that's why. I should've guessed Mamie'd tell you."

Heather's fingers wove my hair. Bits of metal she'd found while wandering the fields — part of a spoon, a coil, a lost buckle, a green glass circle from the bottom of a bottle etched with her birthday of March 27 — were strung on a silver necklace and jingled as she moved. She unclipped her chain, chose a nut from some long-vanished screw, and fixed it to accent my braid.

She caught me staring at the stopped clock. "Ivy, don't. It only needs windin'."

"It's a death omen," I said.

"Go ahead. Try to be a little more morbid, really."

"It ain't morbid. It's how things are," I insisted. "Mamie knows this stuff. She said —"

"When did she say?" Heather dropped my hair and crossed her arms.

"It was a long time ago, when I was little."

That was the last time Mamie spoke, before she went into the attic. To live in silence.

Heather restrung her necklace. "I miss her stories too. Even the one about Birch Markle. But they're bedtime stories to give little girls nightmares. That's all."

Heather disregarded our grandmother's tales, but I couldn't. I needed their truth. They were mythic and strange and disarming, as much a part of my life as tending to fields and brushing dirt from the house. To hear the stories over a pinewood fire, the smells of clove tea and floral powder on old-woman skin, was a joy lost once Mamie quit talking. Heather couldn't take it away again.

I liked doing things the old way, the Glen way, and it was worth paying attention to the omens — especially the life-and-death ones.

Suddenly, the clinic's CB radio hissed to life.

A voice echoed through the static. "Timothy, you there?" No private telephones existed in Rowan's Glen — lack of phone lines — but the few businesses kept radios to make calls. The rattles and clicks of disembodied souls talking across the airwaves were common enough background noises at my family's clinic.

I was reaching for the radio when Papa jogged out from his office. If someone called, he usually needed to deliver a calf or diagnose a horse with colic. I often tagged along as his assistant. It was good practice, and Papa claimed I had "the touch," cats rubbing against my legs, dog kisses slathering my cheek and neck. I could calm a Saint Bernard nervous for a nail trim by scratching behind its ears.

Papa adjusted his glasses and clicked a button on the receiver. "I'm here."

"Listen, Timothy." Sheriff Meriweather's voice was deep, grim. "You gotta come out. Something's down by the river."

"Some*thing?*" Papa and ran his hand along his hair, slicked back in the early 1900s style worn by many of the Glen's men.

The radio spewed another jittery clatter before Sheriff spoke. "We ain't sure what it is. Scavengers have made off with some pieces. There's fur."

My stomach lurched. Animals died all the time. I'd witnessed all means of death, from the beloved old cat that shut its eyes for a final time to the runt pup of a litter that couldn't survive. Accidents on the highway. Predators. Living off the land instilled knowledge of life cycles and perpetuity, but I was yet to be comfortable around the dead.

I gulped loud enough that Heather stopped picking at her red thread bracelet. My mother made the women in our family wear them — even those who didn't share her Mexican blood. The bracelet warded off *mal de ojo*. The evil eye. The Scottish side of the Templetons humored her traditions, despite their own peculiar folklore.

"What's going on?" Heather mouthed.

I hushed her with a finger against my lips. Papa glanced at us, hesitating before he pressed the receiver close to his mouth. "You reckon it's one of the missing dogs?"

Sheriff made a noise. "Too big for that. Cliff's guessing a horse. Since you're the animal man 'round here, you gotta take a look. But there's something more. There's blood, lots of it, all over the grass."

Most Glen folk wouldn't cross Promise Bridge. The land was rocky, and little but the occasional dandelion was brazen enough to root on the bank. Promise Bridge was where I washed the linens in the river, but it was also the place Heather and I spent hours searching the shore for old things, drawing, sometimes lying in the marsh grass. The rickety bridge crossed to Potter's Field, a cemetery of unmarked graves sleeping outside the woods. The granny-women, older women bearing herbs and stories, tended the graves. Always returning to the village before dusk, before the forest awakened.

Papa left the clinic with a curt "Be back soon," but as it was near closing, Heather and I locked up and stalked a few beats behind. She wanted to see what was down by the river, and because I always did what she wanted, I came along. We lingered behind a limestone mound and waited for Papa to cross the suspension bridge of rusted chains and wood before we followed.

The water's depth was illusive, deep enough to allow for Denial Mill upstream. For a century, the Denial clan was its caretakers, most recently Flint and his son Jasper. While it once ground wheat, it became a hydropower mill supplementing the Glen's solar panels. Every so often, a branch wedged in the wheel to halt the turning. Someone then had to take on the dangerous task of wading through the water to remove the obstruction and get the wheel moving again. The building's exterior was old stone, the wood trim faded red paint, and when the sunset hit the mill, the walls looked edged with blood.

Heather halted in the middle of the wavering bridge. My vision swam from trying to hold still. I needed to move.

"You hear something?" She pointed back to a bush growing near the rocky bank. "Look."

All I saw was a belladonna shrub forming the buds of purple flowers that would eventually turn to fat, black berries. The leaves rustled. My chest tightened. Black bears wandered the woods, and if some animal was torn up . . . Human skin was no match for bear claws.

I scooted Heather another step and whispered, "Go slow."

The bush rustled again, and a young man emerged to fix the eyeglasses falling down his nose.

Rook.

His hair was coffee-black and combed back. The sleeves of his button-up shirt were rolled to his elbows, and the worn threads of his suspenders were near breaking. His barn boots had seen better days, lots of scuffs marring the toes. The more I gawked, the higher my pulse rose, and then he waved.

"He must've seen us and decided to follow," Heather hummed beside me.

The Meriweather and Templeton families were close. For as long as I could recall, Rook had been there, bringing fresh brown-shelled eggs or stopping by to walk Heather and me to school. Our families laughed over Sunday suppers, and when the harvest was good in the Meriweathers' field, we'd find clumps of radishes or bunches of rainbow carrots in a crate on our step. Sometimes, Mama sent me to their house with a loaf of bread and retired picture books for Rook's little sister. It was good to share with others.

Running with Rook was expected, yet not that simple at all. Two winters ago, I was sick with the flu for a month. Instead of carousing in snow-laden fields, I lay in bed. Once I recovered, Rook was no longer a gangly kid from down the road. He was tall with broad shoulders and a good laugh. When I saw him again — *really* saw him — I understood how much we'd changed. He'd gone from being a neighbor boy to a boy I thought about.

"Call him over," I urged.

"You." Heather's elbow jabbed me. "Since you want him to join us so bad."

My shoulders tightened, and I breathed in before beckoning him closer with a wave. The invitation eased his smile, and the sun caught him in a way I wanted to remember later when drawing. I smiled back. He jogged toward us, undaunted by the rattling bridge. His legs were fluid as he closed in, and then his palm rested on my upper arm. Maybe he didn't notice the way I jumped when he touched me.

"What are you doing? Trailing Ivy?" Heather asked.

A deep dimple cut his left cheek. He cleared his throat and gave a wing-flap wave behind him. "I was checking the belladonna. There's lots coming up. It ain't native, but it likes the soil. We gotta clear it, or the fields'll poison."

Heather once said Rook's voice was honey, but I thought he spoke with deeper tones, hickory roots burrowing earth and bitter moonshine. His voice was made to read books aloud at sunset when we huddled around a bonfire. I'd listen to Rook's stories and Heather's singing. I listened and drew because that was what I knew to do. It was a good way to spend time, an easy way to forget worries.

"Is that t-true?" I asked. "That belladonna poisons the land?"

"Well, it'd take a hell of a lot to actually get into the soil." Rook knew every plant rooted in the Glen's earth, right down to the Latin names. "But my mama makes me clear it out before planting. She ain't completely crazed. The berries are toxic, and only a few can kill. What about y'all? Where are you headed?"

"Your daddy called Uncle Timothy to Potter's Field. They found a carcass," Heather explained.

"Mind if I come?" Rook asked, to which Heather said yes, but he hadn't asked her. His hand found mine, his skin warm, callused, and *thrilling* to touch. We'd grabbed hands while climbing trees many times growing up, but touching him now was like a dandelion scattering inside me, seeds full of possibility.

From the corner of my eye, I spotted Heather crossing her arms.

She wheeled around, tugging my hand away from Rook's hold. "Come on, Ivy."

Helpless but to go, I looked to Rook over my shoulder. He strolled over the swaying bridge. I'd linger with the same leisured pace as him, but Heather was rushing and breathless.

For April in the Ozarks, it was no shock the wood was slick with humidity. Yesterday's rain saturated the settlement, and soon mildew would creep over the horse fences. We'd get out there with vinegar water to clean off the black rot. It'd come back, and we'd clean again. Seasonal rituals and predictability of chores gave purpose and balance.

We reached the other riverbank and trundled down a dirt path. With the sun drooping low to the horizon, an uneasy hush fell over the village. Vultures circled overhead. A rancid smell, like meat that hadn't salt-cured quite right, drifted from Potter's Field. All three of us covered our faces. The loudest sounds were Heather's mouth-breathing and the swish of long skirts.

Potter's Field lay in a valley surrounded by blackberry thickets. We hunkered down in a cove and used rocks to shield us from the graveyard of the abandoned. A half dozen men stood around, foreheads gleaming with clamminess and skin greenish like they were fighting back the sicks. Of the men, the one I knew best was Sheriff Meriweather — Rook's father. He and Papa were descendants of the Glen's founding families. Sheriff wasn't as tall as Papa; he was stockier with hair the color of nutmegs flecked by silver. Despite being head of police in these parts, he was more carpenter, and during growing months, Sheriff tended fields with Rook to supply a vegetable cart his mother took to town. Rook was the spit of his mother's side, lean and pale and dark-haired Irish.

Along with Sheriff, several other members of the Glen's police — hillmen wearing a star pinned to their britches — crowded around something on the ground. The grass in Potter's Field was brown.

Except for one wide puddle of red.

Sheriff's boots slopped through the puddle and revealed it deep enough to soak his soles. "Timothy, as you can see, it's a hell of a mess."

Papa pushed past the barrier of farmers, and I caught only the briefest glimpse of pink meat slick with fluid. He opened his medical bag and snapped on blue exam gloves. They seemed out of place against his modest shirt and vest. Most veterinarians I'd seen in books wore white jackets, but Papa was never like them, instead looking like doctors from over a century ago.

"Gross," Heather whispered and craned her neck over the rocks.

"Don't get too close," I said, and pulled her back.

She brushed my hand off her shoulder. "What? There ain't anything dangerous."

"You'll blow our cover."

Papa took a syringe from his bag, uncapped it, and jabbed the needle into the carcass. One of the men staggered before vomiting beside a gravestone. Sheriff raised an eyebrow. "One of you's gonna need to grab a bucket from the river and clean up that mess. Show the dead some respect."

Papa withdrew the plunger, and the tube filled with blackish sludge. "This isn't normal decay. This carcass is fresh, but you see how the belly's torn open? Decay won't cause flesh to burst for weeks unless it's extremely hot. Ozarks are warm but not enough to do that, not yet. Something ripped it open."

Rook shifted beside me, took off his glasses, and averted his eyes. What could've done this? Maybe it was my suspicious nature, but I couldn't help but feel something bad seemed to have roused and come to our land.

"What kind of animal was it?" Sheriff asked.

Papa coughed into the crook of his elbow. "It's Bartholomew, the Logans' wolfhound."

I covered my mouth to keep from crying out. *Not Bart.* Despite being the size of a small pony, he was just a juvenile. When he stood on his hind legs, he put his paws on my shoulders to dance. Heather reached over and stroked the back of my head.

"Are you sure that's a dog?" another man asked.

Papa bent over, and something moist popped when he poked around the fresh kill. "Those teeth are canine, and I'm sure it's Bart. I did a dental cleaning two months back. See where those incisors are missing? He'd broken them chewing on his crate."

Papa sounded clinical, but that emotionless tone carried him through his notes and kept him working on the clinic's rough days. On those nights, he came home, and Mama opened a bottle of blueberry wine, set out a glass by the fireplace, and murmured to us to keep our distance — not because he had a bad temper. He simply needed time alone.

"What'd you say did this?" Sheriff wondered, scribbling on a note-pad. "A bear? Remember when Holly Fitzpatrick got mauled by the bobcat thirty years back? My old man said the clawmarks on her—"

"This wasn't some bobcat!" Papa rose to his feet. "And not a bear or coyote, either."

"Then what did it?"

"What predator is the worst?"

Sheriff didn't have to answer. I already knew. The worst predators of all were humans.

CHAPTER TWO

We all know Birch put his mama in the grave early, but most folks ain't sure how, whether his hollering in Sunday church finally made her do the unthinkable to herself, or maybe it was the rusty knife he'd begun carrying around with him.

The macabre news of Bartholomew's demise was a whisper, passing from one farmhouse to the next.

You hear how Bart was ripped apart, didn't even look like a dog no more . . .

Sounds like Birch Markle. Wonder if old Birch has come back . . .

A panicked busyness settled across Rowan's Glen. Since I was little, Birch Markle had been the reason children were told to avoid the tree line, why adults looked around with watchful eyes when outside after dark. Though the last sighting of him in the woods was years ago, his screams were still heard now and then, during the hush of night. Mamie once said it was so bad that for a while, after Birch killed a girl called Terra MacAvoy, no one was allowed out after sunset.

What he did was horrible enough to change the way outsiders treated us. The Glen used to be open to anyone. Outsiders paid by the pound for our fresh crops, eggs, and milk. They came to us to have chickens butchered and deplucked.

Then they stopped coming.

Years dimmed Birch's memory, but stories remained. Given the cries from the forest, the story felt truer now than before. We lost the occasional farm dog to the highway, but if Bart was any indication of the fates of the ones papering the clinic's window, something far worse was going on.

With fear came caution. Farmers locked their livestock in barns instead of allowing cattle to roam for hours of endless grazing; the gates and fences were now strewn with copper warning bells. The silence across the Glen was too silent, a breath drawn and waiting.

During the day, we buried the lingering wrongness by going about our business. Goods were taken to the farmer's market, where townies picked over our hand-stitched quilts, wooden toys, and crisp vegetables. They bought our items, but we didn't mix much beyond that.

We attended school as if nothing was amiss behind the Glen's borders. Heather and I had a couple of classes together at Salem Plateau High School. The Rowan's Glen contingent comprised a small cluster of students amid townies and rollers. When I was younger, our church in the Glen had held classes in the basement, but some uproar about it not being official closed our village school and the county opened their doors to us — never their minds, though. We were outcasts.

Shutting my locker, I nodded at August Donaghy, or rather his fuzzy mound of blond hair. He was the only sophomore bearing a full beard, which, paired with his burly frame, gave him all the tatters of a well-loved teddy bear. Violet Crenshaw stood with him, a bandanna covering the crown of her ice-white hair.

"They're talking about us," she said, and slouched against the locker beside mine.

That wasn't a surprise. "They" often talked about us. "They" pulled our long hair or stepped on our skirt hems to trip us.

"It'll die down again," I reminded her.

Violet looked pointedly at August, who balled his hands into fists. His parents peddled tie-dye shirts at the market. The vegetable dyes left his fingertips discolored, so kids teased that he was diseased and his fingers would fall off.

"Tell her what happened," Violet said.

August glanced around. "Some rollers heard about Bart. Said we was practicing animal sacrifice down in the Glen. Heather told them to shut up, but they turned on her."

Away from the security of the Glen, things were different. We'd heard every insult thrown at us: that we were inbred, hippies, or backwoods hillbillies. But if those names got too loud and persisted, then trouble might come. We couldn't have that.

"Is Heather okay?" I asked.

"The name-calling got bad, Ivy," Violet replied. "At least she had the sense to bail before it got worse."

Violet's lips pressed tight. As if by habit, she rubbed her left cheek — the side of her sister Dahlia's face had been ruined after she made the mistake of standing up to the rollers. I reached for Violet's free hand, but she pulled back.

"Heather'll be okay," I said, more to myself than my friends. "She always is."

"Rook went after her," August added. "We thought maybe they grabbed you and headed back to the Glen."

My breath hitched. Rook went after Heather, and no one had seen them since? Anytime Heather got flak from outsiders, she came to me. I listened. We went everywhere together. If she'd left, why hadn't she taken me along?

A pain twinged in my chest when I thought of Heather and Rook without me. I didn't have a claim on him. Neither did she, but she saw my sketchbook. She left comments in the margin about the thin scar on his upper lip and the cowlick he tried but failed to straighten above his widow's peak. She knew what those sketches meant.

"He's p-probably making sure she's okay," I muttered. "I'd know if she wasn't okay."

"Keep telling yourself that." August walked backwards down the hallway. He side-eyed the rollers who chatted with a townie, chuckling at us. "And watch your back."

Violet hugged herself. "Don't let yourself be alone, Ivy. I'd stay, but I gotta get to class."

I didn't know what to say. Normally, I wasn't alone.

With Violet and August gone, I let myself into the stairwell, where the steel door thudded shut. I pressed my back to it, scanning from the base of the stairs to the second story. With no windows for sunshine, the lone halogen light flickered before dropping the stairs into half-dark. A red glow radiated from the EXIT signs.

No one from the Glen went off alone to school. Most of us even walked to class in pairs. The trust that we'd make it up and down the stairs, back and forth through the hallways undamaged was a farce. Threats and taunts were just that until they weren't. Dahlia Crenshaw needed a scarf to cover her scars. Those boys were arrested, but Dahlia never came back to school. She rarely left her home at all.

I climbed several steps. Without any ventilation, the stairway was a hot box. Sweat beaded on my forehead, yet cold walked down my spine.

As if someone came up behind me.

I felt fingers stretching to touch me, coming closer. Praying I wouldn't turn around.

I pivoted to face the door at the bottom of the stairs. The echoes were loud here and the walls tight; a claustrophobic panic froze me.

From below, the door banged. It was a boy wearing a flannel shirt and jeans with a hole in the knee, his jaw-length hair faded into once-bleached blond. He was a roller, but that was about as much as I knew. That and he spent English class texting on his phone.

I kept my eyes on the banister while waiting for him to pass, but he stopped beside me, his shadow creeping over my body. He was tall, all legs and arms like the rope of a tire swing.

"You're from Rowan's Glen?" he asked.

He was talking to *me*?

"You know, the cult outside of town?"

My eyebrow quirked. A cult. That was one of the nicer things the Glen was called.

He snorted. "You friends with that Heather chick? The redhead?"

My muscles tensed. Who was this boy, and what did he want with Heather? How did he know her? If he'd made her run out of class, so help me God . . . I cringed because, really, I'd do nothing. I paused on the wolf-blue of his irises, then his full lips that'd be pretty on a girl but were strange on him. An overbearing cigarette odor choked me.

His sneaker's toe pushed mine. "You deaf? Or are you ignorin' me 'cause I ain't one of you?"

"I-I just th-think you're crass."

His mouth arced in a smirk.

"What do you want with Heather?"

"So you *do* know her." He inched closer yet, barricading me against the railing with his arms. My shoulders clenched. Someone else should've come through the door at the bottom of the staircase by now.

I tried to wriggle out from beneath him. "I gotta get to class."

He didn't budge.

"Tell Heather I need her."

"She won't know who you are." I jutted out my chin, but all the bad things that could happen while trapped in a staircase niggled at my mind.

He snickered. "Oh, she'll know."

I coiled my fingers around my sketchbook. The stairway door squealed, and boots tromped up the steps. *Oh, God, another roller.* My gut twisted. The herb salves hadn't stopped Dahlia's wounds from infecting. I knew what was said, how the rollers and townies claimed she'd brought on the attack.

"My name is Milo Entwhistle," the roller said in my ear. "And you are . . . ?"

"The name's Go to Hell."

My breath released as Rook shoved the roller's hands off the rail. But I'd thought he'd left school. He was still here, which meant — where was Heather? Was she all right?

Milo climbed a step and shook away from Rook's hold. I placed the last name, sort of. A girl a couple of years older than Heather and me. She left in the middle of her senior year. He looked like her.

"Jesus, we were talking," Milo said.

Rook's voice was a sharp bite. "Why? So you can laugh later? Your kind says we sacrificed the dog since virgins aren't the devil's kink."

"You were there, man. I didn't say that."

I peered back to see Rook's jaw set hard and his eyes narrow behind his glasses. "You laughed. Go jack off somewhere else and leave her alone."

Milo stepped aside. "You've got some serious anger management issues."

"Go!"

Rook pointed to the top of the stairs. Milo trudged up the remaining steps before he disappeared through the doorway. Like a plug pulled on a drain, the tension spilled from me.

"Heather," I blurted out. "Where is she?"

She was all that was on my mind. Why she'd left. Where she'd gone. Why Milo wanted her.

"Ivy?"

The way Rook said my name, careful as if it were some half-broken creature cupped in his hands, brought me back to focus.

"I'm okay," I said.

Rook eased my sketchbook from my arm and rested his hand on the small of my back. His hand was warm through my shirt, my body warmer still from my speeding heart. "I get worried about you."

"August said you left with Heather."

We ascended the staircase, Rook stopping me a few steps from the landing. "She wanted to leave, but I convinced her to take a breather in the library. I ain't goin' back to the Glen without you."

He wouldn't go without *me*. I looked at his boots. "It's 'cause of the animals, right?"

"It'll be safer if someone goes along with you, least till things get back to normal. My pops told my mama he owes it to Dr. Timothy to keep you safe and is ridin' me about it."

Keep me safe? Why would Sheriff owe that to my father? I didn't want Rook escorting me only because Sheriff didn't give him a choice. Besides, everywhere I went, Heather went too.

"Folks say it's Birch Markle come back. What do you think?" I asked, taking a few more steps.

Rook gave a heavy sigh. "I think people run their mouths."

"What's that mean?"

"Nothin'." He pressed his back to the door for the art hallway so we faced one another.

"Rook, come on."

"Just bothers me when rollers talk shit." His mouth twitched into a frown. "They were saying stuff in history. They're clueless about the Glen."

He rolled his eyes and leaned his head against the door. I stared at him harder, like I could will him into speaking. "What'd they say? Something about Heather?"

He looked down.

"About *me*?" I asked.

He hesitated. "All right, I'll tell you. They were talking about how your daddy's the vet, and if someone's killing animals, then it's someone who's done it before. Like Dr. Timothy. Because as a vet, he puts animals to sleep."

The hair on the nape of my neck tightened, and a prickle crawled over my scalp until my hair and skin were a weave of dread. "My father wouldn't."

"That's what Heather told them, and they went after her instead."

Would Heather have told me that if Rook hadn't? She'd stood up like Dahlia had. Their cruelty was for me, and she'd smothered it. She did what a sister would. A bitter-tasting guilt puckered my mouth. I wanted to believe I'd do the same for Heather, but the truth was I didn't know. I wasn't that brave.

Once we reached the art room, I settled into my usual spot. The room smelled chemical — glue and acrylic paint — mixing with the earthen slop of clay. The art room was safe. Everyone was too into their projects to bother with us but for a few wary glances when Rook wandered over to the bin loaded with red mud. The townies' cluster went silent as he neared. Then they veered inward, whispers floating above their sacred circle.

" . . . dog . . . in pieces . . . You think they were there?"

Rook shot them a dirty look before claiming his seat beside me. I broke apart some clay to roll out snakes for a coil vase with a perilous tilt to the left. I had no illusions — it was ugly as sin. While drawing came natural, sculpture wasn't my gift of the spirit.

A glop of clay squished between my fingers. "What do you think that guy Milo wanted with Heather?"

"It's always Heather, isn't it?" Rook grunted and rolled out the clay for his own vase. "Milo's scum. If Heather's got some deal with him, she'll tell you, but from what I know, nothing good comes when that guy's around."

"How do you know?" I asked. "It ain't like you run with any rollers."

"No, but I know trouble when I see it."

Crash!

The bang ended with the shatter of glass. I jumped from my seat, and all around, the other students searched the walls with startled expressions to see what had fallen.

"What was that?" Rook asked.

I spied a broken picture frame on the ground. My stomach dropped as I knelt beside the shards of glass covering my pencil drawing of Whimsy from last year. Mrs. Fenton had liked it so much she entered it into several contests. I won a couple. Now the remnants were splintered on the floor, and I stooped to clear away the broken pieces. It shouldn't have fallen. That was bad luck.

Worse than bad. Fatal.

"Miss Templeton," Mrs. Fenton said as she rushed over. "Are you okay? Oh, your picture!"

Rook approached with a broom and dustpan. "I bet it can be re-framed."

"It ain't the picture." I tamped the grains of glass into the dustpan and waited until another student distracted Mrs. Fenton before I whispered to Rook, "Mamie says a picture that falls without warnin' brings death in the mornin'."

His expression stayed neutral, and even though he didn't tell me I was off my rocker, heat circled around my neck and spread to my jaw. Rook dumped the glass into the trash, returned the broom and dustpan to their place, and found his seat. God, I must've sounded so insane he didn't know how to respond. Yet he crooked his finger to beckon me to our table.

He murmured, "My pops gets wily if a bird flies into our house."

A bird in a house means death is flyin' about. Mamie's once-strong voice echoed in my memory. She'd comb my hair with one hundred strokes and tell me the hillfolks' lore, stories of the backwoods. Mamie went quiet when Gramps died, but when I was small and needed coaxing to sleep, she recited the tales. The words she spoke wove themselves into the ribbons of my veins and knitted together my very soul.

Rook knew the stories too, and he didn't outright dismiss them. Not the way Heather did.

The front of his throat bobbed. I didn't want to look like I was studying him, but I was. Because I drew everything I remembered, there'd be more pages of him in my sketchbook.

A loud laugh broke my focus. Heather beamed under the unforgiving hallway lights, laughing with someone away from the door's view. She was willowy in a green halter laced to show off her slim waist and small breasts. A gauzy black shirt beneath was painted on like a second skin. When she lifted her arm to push away whomever she talked with, she was like a cattail bending from the breeze.

I looked at my blue peasant top. Heavier with hips and breasts, I was dowdy and cloaked, nothing like the bright star of my cousin. Papa and my aunt Rue were Templetons, Mamie's children, and Heather had Mamie's once-scarlet hair, our grandmother's hair so red she'd even been named Ginger at birth. I was darker, with wide lips and shadows under my eyes, which were as black as ebony wood. On the surface, there was nothing proving Heather and I shared blood. I was three weeks older than she, the only days I'd lived without her.

A boy's hand, all I saw of him, brushed his fingertips along Heather's arm. Milo? I couldn't be sure. With a giggle, she tossed her curls. His hand lingered in the air as if the touch was unfinished. Whatever had upset her had dissolved. I was mesmerized and unblinking, not from envy or anger but because she was magic and life and joy.

"Hey, you all right?" I asked once she joined our table. "I heard what happened. Thank you."

She pushed my hair from my face. "It's fine, Ivy. Like I'm gonna let anyone talk bad about my kinfolk. Those kind of guys are what's left after Uncle Timothy castrates the bulls — useless dicks."

Rook snickered, but I tilted my head. How could she be cavalier? She wore a brave face, but I had to wonder if she was so brave when alone.

"Who was that?" I asked. "Out in the hall."

"Some roller." She lifted her bag off her shoulder and opened the flap. Inside was a paper bag with the top parted to reveal a dried lump of herbs.

I squished some clay between my fingers, sighing. "Rose Connelly has a whole pot field growing behind her house. If you want weed, don't go buyin' it off that Milo creep."

"Milo?" Heather's eyes widened, and she slapped her bag shut. "What do you know? Were you spying on me?"

"He cornered Ivy in the stairs," Rook intervened.

"What'd he say?" She cuffed my wrist and held tight. I pulled back, but she squeezed harder. The half-moons of her fingernails paled my skin. What a sudden shift in her.

"Heather, what's your problem?" I asked. "He only said he was looking for you."

She dropped my hand, then wiped her palm on her shirt. "Well, I guess he found me."

Her ass wiggled in her seat as if she was contemplating bolting from class. Before Heather could get up, Mrs. Fenton came around to survey our work and take attendance. The teacher took one gander at my leaning vase and huffed before moving to the next table.

"Heather," I pressed.

"Ivy, not now."

Her bag lay on the floor between my shoes and hers. She nudged it beneath her chair, the toes of her sneakers bumping mine as she kicked it back.

Kept it away from me.

CHAPTER THREE

Animals 'round the Glen started missin'. First, the barn cats. Jackdaw Meriweather'd find 'em in the dirt road. Maybe one got under a wagon's wheels, but two? Six? No one knew how many. Then folks noticed birds and fur 'round the Markle house and the bones hangin' in the trees.

My hands dove into soapy water. Warmth swirled around my forearms while I drew the washrag in circles over the plate. My parents and I had arrived at Mamie's home before the skies cracked and gushed rain, bellows of thunder rattling the windows.

From the sink, I had a view into the dining room, where the grownups relaxed around the table. Mama, Papa, and Heather's stepfather, a hillman named Marsh Freeman, sipped wine, while Aunt Rue rubbed her belly, round with a June baby. Taking the evening meal with kin was common in the Glen. I liked the closeness of our families. For some folks, there were so many members, they dined in a barn around a harvest table filled with dishes of mashed potatoes, cornbread, roasted chickens, and salad greens piled high in bowls.

Most years, the Glen's growing season was good, and we shared the bounty.

Mama's fingers walked across the knotted pine to rub Papa's arm, her bracelets singing as she moved. He'd been in a quiet mood since examining Bart's remains. Mama exchanged a nervous glance with Marsh. Few people read Papa's moods like Marsh — he'd been reading them since they were ten-year-olds with Sheriff trying to hook a catfish that supposedly ate a pony in the river.

"Rue and I had tea with Iris Crenshaw." Mama ventured a conversation. "*Señoras* are planning a May Day celebration for the Glen. Iris says it's 'cause of all the horrible things happening, that it might bring some joy."

"Luz, you have no idea how wonderful the old May Days were." Aunt Rue beamed. "The parties went all night. There was singing and dancing. We haven't had one in over twenty years, but I can't wait! It'll be such fun!"

Mama nodded. "It all sounds very sweet."

Aunt Rue continued. "We hung flowers on the houses. Oh! And there was a maypole and a parade!"

I dried my hands on my apron and met Heather's eyes. She stopped braiding her mother's hair and shrugged. We'd heard tales about the May Days of Rowan's Glen, but all that ended because of Birch Markle. Maybe, though, enough time had passed that folks were willing to try again without the specter of murder haunting the celebration.

"Ivy and Heather, you *señoritas* will have a good time," my mother said. "Iris said she was May Queen one year. Maybe one of you will be queen."

Aunt Rue gave a stiff smile. "Maybe so. Either way, you'll both be in the parade. We have Mamie's old dress. One of you should wear it."

The May Queen. I'd seen old photographs in Mamie's album, girls in long dresses with flowers in their hair, girls dancing with spring mud between their toes. They were new growth. The one chosen as queen was the Glen's very best, the embodiment of hope for prosperity and harvest. With death haunting the fields, maybe a prayer and dance for life would chase off the sorrow.

Perhaps I could be May Queen. Maybe. It'd be nice to be chosen. I'd come out from my shadow and show how green and vivid I could be.

Heather twisted a curl around her finger and asked, "So how does it work? Do you just randomly pick someone to be May Queen?"

Aunt Rue sipped from a mug of tea. "Any girl sixteen and older, not yet married, can be May Queen. The women choose by a secret ballot. The girl's gotta be the brightness of spring. Back in the old country, after our clans became Christian, the May Queen also reflected Mary and her holiness."

Heather giggled, but her mother gave her a cross look and continued, "It's been done this way for centuries, and I don't reckon it's funny. The May Queen's important. She's gotta be gentle, virtuous, and love the land and folks here. After years without one, I'm glad to see a return."

Papa poured a fresh glass of wine, his mouth twitching with what seemed half a dozen thoughts before he blurted out, "It's a terrible idea."

Mama tore a chunk off a loaf of bread left on the table, popped it into her mouth, and chewed as she spoke. "*Qué?* I don't see a problem. The way Iris and the others talk, they miss it. Things will be different than in the past."

"Did you forget why we stopped?" Papa asked.

All the family focused on him. He didn't sound angry or unreasonable, rather hushed. He tipped his chair onto its hind legs and folded his hands behind his head. "The townies, if they got wind of a May Day 'round here, they'd send their preachers and pitchforks. We don't need that kind of trouble again."

He walked over to the window to watch the storm blowing through the village. Mama reached for the wineglass he'd poured but hadn't touched, and she swallowed it herself without stopping to breathe.

"Timothy, Iris took it to council," Aunt Rue declared. "It'll be good for the Glen."

My father turned halfway from the window so the storm reflected off his glasses. "So that's it? It's a done deal? May Day ain't just a bad idea. It's *cursed*. You know bringin' back May Day is trouble, and we got enough."

My aunt cast her gaze to her belly while her husband approached Papa and placed a hand on his shoulder, his arms strong from kneading bread dough. Shadows drawn by the rain spilling down the glass formed wavy lines on their faces. Marsh had married my aunt two years before, some six months after her first husband, Heather's father, departed from a tobacco habit that put cancer in his mouth.

"C'mon, Timothy," Marsh murmured. "All that's buried. Let it rest in peace."

"For twenty-five years, I've left it buried. Y'all had stories about Birch Markle, and they damn near ruined the Glen. The way the county police came in, tromped all over our land. They got the outsiders talkin' 'bout us and wonderin' what we do. It took a year before we could sell anything at market in town. I don't wanna risk that, all 'cause Rue wants Heather to get some attention."

"That's not —" my aunt protested.

"Really?" Papa asked. "'Cause you know Ivy can't be May Queen. Did you tell Luz that?"

My gut tumbled. So it wouldn't be me. Some other girl. I glanced across the room to Heather, who stared at me, her expression oddly plain. Mama saw my frown and asked, "Why not? You won't let her name be on the ballot?"

"She *can't* be on the ballot," Marsh said. "Both parents of the May Queen gotta be Glen born."

A flush came over Mama's cheeks. *"Mierda."*

The tension in the house thickened, foglike in its depth. My mother, the peacemaker in most disputes, ducked into the kitchen while my father glowered. This was more than hackles raised. Some history, some secret Papa wanted untold, moved from a forgotten thing to one with substance. It spread to the corners and rose along the walls.

I followed Mama and asked, "Why's Papa so upset? Is it 'cause of what they said about how I can't be May Queen?"

She dropped the rosary working in her fingers, a remnant of growing up Catholic. I picked up the chain of freshwater pearls and lingered on the crucifix before handing it over. Mama tucked the rosary into her apron. "If that's all it was, *bonita. Señoras* were so excited about May Day . . . I thought Timoteo would be too, but the past still hurts. I wasn't here then. Sometimes, Ivy, it feels like no matter how long I live in the Glen, I'll never belong."

The sadness in my mother's face pained my chest, and I didn't know what to say. Sometimes even silence felt like a falter.

She patted her apron pocket. A loop from the rosary strand peeked out from the eyelet trim. "Jay called on your father today. Another dog, this one only bones."

The subject change wasn't a relief. I prayed it wasn't a dog from the clinic — maybe some farmer's hunting hound — but if the poor beast was only bones, we wouldn't know which owner to visit.

"The skull was missing," Mama went on, though the distant look on her face made me wonder if she was talking to me or speaking to rid her mind of the image. "Can't imagine who'd do such a horrible thing. I don't want you and Heather down by that water. Too much blood in it."

The crude electrical wiring in the Glen couldn't support a washer or dryer, so going to the river was a constant task. All the times I'd done laundry in the river, listening to Denial Mill's churning wheel, and the times Rook, Heather, and I went fishing, the water was clear when it skimmed through my fingers. Now my mind made it sludgy red, with bits of fur and meat clinging to my skin as the blood oozed past.

A sudden thump from the room above the kitchen shook the light. For a while after Mamie had gone silent, she sat with the family, taking in the clunky sounds only happy busyness made. She'd knit, a muted but steady presence. Not now. Perhaps her silence finally removed her from the living world.

Footsteps gave way to the squeal of a door opening and a fork scraping a plate as she set it on the table outside her room. I started up the stairs between the kitchen and dining room. Mamie's door was shut, and her plate was nearly full on the table.

I let myself into the room. My grandmother sat in a rocker beside a window overlooking the Glen's fields. The kerosene lamp on her desk spread a gold glow across the dark. In the corner, Gramps's shotgun was propped against the wall, unused since his death years ago but still within reach — ready for those nights if the screaming from the woods got too close. Some nights it sounded as if Birch came out of the woods and into the fields, but I'd always been too scared to look out my window because *what if he was there?*

"Mamie, everything all right?" I asked. "You didn't eat much."

She didn't move from her rocking chair. Her profile split the window, the sharp nose and high cheekbones common in Templetons — but not me. Blue lightning bloomed around Mamie. Some sandy wisps sprouted near the wings of her red hair, which she kept in a bun. She'd worked the land as a girl, and the once-creamy skin had ruddied under the sun. But in the few pictures that existed, ones where she was young, she looked like Heather.

Mamie gave me a good study, her face a lattice of wrinkles. Her china-blue eyes narrowed as she assessed me, and then her hand shot out, grabbing my red thread bracelet. That grip was tough, no gentleness, while she flipped my hand from side to side and bent my fingers this way and that.

Then for the first time in years, Mamie's tongue loosened enough to make a sound.

"Hmm." It was a grumble of a noise, but it was something.

Something she didn't like.

She dragged me by the wrist over to her desk. I smelled the mustiness of time past and held still while she pulled off the glass chimney from the oil lamp and unscrewed the burner and collar. She tugged the red string with one of her burled fingers, breaking it so it fell to the floor. My wrist felt naked and slippery, but Mamie seemed intent on not letting that last long. Her hand dove into her apron pocket, and she snapped a new length of red thread from the spool with her teeth and dredged it through the oil in the lamp where a small string of red wool already drowned.

Use the oil, girl, Mamie had told me when I was no older than five or six. She'd brought me to her room with the promise of making a Victorian-style silhouette, but instead, she thrust me in her rocking chair and knelt on the floor with her kerosene lamp in pieces on the desktop. *Can't go runnin' 'round these parts with no oil on your strings. That Mexican mama you got keeps them evil eyes off you, and while her ways are fair enough, you gots to have the oil to slick off the bad spirits and bad intentions. May no violent or poisoned death come your way when you're oiled well enough.*

Now she tied the soaked string on my wrist. "Mamie," I said, "is there something else?"

She crisscrossed her hands as she waved me off, ushering me out of her room to the steps.

"Mamie, please?" I begged.

Her gaze held mine. A flex in her lips, twitch of her eyelid.

Nothing. She didn't — couldn't — speak.

As I carried her barely touched dinner plate down the stairs, oil leaked from my wrist to drip off my little finger. At the base of the steps, I heard the click of Mamie's door as it shut.

Outside, the rain eased. Heather bounced on her toes in the kitchen and checked the window in the back door. She tugged her own red thread bracelet and moved with an impatience so palpable I could've grabbed it.

"You're wound up," I said.

"Waitin' for the rain to stop," she explained. She cocked her head. "You upset about the May Queen thing?"

Yes, I was jealous, though it was hard to admit. "Maybe a little."

"It's stupid, to have it based on who your parents are. It's gonna be a popularity contest," she scoffed. "Look, I'll tell my mama that I refuse to be nominated if you can't be."

"Don't do that. You deserve to be on the ballot," I said.

"So do you! You love the Glen, Ivy. If anyone should be May Queen, it's you, and that you can't — No, I don't want it. Give it to some other girl. Maybe Violet."

The gesture was thoughtful and lifted the corners of my mouth.

Heather hugged me and kissed my cheek before she took a hooded shawl from the wall hooks near the door.

"Wh-where are you goin'?" I asked.

She slipped the shawl over her shoulders and drew the hood to hide her curls. "I gotta go. Cover for me?"

Heather, come on. You can tell me what you're up to. You tell me everything 'cause you're almost my sister. I didn't say that.

"They'll notice you're gone."

"They're drunk on honey wine, and Mama has baby brain. It's all she thinks about." She giggled. Her face was soft, but her voice needy. "Do this for me, Ivy."

"Will you tell me what's going on?"

"So many questions. Now, I've gotta go, so please? I'll tell you about it later."

I should've pressed harder. Instead, I sighed in tacit agreement. "What do you want me to tell them? If Marsh notices —"

"He'll what?" Heather snorted. "You're assuming he remembers I exist."

She frowned, and I rubbed her arm. She was her daddy's girl, no surprise since she was named for Uncle Heath, but that Aunt Rue remarried so soon after burying him was tender yet. It didn't matter much that Marsh was all but family for years, being close to my father and all. On good days, Marsh and Heather were cordial at best. On most days, they didn't speak to each other.

"*If* that man realizes I slipped out, say I'm checking the horses."

"Heather, with the animals gettin' killed, I'm worried."

"All the more reason for someone to check the horses, don't you think?"

"No!" I winced at the loudness of my voice, and Heather went to the doorway to make sure our parents were still occupied while I trailed behind her, whispering, "Let Marsh do it, or my daddy, if you're so worried." She glared over her shoulder, and I realized she wasn't concerned about the horses at all. "It's night, and isn't safe."

Her lips perked in a coy smile. "Sometimes you gotta face danger to find what you're looking for."

That was where we differed. Heather wasn't afraid. I was terrified.

I closed my eyes with a sigh. She gave me a swift kiss, and then disappeared out the back door without a sound.

I should've tried harder to keep her.

The rain hitting the windows paused, but the sound of water draining off the tin roof and trickling over the gutters remained. It was too dark to make out Heather's shape once she climbed the horse fence separating her garden from the neighbors'. I found a broom in a closet and swept all traces of crumbs and dust into a neat pile before brushing it out the door.

In a way, it wasn't fair that Heather could run off and be Heather. She might end up being scolded for gallivanting through stormy fields when someone was murdering animals, but her punishment never lasted. It was impossible to stay angry with her. She'd kiss and swear she meant no harm — and she didn't. She wasn't cruel. What Heather wanted, Heather did. She wasn't uncaring. I suspected she simply didn't notice what impact she had on me, on others. How freeing to be so unaffected.

Suddenly, a flare outside the kitchen glowed like the negative of a photograph. The deafening boom made me jump while the pendant light above the sink blinked out. From the dining room, my parents and Heather's shuffled in search of candles. I fumbled along the cabinets until I came to one holding extra candles and matches. Between the mill and solar panels, the Glen had electricity, but the houses' wiring was rudimentary. Blackouts weren't uncommon, even in good weather. Most of us still used kerosene lamps for that reason.

I scratched a match. The rotten-egg smell of sulfur was fleeting as I lit a candle. Mama appeared in the doorway. "You *buena*, Ivy?"

"*Sí*."

Thump.

The noise came from the window. I glanced at Mama. "What was that?"

"The wind, probably," she answered.

Thump.

Thump. Thump.

That wasn't wind. My pulse quickened. I cupped the candle and stood on my tiptoes, holding the flame to the window.

THUMP.

I jumped back from the jolted windowsill. In the living room, Marsh called to check on Mama and me. By now she was beside me, candle in hand, as we tried to see what was outside.

THUMP! THUMP! THUMP!

My heart rode into my throat. It didn't sound like hail. The bangs against the glass were too sporadic, frenzied.

"Luz?" Papa yelled. "What the hell's that?"

Against a faraway gleam of lighting, a black mass reeled from the window as if taking a breath before soaring straight for the glass again.

THUMP! THUMP!

I couldn't move. The dark thing outside whisked from side to side. It pulled back and —

CRASH!

With a yelp, I ducked the flying glass. Mama rushed over to the wet, black thing flopping on the floor and, crying out in Spanish, backed away. The glow of the candles revealed a blackbird. It wasn't dead, but from the way it flailed and twitched, it would be soon. My scream stunned into silence, all I could do was watch the bird in its death throes. Its crooked wings strained to lift, but its bones were shattered.

Papa reached the kitchen, saw the dying bird, and recoiled. "Stay back," he ordered Mama and me.

I didn't want to look, but the chaos of the bird desperate to remain alive in spite of its gnarled body was impossible to ignore. Papa knelt, his face a mixture of revulsion and pity, and took the bird into gentle hands. His thumb stroked the tiny creature's wing.

Then he wrung the bird's neck, its bones crunching.

For a minute, the only movement was the waver of the candle's flame pulling and pushing the shadows. Papa's eyes closed, and I was quite sure he said a prayer. Maybe to spirit away the bird. Maybe to ask forgiveness for what he'd done. To bring death sometimes was a kindness. He opened his hands.

"Oh, God," I whispered.

The bird wasn't one but two, a bird with a conjoined twin. One body with two beaks, a single head with four beady eyes. Two birds so close they were one, and one's death killed the other.

I went after Heather.

Marsh ordered me to find her, too occupied with repairing the kitchen window to chase her down himself. I was glad to leave. I couldn't stay knowing that *thing* had shattered the window and died at my feet. The danger outside didn't feel as real as the danger of where my thoughts would go if I stayed in.

Where Heather went was a mystery. The storm moved northeast, though the clouds still dashed white then dark. I hugged myself as I forged down the muddy road. The Glen's electricity was out, the candles by windows ember-like in their dimness. Sheriff's men relit the torches along the fences. Nothing felt right, nothing safe. Something close flapped in a gust of wind. A figure loomed over me, taller than anyone I knew.

"Wh-who's there?" I called, wishing I didn't sound so meek.

A shriek tore out across the sky, a high-pitched cackle from deep within the woods.

I rammed into the crossbeam of the scarecrow. Its body was mounted on a pole with its arms outstretched, its shirt weathered. A puppet to frighten off birds from scrounging the Thomsons' strawberries. Each family had its own way of crafting scarecrows — a few with pumpkins or old leather sacks for heads, some bodies stuffed with wheatgrasses, whereas others were filled with dried corn stalks. The birds came in plague-like numbers once the berries ripened, but during the dead months when nothing was harvested, one gazed to the fields to view scarecrow after scarecrow guarding the barren land like impaled corpses left to rot.

This scarecrow's head was a bag of dried beans. Desiccated sprouts from last summer poked through the burlap only to curl back inside. Soggy with rain, the bean sprouts beaded water, the head sack slumped, one button eye lost and marked only by an X in black thread. Its mouth was crooked, sloppy paint, most of which had flaked away, giving the scarecrow a gray expression.

A second whooping cry sprang from the woods, raising every hair on my neck and arms. I whipped around and surveyed the distance. A horse neighed. *Whimsy.* Heather told me to say she'd gone to check on the horses. There might be some truth in that. I peeled away from the scarecrow's path, cut through the mess of mud to the pasture where my horse lived with a small herd. While most of the herd was likely dozing, one spooked horse could infect the others and cause an accident.

At the pasture, the six steeds at this end of the Glen were quiet, their long necks drooped forward to lower their faces while they nibbled grass. They should've been in their stalls with buckets of oats, safe from the storm, yet light leaked out from the barn.

I climbed the fence and pushed closer to the stable. The air was heavy with the aroma of wet horses and sweet-pungent manure. A chestnut gelding gave me a curious glance, and I nodded, hoping he wasn't apt to startle.

Whimsy's black coat camouflaged her, but her habit of kicking the water trough gave away her location. She lifted her head, and her ears perked, large eyes reflecting the light slivers coming from the stable. The mare ambled behind me, her breath hot and constant, puffing from her velveteen muzzle.

From inside the stable, a laugh rang out, a girlish chime.

Heather.

I edged around to the front, to the closed door, where I leaned against the wood, my face pressed to a knothole. Inside was a glowing lantern. Heather's skirt was all shadow as she twirled, her back to me shining pale and naked. She stretched out her arms and spun again, her necklace of found things rising and falling between her bare breasts. Beyond her, out of the lantern's gleam, someone shifted. The scuffed toe of a boot and nothing more.

My heart plummeted, a gasp in my throat.

Heather jerked her head. Her lips pursed. Her hair parted and covered her breasts while each step she took toward the door was deliberate.

"I know you're out there," she snapped.

"Wh-what are you doin'?" I whispered. "Who's with you?"

She lowered her face and fixed her eye on mine. "Go home, Ivy."

"I need you. It's not safe out here."

"Then leave."

More shifting behind her. I tried to see past her, but she filled my sight. Heather was everywhere I looked.

"Ivy . . . please." A note of desperation crept into her voice.

"What's going on?" I asked. "You tell me everything."

"No, I don't. Now, stop. You need to go. You didn't see me."

How was I supposed to act like I hadn't?

"Heather, come on. Something terrible happened, and I don't wanna be alone."

Her eye disappeared from the knothole. A moment later, the stable door creaked and she came out, arms crossed. "Are you okay?"

"Th-there was a bird. And the w-w-window." Putting together the horror of the bird was harder than my throat would allow. "It was bad."

Heather peeked inside the stable as if waiting for her lover to emerge. Her fingernails tapped against the bare arm covering her chest. "I'll be home soon."

"You ain't coming now?" I heard my whine and cringed. I didn't want to be that girl, the tagalong who didn't realize when her friends had outgrown her. Was that what had happened? Not long ago, it would've been me she snuck out with.

Her and me. Cousins. Nearly sisters.

Forever.

She reached out and touched my hand. "I'll be home. Soon."

My throat was thick while I trudged back from the stable. Whimsy's hooves padded the earth as she moved closer to me. I stroked the side of my horse's face and tucked my hand into my sleeve to wipe away the hot streak of tears. Heather stayed behind. How could she pick another over her family when we needed her? Over me?

I hurried through the pasture to the wet road. When I turned and looked over my shoulder to the stable, the light was out.

CHAPTER FOUR

The flies always buzzed 'round Birch 'cause flies always come when death's close.

I awakened to tapping on my window. When I peered through the gauze of twisted wing and double beak dreams, Heather's hand pressed to the glass, the red thread knotted around her wrist. The rest of her ghosted pale from the dewy film on the pane. Behind her, starlight brushed the sky, the sun unready to rise.

"Ivy . . . Ivy, girl, c'mon." Her voice was a songbird's melody. "Open the window."

Never open the window when it's dark, Mamie used to say. *Even to someone you know. Wickedness takes the shape of what you love.*

I pushed back the quilt Mamie made when I was born and flipped my braid down my back. That I was drowsy gave me time to linger and remember the previous night — the bird, the ache of being sent away. Now Heather had returned.

"Ivy," she sang through the glass.

My feet hit the cold floor. My blue nightdress skimmed my ankles, and I bunched the fabric in my fists. I was angry yet relieved she'd come — ready to choke her yet yearning to hug her and make her promise she'd never shut me out again. Her fingertips squeaked on the wet glass as her hand dropped. Through the spots left behind, I watched her chew her lip. I flicked the metal lock and opened the window.

"Oh, thank you," she cheered and reached through the opening to clutch my hands. Her skin was warm, despite the morning chill. She smelled like Aunt Rue's homemade lavender soap. "I'm *so* sorry I couldn't talk to you last night."

All at once, I became a dull piece of ash compared to the glow of Heather's embers. She had fire and heat, and I was cold and so flimsy the wind could whisk me away without remembering it ever carried me.

"Heather, what time did you get home? It was after we left," I said.

"I know. Did you tell them I was taking care of the horses?"

"Yes. I didn't know what else to say."

"Did they believe you?"

"They have no reason not to."

We stared hard at each other. Heather averted her eyes first. She hesitated before a flush bled pink into her freckled cheeks. "Thank you. Can we talk?"

"Is it about what I saw in the stable?" I asked.

She went redder yet. "I want you to be happy for me. If it were you, I'd be so happy."

Whoever was with her last night had left her breathless.

Heather was in love.

I didn't know what that felt like.

But she did, and I could only guess from the way she behaved that the feeling was a kind of magic. It must be wonderful. A dream. A wish. A promise shared. She was blessed if the one she loved felt the same, which, of course, her mystery suitor must. Heather was easy to love.

"Wh-who did you see last night?" I asked.

She twisted her fingers through a tendril of my hair. "Come outside. I don't want anyone to overhear."

I shut my window and changed into a brown skirt that I matched with a gray shawl Mamie didn't wear anymore. Unease squirmed through my stomach, a worm wriggling through damp earth. Heather avoided my question, like she had last night. Was it on purpose? Was she worried how I'd react? If it were the latter, who could she love that'd upset me—

A boot with a scuffed toe. I'd drawn that boot.

Rook.

Cold started behind my skull and spread along my neck. August had seen them going off together. I wanted Rook to notice me. Anytime I saw him, Heather was around too. I was an idiot, fooling myself into thinking maybe he'd noticed me as well.

But even if Rook didn't know how I felt, Heather did. How could she do this to me?

I didn't want him to pick Heather over me. I loved my cousin, but right then, I was a fragile stem yanked from the earth, roots stripped and separated.

My hair slipped from its braid, and I combed the black waves. Nothing fussy, but it was time enough to steel my face.

"You okay?" Heather squeezed my shoulder as I met her on the porch. She wore a handwoven duster so big only the tips of her red sneakers stuck out, and her hair was pinned up. "You look like you've got the sicks."

I waved off her comment and sat beside her. "Must be something I ate."

She grinned and hugged me close against her. My arms were heavy, but I managed to rest one around her waist. How could I not want her to be happy? How could I stop from wanting what she had? I would listen, smile, and be happy for her no matter the ache inside. But I could have secrets too.

"Please don't be mad," she murmured into my ear.

I shook my head, unable to find my voice.

I'm furious because you were with him.

"N-n-not angry," I replied, and stepped out of the hug. *Don't sound jealous. Be her friend.* "Why are you sneakin' around?"

"It's special, Ivy, and I'm still figuring out what it all means."

Heather turned her face to the dawning sky, and everything about her softened — her smile, the pinch around her eyes. "It's all I want, but nobody would understand."

"I might."

"No, Ivy, I don't think so."

"You know I'm here for you."

"Don't, please. Don't guilt-trip me."

I bristled. "I'm not laying on a guilt trip, but you've never held anything back. So why now?"

Because she's in love with the same boy you are, and she doesn't know how to tell you that he loves her, not you.

Her cheeks were no longer pink with the bud of first love, but her nose went red, eyes shining wet. She reached out her hand, and though I had unanswered questions, we laced fingers.

"You'd tell me if someone kissed you, right?" she asked.

I forced a laugh. "I'd tell you immediately. Hell, you'd probably know before I did." After she'd let the pause draw out too long because we both knew no one kissed me, I said, "Tell me about it."

Heather had to tell me everything. She *had* to, or I'd never stop thinking about it.

"It's like trying a new fruit." She didn't look up. "At first, you're sorta shy about putting your mouth on another person's, but all you feel is softness and warm and wet. You open your lips wider, and once their tongue first flicks yours, it seems like your heart could flutter right up your throat and come outta your mouth into theirs, and they'd have your heart forever."

I didn't want to picture her kissing Rook, each of them guessing what to do, feeling good together.

"And there's more than that," she said. "Fingers pull at your shirt, tickle your waist, then move higher. It's handful after handful of sweaty skin, and your mouth hurts from kissing."

No, no, no, I didn't want to hear this.

But I would.

I wouldn't hold it against her. She deserved falling in love. Everyone did. Including me, someday. So why did my chest expand with panic as if a million butterflies were shivering against a screened window, waiting to burst through?

"Ivy, last night, it started innocent, and the kisses went to my neck, down my chest, from one side to the other." She motioned between her breasts. I closed my eyes and willed myself not to see what she described, Rook's dimples as his lips touched her skin. Had he taken off his glasses so they wouldn't be in the way? I wanted to stop my mind, yet the more she talked, the more detail she felt compelled to give, and I listened because that was what good friends did. "I didn't know I could come from touching and kissing, but Ivy, I did."

The silence between us was so solid, I didn't know if it'd break.

Not knowing what to say, I asked the obvious, to know and get it over. "You had sex?"

Heather nodded. "Yeah."

Her bluntness surprised me. She didn't hold back even after my jaw dropped.

"You know how they say it hurts the first time?" she remarked. "It ain't like that at all."

I didn't want more details. It'd be too much. There were other things I wanted to know. "So who is it?"

She didn't answer.

I pressed again. "Is it Rook?"

She let out an exasperated breath. "*That's* what you ask?"

But she isn't answering.

Everything hinged on this one admission, and she kept it from me. Was she that afraid of how I'd act? I wouldn't slap her. I wouldn't stop talking to her. But maybe she knew that. Maybe she knew me so well that she expected me not to react until I was alone.

That same bewildered, sick feeling hit me hard again. I didn't dare move away or let a muscle in my face twitch. I should be heartened she'd chosen me to share this with first, and yet I ached to run past the scarecrows to the fields and flop in a vegetable plot to cry into my skirt. I hadn't known we were both racing to the same finish line until she arrived first.

"Nothing's changed, Ivy. Not between us," Heather swore.

Everything had changed.

She'd left me behind, and she felt it as well, or she wouldn't have said anything. She reached over, our pinkie fingers twined around each other, and she watched me, an expectant look on her face. I needed to come up with something.

"Is it worth all the secrets and sneaking around?" I wondered.

Heather sat on the step with her knees drawn to her chest. "You know, Ivy, I think it is."

When Heather and I stopped outside her house, she tugged me into a hug. The abruptness of it, the tightness, startled me.

"Thank you," she whispered, "thank you so much."

I took her weight of secrecy. It became mine. My silence. My sadness. So she'd be happy.

My hand twitched, the red threads on our wrists side by side, an infinity loop. Heather broke away with a wave and disappeared inside. School was a good two hours off, and the night only began to dissolve into daybreak. The first violet ray of dawn crept over the horizon, and smoky blue drenched the Glen. My feet tromped the ground, and though I was aware of houses and farms, I was blind.

The rustle of leaves and stomp of boots caught my ear. Ahead of me lay the Meriweathers' vegetable plots. The soil was tilled black. For now, the seedlings took refuge inside Rook's greenhouse built from windows and glass doors reclaimed from the hollow's demolished buildings. He and Sheriff retrieved the discards from the roadside and fastened parts together until they had a curious building of pieces unwanted by others. Through dusty glass, I spied two shapes moving about the greenhouse, one burly and the other leaner and athletic. The second silhouette appeared in my sketchbook dozens of times. The sight of him caused me to break into a cold sweat.

How could I speak to him now? How could I not feel something rip in me?

I lifted my skirt's hem to run, but I hadn't made it more than five feet before he called.

"Ivy!"

Don't face him. Despite my brain's begging, my heart demanded I stay.

Rook waited outside the greenhouse. His brown shirt and trousers were dingy, and his hands, protected by gloves, held a snarl of branches dotted with dried black berries. Belladonna. He weeded it from the fields each year, and some must've taken root in the greenhouse last fall.

"Why are you over this way so early?" he asked.

"I went for a w-walk." I fumbled the words.

"Alone?" He threw down the belladonna, stripped off his gloves, and moved toward me. His gait was an easy jog, and the redness in his pale cheeks a combination of working and the brisk morning.

Behind him, the second shadow exited the greenhouse. August remained in the background, knee-deep in belladonna and called, "Rook, what's goin' on?"

He ignored August, his focus intent on me. A day ago, I would've craved his determined gaze. "Ivy, I told you what my pops said 'bout not going out alone."

"I was with Heather."

So were you.

I bit back the venom of my wounded feelings. He'd made his pick, and I wasn't it. If Heather had found anyone else, I'd have danced with her in dizzy circles. Because it was Rook, a tremendous guilt filled my belly for wishing it wasn't.

He crossed his arms and looked every bit a self-appointed big brother. Maybe he never had seen me as more than a sister. "You should be more careful. I don't think you get how serious Pops was when he said not to go off on your own. I mean it — if you're gonna be wandering 'round, take me with you."

Something in my head snapped. It cleaved open the last bit of will holding back my hurt. He was a hypocrite, telling me to watch my back and be safe while he and Heather snuck around. All the soreness clamping my heart, the anger and sourness, rose from me.

"Screw you, Rook! I ain't the one runnin' around half the night!"

He staggered back into a horse fence. "Ivy, what the hell?"

My mouth fell open, and I tried to come up with more to yell. My thoughts were colors, shades of red, alarming and enraged.

He peeled himself off the fence and reapproached me. "I have no idea—"

"Don't give me that bullshit," I growled. "You treat me like I'm a kid! I'm *older* than Heather! You pull this on her?"

"You think she'd listen if I tried? No! She'd laugh in my face." He jammed his fingers through his dark hair. "Heather'll take care of herself, but you depend on her for every—"

My hands slapped against his abdomen and knocked him backwards, but he regained his balance. It made me want to throw my weight into him again. I lunged for him. He caught my wrists, and we twisted together, me trying to strike him and him deflecting me no matter how rabid I was.

"Stop!" he ordered. "You're gonna get hurt!"

"I'm already hurt!"

His grip tightened around my wrists, and he stared so intently I wondered if he was trying to crush me. I wanted to be dust.

"Rook, let her go!" August grabbed his friend to separate us. "Jesus, she's crying! You see that?"

I lifted the corner of Mamie's shawl to wipe my eyes as I bolted toward home. Behind me, Rook and August yelled back and forth, but I didn't hear what they said. My breath rushed out too hard. Yet within a few paces, fingers snagged at my sleeve.

"Wait!" Rook called.

I wanted to leave. I wanted to make-believe that everything, beginning the minute I'd found Heather in the stable to discovering her secret, was nothing more than a fever dream.

"For God's sake, girl, stop runnin' from me!"

The driving force to flee emptied from my legs. But I wouldn't face him. I didn't want him to see me looking like a mess from sniveling and my hair ragged. He stood so near that his body heat reached out to me. With a deft gentleness hard to imagine from someone who worked in fields — let alone someone who had every right to be angry with me — his touch slipped down the length of my arm.

"Ivy, what'd I do?"

I sniffed back a sob, but the noise was half strangled. Rook circled in front of me. He was over six feet tall, and the top of my head didn't even reach his shoulder. Though I tried not to look at him, it was too late to stop a fresh well of pain from springing. Warmth kissed my cheek, his palm cupping my face, the pad of his thumb blotting away a tear.

Yet no matter the heat exuding from him, the coldness returned to my body, starting with my feet. The longer I stood with Rook under the predawn sky, the cooler the earth beneath me grew. The fire of my temper, which sought to burn and blister, Rook abruptly snuffed. I was burned out and numb. A stench reminiscent of deer-hunting season when the carcasses were bled at nearly every farm gagged me.

"What is that?" I asked.

Rook lifted his collar to cover his nose. "Something smells dead."

I squinted and looked out past the horse fences. Something pale with curves and hollow caught a few fickle rays of light from the torches. Ribs. Leg bones. Something *was* dead and stripped of its flesh, leaving a skeleton jutting up from the field.

"Oh, God," Rook blurted out. "What do you think it is?"

"I don't know," I said. "Go get your daddy."

"Hang on a second."

Rook pulled himself over the horse fence. I tucked up my skirt and climbed over after him. The closer we drew, the easier it was to see the carcass. Bits of meat still clung to the pearly bones. Tufts of coarse brown fur lay on the ground, half submerged in a thick puddle of darkness spreading out from around the skeleton. It had cloven hooves. It was a goat.

Its head was missing.

CHAPTER FIVE

You'd smell Birch before you saw him. He never bathed, or if he did, the water was tainted by blood. He took animal skins and wore 'em. Once, he cut open a deer and wore its belly chains 'round his neck like some kinda unholy shawl.

My feet were cold, my shoes seized by Sheriff and zipped in a bag marked EVIDENCE. They had to know which footprints in the field came from me.

Women came outside wearing aprons, interrupted from preparing the day's first meal. Some carried baskets of speckled eggs plucked from hen houses moments before the commotion began. The men forgot to fasten their suspenders or slick back their hair once Sheriff and his men knocked on their doors to account for folks' where-abouts.

Absent from the souls milling in fear was Heather.

Across the road, Rook was sequestered at a harvest table. Beside him was the bag containing my shoes. Rook's boots were in another bag. His head lifted, lips parted as if about to call to me. He didn't. Instead his mama, Briar, crowded him, smoothing his hair with a hand meant to steady, to wipe away all the horror he'd seen. All while his little sister, Raven, jostled her free hand.

Mama hurried close and offered me an extra pair of shoes, but I didn't budge, too stupefied to move as she knelt and eased my feet into the sneakers.

"So what d'ya think, Timothy?" Sheriff asked, his head angled so close to Papa's that I strained to hear.

Papa stooped beside the viscous puddle, holding a vial with a sample. "No animal did this, if that's what you're askin'."

"You think it's the same fellow who did in the dog?"

"Maybe."

No tracks on the ground except for Rook's and mine, nothing to yield answers to multitudes of questions. The rising sun cast a rosy glow, dawn's promise, yet in that glimmer, the darkness of death was fathomless.

Near the puddle, Sheriff's men guarded a sheet, once white, now painted with rusty splotches, covering the remains. Dale Crenshaw, a deputy and winemaker, wiped his forehead with a handkerchief.

"I reckon it's time to call in the county officers, ain't it, Jay?"

Sheriff looked toward Papa. Some expression I didn't know on my father's face worried me, how his eyes widened and cheeks paled at the mention of outside police. They weren't to be brought in, Papa always said. Nothing happened in the Glen that our own people couldn't handle.

"You're jumping to conclusions, Dale," Sheriff said. "We don't know what we got going on, and you really think the county's gonna give a damn about dead livestock?"

When livestock died, folks removed the carcass before the flies and death smell came, ideally within twenty-four hours. That meant hauling the dead south to the bone land. Coyotes took care of the flesh. But if Papa found the creature diseased, the carcass was burned, and there was no escaping the odor, no matter which way the wind blew.

Sheriff and Papa both peered under the sheet covering the skeleton and skin. A fly buzzed near the corner, dipping inside, zooming out a second later. A whimper escaped my lips, and I tucked myself against Mama. She pushed my hair down in front of my eyes, and her hand spread warm on my cheek as she turned my face.

I breathed to calm myself, but a metal taste crept up my throat and lay flat on my tongue.

My mother murmured, "*Ay, Dios mío, bonita,*" as she rubbed my back. I had to get away, walk around, or do something, so I stepped outside of my mother's reach and closed the gap separating me from Papa and Sheriff. I stayed on the fringe, not wanting to hear and yet a morbid curiosity forcing me to listen.

"Sheriff," Dale said, "you gotta catch this killer before he goes after some person."

The crowd split and wandered away, but Sheriff caught my father's shoulder and hissed in his ear.

"I don't like havin' that son of a bitch Birch Markle on a killin' spree. I'm worried Crenshaw's right and we'll have more than dead animals soon. But I ain't turning it over to county police. Not after how they mucked things around last time."

Papa shrugged off Sheriff's hand and buckled his veterinary bag. "Jay, you truly suspect Birch?"

"You yourself said some animal didn't do it," Sheriff said. "Woods are wide, Timothy. People get lost and don't come out, but who's to say a few don't come out on purpose? And after what he did to Terra—"

"Jay," Papa interrupted. He stared at me. "How much have you heard?"

"Enough," I said. "I know the stories."

My father sucked in a sharp breath while Sheriff walked to a fence and snatched an oddly discarded spade lying nearby. The blood soaking dark into the earth thickened on the dirt's surface.

"There's truth in the old stories, Ivy," Sheriff declared, his words punctuated by the metallic singing of the spade striking rock. "Get on home. Get there fast and safe."

A child's nightmare came to life. The monster in the woods, the howler at night, was real. With the spade, Sheriff scattered fresh dirt over the blood. He'd dry it out best he could and bury it deep. No one'd know it'd ever been.

Heather walked with me to school the following morning, but upon reaching the trailer park, she broke away.

"I gotta make a quick stop." She bounced on the toes of her sneakers and looked over both her shoulders as if to see who might be watching.

No one from the Glen went to the trailer park, but Milo was looking for her the other day. What if it was for something more than just weed? How easily could he slip across the Glen's borders and go unnoticed except by a girl meeting him in the stable? My heart skipped. I half smiled. Maybe Rook wasn't Heather's lover after all.

"So, tell me more about Milo," I said. "Was it him you were with in the stable?"

She shook her head and laughed. "I swear, you're still so hung up on that. Come *on,* Ivy. I'm making a quick stop. That's all."

The soles of my shoes ground on the gravel road. I pretended to study a dandelion. "Can't you just walk with me?"

"I gotta go. Promise me you won't tell. If you do . . ." Heather's threat stayed in the air, unfinished with the imagination of what could be painful enough to hold me silent. I hated being alone, left to watch as she crossed the road and checked a metal pail hanging near Milo's trailer before removing something to shove in her bag. She'd never show me. Maybe before, but not now.

By that afternoon, she leaned on me as we sat outside her house. I drew a picture of Rook's greenhouse. Heather embroidered blue flowers on a handkerchief and tucked it inside her shirt when she finished, setting about to braid my hair.

"Your time will come, Ivy," she said.

I closed my sketchbook. My time, I had always believed, would be with the boy who built that greenhouse.

"You know all you gotta do is open your mouth and talk. You've got a lot of good stories, Mamie's stories, if you'd get over being so shy."

"I ain't changing who I am," I said. I was Ivy. I was the quiet one.

Heather pulled another lock of my hair into the braid. "You need to have more than only me."

It's a warning, I heard Mamie say in my head. *She's movin' on, and you're stayin' behind.*

The next morning, I knocked on Heather's door, only to surprise Aunt Rue. Heather had left hours before, claimed she was up early to bake muffins with me as we often had. I wasn't quick enough to come up with a lie for my cousin and ran away. As I passed the Meriweathers' farm, neat bundles of belladonna were stacked, a sign Rook had been there, but he was gone too. My left eye twitched, wondering. Why didn't he wait to walk with me?

By the third morning, I stopped looking, knowing I would see Heather at school. Knowing she was hiding things from me.

My shoes, some new-to-me gray Chucks Mama traded for at the thrift store, sank into the earth. The only sound was the faint chime of bells sewn into my skirt. My schoolbooks nestled against my chest, my gaze fixed on the path. The wind's cool wisps traced my bones. I was alone, exactly what I was warned never to be. I wished I cut a more imposing shadow, but I was short and not at all a savage thing.

I heard heavy footfalls nearby and stopped.

Someone lingered close behind. My fingers tensed around my books. A rusted weathervane of a blackbird spun, metal whining as it spiraled. My heart slithered up my throat.

I spun in a hesitant circle. A chicken pecked at grubs in the dirt. My eyes lifted to the glower of a scarecrow's black-button eyes. *Only a scarecrow . . .*

Yet someone was out there.

"Ivy!"

The *whup-whup* of August running accompanied the flop of his curly hair. His barrel chest heaved. "Wait up!"

My muscles unwound. Hay and manure from mucking stables flecked his boots while the sweetish odor of horses emanated from his shirt.

"Rook asked me to walk with you," he said.

I raised an eyebrow. Why should Rook be thinking of me at all? "I've been walking by m-myself. No one's talking to me."

"No one knows what to say, Ivy."

Hearing that reply, however honest, angered me, though my stammer tried to block my tongue.

Speak steady, Ivy. Think about your words, and they'll not trouble you.

Yes, Mamie.

"Why?" I asked. "'Cause I'm a third wheel?"

"What? No." August pulled a dusty St. Louis Cardinals cap from his overalls and tucked his perpetual cowlicks beneath the brim.

"Don't be such a head case. Seeing that dead goat, Rook's freaked. He's got nightmares. And if he's bad off, I can't imagine what it's like for you."

"At least he has someone to talk to. Heather keeps going off," I muttered.

"Heather'll find herself trouble."

"No, she won't. I'll cover for her 'cause that's what I always do."

My voice thinned. The last thing I wanted was to cry in front of August. Did he know how it hurt to think of her and Rook together?

We landed on the country highway leading into town, where the lush barricade of oak trees was gone, replaced by wild oat grass tolerant of the Ozark heat. The gravel road through this hollow didn't find much traffic, yet a big rig barreled through and kicked up a dust cloud.

The trailer park was across the road. Each unit was a pastel color: robin's egg, canary, salmon; all with white roofs and mold crawling up the sides. A pink trailer with a sunflower pinwheel was closest to the road. The ground was dead earth, no green or yellow sprouting from it. A child's slide and tricycle faded under the sun. My nose burned as I crossed a plume of cigarette smoke — it was like someone had plunked against one of the emaciated trees and inhaled half a pack of cancer sticks in a single go.

A screen door banged, then a girl laughed. "Oh, Milo, you're terrible."

My neck went stiff. The lullaby lilt of Heather's voice was unmistakable.

"What's she doin' here?" August whispered.

Not now, August. I needed to hear what she and Milo said.

"I'm just sayin', you know you can't get enough of Mary Jane," Milo teased.

I crept closer. He was talking about weed. I'd heard rollers at school calling marijuana that. It seemed Milo was a dealer, while Heather his latest buyer.

I slunk past August's arm and inched along a chicken wire fence. Milo was sitting on the steps of a pink trailer, puffing on a cigarette. Heather stood by him, one foot wrapped behind her other ankle like a flamingo. The way she leaned toward him, she knew him. Her hand was out as he took a case of folding papers from his shirt pocket, removed one, then doled out some weed from a bag he'd tucked in his jeans. He rolled a joint, his eyes on her as his tongue slicked out to wet the seam and seal it.

"A little Mary Jane to start your morning?"

"Oh, hell, yes." Heather put the joint between her lips, bouncing when he brought up his lighter to give her a spark. During afternoon picnics by the riverside, it wasn't that uncommon for Rook, Heather, and me to pass one around until we laughed and sprawled, skirts and limbs flopped over each other like a snuggly litter of puppies.

Dragging on his cigarette, Milo folded his arms. "You know, the rest of the trash livin' in this dump would string you up by your long skirt if they knew what you really came here for."

"I. Don't. Care," Heather said, and blew out smoke with each word.

"People 'round here have heard about what creepy shit you heathen weirdos are into."

Heather laughed again. "You watch your mouth, roller scum. You know well as I do that we ain't heathens, just simple folk."

"In some places, simple means dumb."

He gave her a crooked grin. She raised her middle finger, laughing and smoking. "You think you know me so well."

Milo leaned against the trailer door, his hand coming down to smack the red lid of an orange drum beside the front stoop. It was marked with a big label reading BIOHAZARD. "You're smart, but you do dumb things. Like hang out here."

She shrugged. "I gotta get my fix."

The quirk was gone from his mouth as he sucked the last of his cigarette, blowing out the smoke from his nose in twin streams. "You always get what you want, don't you? 'Cause you're you, and no one's gonna say no to you." His eyes went dead as he fixed on my cousin.

"Milo."

"I just don't want nobody to get hurt, that's all," he said, a touch of tenderness creeping into his voice. Then he dropped his cigarette butt to the ground.

Heather squashed the filter under her foot and picked it up, discarding the wasted filter in his palm. "Keep that poison outta the soil."

"I'm mighty sure there's worse comin' for me than a few cancer cells."

With a jut of her hip, Heather waved off, ducking under the trees and slipping through a gap in the fence. August and I stayed frozen, my eyes trained on the red fire of my cousin's hair as she sauntered down the road.

Standing in a cloud of smoke, my legs grew heavy. "I don't like this."

August's nose wrinkled. "Stay away from him."

"I doubt Milo gives a damn about me." My knees buckled, and I slumped beside a tree. "Milo's got his sights set on Heather. Like everyone else."

"Don't be like that."

"L-like what? Like I'm sick of being forgotten? So what if I don't laugh as loud or talk as much? It's always her and what she can get, and since I'm her cousin and her best friend, I gotta be h-h-happy. If I say I'm not, I come off like a jealous bitch."

August knelt beside me. Why I'd poured out all that to him, I didn't know. Because he was there? Because he wasn't threaded in the knot that Rook, Heather, and I had become?

His dye-stained fingers withdrew a necklace of a leather cord strung through an acorn from his pocket. "Heather doesn't get everything."

He lowered the necklace into my palm.

The acorn cap was still warm from his pocket. "August, this is sweet."

His mouth cracked in a smile. "Let me put it on you."

He swept aside my hair to expose my neck. His thumbs treaded down the bumpy ridge of my neck bones and then he looped the cord and tied it. The acorn fell just above my breasts. Acorns came from oaks, trees that were sturdy and hard to break. They didn't have to grow in a grove and did fine all alone.

A red curl hopped along the oat grass field, bobbing low, then high, an undulating wave.

"August?"

"Hmm?"

"Did you . . ." I trailed off, brushing dirt and roots from my skirt as I clambered to the road. I felt the red curl's pull, and I followed.

Heather should've been far, far ahead, yet I saw her. Red hair. No one had hair like hers, so wild with braids and metaled with beads. She walked down the hollow's road, sunshine so harsh I shielded my eyes, but I knew the sway of her hips. Her feet were bare. They shouldn't haven't been bare.

"Heather!"

She walked on.

I dug my shoe into the gravel, sprinting forward, chasing her. What was she doing? Why wasn't she going to school? Something wasn't right.

As I closed the gap to twenty, fifteen, ten feet, I spotted two old silver coins in her palm, the kind of coins dating to well over a century ago that we sometimes dug up on Glen land. It was corpse money, pieces of silver to lay over the eyes of the dead. Mamie kept a set on her dresser for when the time came. I slowed my gait and studied the hand holding the coins. Her skin was gray, her fingernails purplish-blue and slipping loose from their beds. The fingers were bloated, while the fat part of her palm's heel was split, the skin peeling back in a translucent flap. My shoes ground to a halt. Gravel spit out from beneath my soles.

That ain't Heather.

Yet it was.

She moved in a herky-jerky dance as she pirouetted to face me. I shrieked, covering my mouth. My legs turned coltish, and I couldn't move to run. My skirt wrapped around my legs, cocooning me.

Heather's mouth was too wide across her face and curled to twist upward beneath her eyes. All her teeth showed at once, gums visible. Her lips were gone.

Gone.

Removed, not hacked off in some juvenile fit like the massacred animals, but sliced off with precision to preserve the Cupid's bow at their peak. Her face was a death pallor, blue and white to make her freckles stand out like specks of dried blood. She grinned, not because she wanted to, but rather from the corrupted smile slashed into her face.

My throat was raw, scraped out by screams. I should've broken away, tailed back to August under the tree, yet I waited by this dead walking Heather.

Blue-black veins bulged near her temples and hid beneath the surface only to burst forth again in thick cords at her neck. Her clothes whispered of some unspeakable thing. The fabric slashed open, with dark, curdled sludge spilled down the front. It plunked on her bare feet and rolled over her skin to the gravel.

Ting, ting, ting. Her fingers twitched, the coins clinking together.

I whimpered, "H-Heather . . . wh-what happened?"

She cocked her head. Her hair slung over one shoulder in a wet heap. She was soaked. From her too-wide mouth and her nose, dirty fluids streaked down her skin.

My pulse battered the space between my ears until my sight went hazy. I fell backwards on the road. Jagged pebbles dug into my back, and the sun's rays were so sharp and bright they blinded me. Then Heather's dead face loomed over me. She was closer, dripping cold and wet on my forehead.

Then, the sound of tires skidding on gravel.

"Ivy, look out!"

CHAPTER SIX

Pastor tried praying for Birch Markle's soul. He brought us women healers and our herbs and stones to draw out that darkness from the boy, but he laughed. It was a terrible sound that I still can hear. Birch didn't want no saving.

August grabbed me out of the way of a truck. The driver's horn blasted at us while it passed, and tires kicked stone pellets against my skirt and arms. I didn't see it coming, my head lost in a mist of terrors and tradition.

Like others in the Glen, I grew up throwing chicken bones to divine the future and predicting rain by when dandelions closed their yellow heads. I knew a frost's arrival by the cicadas' buzz. What happened, that horrible monster I saw on the road, was a nightmare thing. Stories of old claimed that shadow selves wandered the hills and emerged once death circled near. It wasn't something you brought up over the dinner table while passing the butter dish. You waited until night fell and the hearth fire wearied. The hiss of pinesap in charred wood coaxed secrets you'd never share with sunlight on your face.

Long before my birth, a shadow self visited my family. Gramps was still a youngish man. He'd claimed October that year was blisteringly cold, winds from the north bringing such an early chill the Glen feared for its autumn harvest. The story went that he minded the fire while Aunt Rue, then a toddler, skipped around the long table. Upstairs in the little house, the midwives had shooed away Gramps. He was to have clean towels and hot water ready. Mamie — or Ginger, as she was called then, before she had grand-children — was in the labor pains, and that was granny-women's business, no room for a sheepherder like him.

The clock struck ten o'clock, and a draft whisked through the home to stir the family Bible's pages. Gramps clutched the cracked leather cover and, by the fireplace across the room, saw Mamie's silhouette. She wore her birthing gown, her red hair unpinned in sweaty curls. In one hand, she held the iron poker and prodded the fire's embers until orange tongues unfurled as hot as possible. Mamie's other arm coddled a newborn wrapped in blankets. She focused on the baby, a baby that made no sound.

For as long as Gramps lived, he swore what happened next was God's truth. Mamie's skin was as thin as tissue paper, veined black. Gramps set aside his Bible and called to her, but she didn't flinch. The only movement was a twitch of her lips, which were blue but for the fat part of her lower lip where her teeth had gouged as she pushed out the baby. She didn't notice Gramps and stoked the fire until it was so hot he yelled to stop or sparks might escape and burn down the house. Then she dropped the iron poker, metal clanging on rock, and drew one fingertip along the curve of the baby's cheek. She threw the baby in the fire where it landed on the logs like a squirmy grub. The flames scorched the swaddling and turned dead-white skin to ash.

That was the night Mamie gave birth to a stillborn daughter and nearly bled out herself on the bed.

To see a shadow self was to see the walking soul of someone whose back was in the grave while they faced the living. What I saw on the road could've been exhaustion, stress, a nightmare, or — as August suspected — some hallucinogenic accident because I wandered too close to smoke from Milo's Mary Jane.

Excuses didn't make what I saw less of a warning.

August swore he wouldn't speak of it. I believed him, but I wouldn't find peace of mind until I saw the real Heather.

I finally found her outside by the football field at school with a joint between her forefinger and thumb.

I held my sketchbook to my chest. "W-we need to talk."

"About?" She puffed on the joint and offered me a hit, but I shook my head.

"I'm worried. I saw something when you left the trailer park —"

She held up a hand. "Hold up. You followed me to the trailer park? Ivy?"

"I didn't follow you."

She tipped back her head and took a few noisy breaths. They were supposed to be calming breaths, yet her shoulders went high at her neck. "So what is it?"

"You're in trouble," I said.

"Did Marsh see me? Uncle Timothy?"

"No, *danger* trouble. Mamie's stories 'bout shadow selves and how they're death omens? I saw yours, Heather! You know what that means!" I felt silly saying it, knowing how easy she would dismiss it as foolery. Still, I had to warn her in the hope that maybe — not now but later, once she was alone — she'd hear me and be careful.

She gave a smoky laugh, then a doubtful scan from my face to my toes and back to my face. She knew I wasn't joking, but still she scoffed.

"You gotta be kidding me." Heather finished her joint, grinding out the cherry on the metal overhang of the bleachers. "You're all worked up over nothing."

"Will you please listen?" I begged.

"You know what your problem is, Ivy?" she snapped. "If it were up to you, everybody'd only listen. Well, I can't listen anymore. Some things I gotta *do*."

"Can you at least be careful?"

"I'm with someone who makes me feel safe."

A lump formed in my throat. Who always kept an eye on us? Who was always the protective boy-next-door? And if Rook knew she'd gone back to Milo for more weed, he'd be hurt.

I was hurt.

"I'll be fine, Ivy," she promised.

She stepped out from the bleachers and into the grass, the jingling of her necklace of found things loud against the stillness of the parking lot.

I prayed what I saw was nothing. Because I couldn't save her.

After school, I'd been at the clinic only a few minutes when Papa finished checking a coydog named Ratter for ear mites. Papa waited until Ratter's owner left before he placed his palm against my forehead, then untucked his stethoscope from his collar, pressing it to my back while I breathed for him.

"You feel okay? You're pale," he said.

I didn't get pale. Not with my mother's Mexican blood in me. "I'm fine."

I reached for the jar of dog treats on the counter and knocked off a pair of scissors. Papa eyed the metal blades, open with one pointing toward the entrance and the other pointing at me. Neither of us could retrieve them. It had to wait until a guest arrived. Otherwise, bad luck would come.

"I'll have my next appointment get them," Papa said. "You go home. Get some rest. I can walk you there."

"I'll go by myself," I said.

Papa frowned, but I brushed past him. I sensed him still frowning as I exited, walking past the weathered LOST DOG signs. There was no escape, not at the clinic, at school, not anywhere. It didn't matter where I went, dread followed, wraithlike.

Death's a-comin', Ivy. Watch the signs.

I shook Mamie's voice from my head. Superstitions weren't worth a dime if the person they meant to warn didn't heed them.

I started on the path and looked back once to see Papa waiting by the door. He'd built his practice close to the road to attract farmers and the occasional townie who liked the idea of the country vet. The distance wasn't long to the heart of the Glen, where the homesteads lay, and the dirt road was well-beaten by hillfolks' boots, their carts and horses. But I didn't stop once I reached my house; I went deeper into the fields, until the road crumbled away, overtaken by patchy grass. Above me, the sky held its breath, turning dark blues and grays, spring storm colors that made the trees' new buds seem all that much greener, the red of the barns that much more vivid.

I arrived at the horse paddock and peeled away a pernicious vine rooting near the rusted gate, and then I nickered at the horses. Between a sorrel and bay, Whimsy lifted her dark head, ears forward. She plodded forth and met me. My hands stroked the sides of her muscular neck and the silken coat as she warmed me.

"I'm gonna ride you today," I told her. "I'm gonna forget everything. We'll trample the ground. I'll take you down to the river, and we can go as deep as you want."

Her big nostrils puffed, her whiskery lips loose. I had reached for her when she reared three steps. Whipping around, I glimpsed brown trousers and dark hair disappearing behind a cart loaded with hay. I left Whimsy's side and rounded the cart, covering my mouth in surprise.

Rook didn't look right. Stubble scruffed his cheeks. Some curious part of me wanted to run my hand over him, his roughness. By the gray light, his skin was pasty, the natural flush of his lips even redder. He was handsome and spooked.

"I haven't seen you in days," he said.

Which was true. Rook hadn't been in class. August claimed what we'd found in the field had left him bone-sick. Looking at the sad hollows of Rook's face, I saw August hadn't lied.

"What's goin' on, Rook?" I asked.

He gestured to the horses. "Wanna ride?"

I had reasons not to go: the danger of being outside at dusk, fearing what he might tell me — and what I might say, hurting Heather.

But it was Rook asking me.

I slipped inside the stable with him. Dust danced in the sunbeams where light poured through the barred windows. His boots scattered hay on the concrete floor while barn swallows nested. Rook lifted two bridles from the tack room, and it was all I could do not to picture him sitting with his legs apart as Heather spun topless before him. Bile stung my throat.

He slung the bridles over his shoulder. "I wanted to see you sooner, but my pops said you needed space after . . ."

His words trailed off as he handed me Whimsy's bridle and I eased it over her head. If he saw how my hands shook, he didn't let on. He followed with his blue roan gelding, Journey. We rode bareback down the Glen's far northwestern edge, wandering near the riverbed. I listened to the horses' hooves against the earth, their tails whisking in tandem.

"My folks say if you dream of someone, they're awake and pacing," Rook said as he negotiated Journey around a swath of belladonna. "Do you have trouble sleeping, Ivy?"

I slowed Whimsy's gait. He dreamed of *me?*

Heather, Heather, Heather . . .

Yet I didn't want to break the spell by saying her name.

Rook steered Journey in a half circle to peer at me. "I shouldn't have said anything."

"Why'd you come out here with me instead of Heather?" I asked.

"Why would I be with Heather?" He seemed puzzled. "You're the one I want to talk to."

He dug his heels into Journey's sides. He wore new boots, not the ones with the scuffed toes. The horse sauntered onward. I kicked Whimsy forward and launched into a posting trot, my hips moving up and down with her rhythm.

The wind blew my skirt even higher above my knees. I listened to the rush of the river and groan of Denial Mill turning. Behind us were more fields and barns succumbing to decay. A scarecrow leaned on a post, his overalls stuffed with hay and a tattered leather hat hiding his sack face.

Alone with me, Rook watched the dark river water sloshing over the rocky shore. His fists wound in Journey's reins until the knuckles protruded white. "I'm tired, Ivy. Too damn many nightmares."

"T-tell me what you dream," I said.

I motioned to a sizable chunk of limestone half submerged in the water. It was big enough for the both of us to sit. We weren't prepared, no blanket to protect against the rock's scrape, no lantern to light the way once it grew dark. We'd made a stupid move coming out alone when death roamed the Glen. Yet my blood tingled. Alive. So alive. Scared. So scared. Of what I'd hear. Of being with him.

I dismounted Whimsy and took her to the water's edge, where she drank. Rook brought down Journey, and we unclipped the horses' reins and climbed onto the limestone. Rook's legs dangled over the rock's edge, his body deflated like his insides were no longer ripe with blood. The wind was cool, but his heat radiated against my arm. Questions rolled around my mind, and I couldn't ruin the hush by speaking. Because I liked that moment. I couldn't bear to think about its price.

Rook cracked his knuckles, blurting out, "I'm thinkin' 'bout leaving the Glen."

"What? No!" I felt as if kicked from behind and teetering on the rock's edge. "Y-you can't!"

Before I could stop myself, I reached for him, as if by latching our fingers, I could stop him from running. Heather had already pulled away. I couldn't lose both of them. I squeezed his hand, tight and tighter.

"You're Sheriff's son," I persisted. "That's gonna be your job someday."

He looked at our hands, blinking behind his glasses. "I dream the goat's blood turns into a puddle beneath our feet that gets so big it sucks you down. I look but can't find you. Then we both drown in blood. I sound like I've lost my mind."

A whimper peeped through my lips.

"No," I said, "you sound like someone who's seen something awful. But you can't run away, Rook. *I* don't want you to go."

He stiffened. Every inch of him tensed. I unwound my fingers from his before placing my hands on his shoulders, broad shoulders he had yet to grow into and yet seemed like they could withstand the chaos inside me. His neck bowed forward. A wisp of his black hair fell and twisted into mine.

Stay, Rook.

"The Glen can be safe again," I promised. "Our families built this place to keep the outside world away. What's happening now? It's that monster in the woods."

"Birch Markle?" Rook scoffed.

"They said the Devil got him," I said. "He could've come back."

"More reason to get away from here."

I fought the lump in my throat. "You can't go, 'cause I can't stand the idea of you leavin', of you bein' with someone else!"

I clamped my hands over my mouth. I'd said too much. He was with Heather, not me. Guilt flooded my blood, dizzying me. Rook's eyes widened. That hint of movement was the only indication he'd heard me. His face was like a full moon, haunted and stripped of all its shadows. But me? My skin burned from my chest all the way up to my ears.

Then Rook took my hands. "What d'you mean? You don't want me with anyone else?"

"Just ignore me. It don't matter." My face was so hot, and I wished I could fan myself, but he didn't let go.

The tip of my nose grazed his cheek as his forehead pressed to mine. His breath drew in. I ached to feel his mouth, to fold my lips between his. I didn't want to hold back, but going forward would be wrong.

He tucked my hair behind my ear and balanced his mouth over mine. I turned my face. "I can't."

"What's wrong?" he asked.

"I know you're with Heather."

"No, I ain't. I wanna be with you, Ivy."

I sniffed. *What?* "Wait. Heather was with someone in the stable. Wasn't it you?"

He furrowed his brow. "No. Of course not."

My heart pounded in my ears, and I stared at him in disbelief. What I'd thought was true, how I'd been hurt so badly, it was all a mistake. His fingers stroked down my neck, twisting the cord of August's necklace between them, and right before he found the acorn, I tucked it inside my shirt collar. I should've never taken it from August, but it was nice at the time.

Rook's mouth skimmed mine. "I like you, Ivy. I've always liked you."

His lips were gentle as they touched mine. It took several passes of our mouths before we warmed to each other. His hands cuffed my arms and then slipped around to my back. He eased me onto his lap and kissed me again. And again. Everything I ever wondered about how his lips felt — the truth was softer, wetter than I imagined. His hands wandered down from the middle of my back to my hips, to my thighs. My chest rose from holding my breath, but his lips didn't leave mine. This time, I didn't hold back and allowed the kiss to widen. The relief of knowing I'd been wrong kept me floating. The way he touched me grounded me, held me still.

We sat with Rook's arms draped around me, my body tucked against his. I reached up to stroke the back of his head, pull him in for another kiss, threading his dark hair through my hands. Being next to him felt good. Better than good — as if my body smiled.

Rook's head rested on my shoulder. "About two years ago, you left your sketchbook in the art room at school. You draw really well."

"No . . ." I swallowed back an embarrassed groan. He'd seen my drawings, not just the ones I'd drawn in front of him that he knew about, but now the others from when I was alone, daydreaming, wishing. So many of him. The only person I allowed to see them was Heather. If Rook had seen all of them, there was no denying how I felt about him.

"Don't get like that," he said. "I have drawings of you, too."

"You do?" I asked.

"They ain't good, not like yours."

Who knew how long we could've gone on, too afraid to grab the other's attention? When all that time I hoped Rook noticed me, he had. Now that he pressed kisses along my jaw, I didn't want him to stop.

"Please don't go," I whispered. "Promise me you won't leave the Glen. Heather's already leaving me behind."

Rook pulled back. "What do you mean? She's always with you."

"Not anymore. She's running off all hours of the night. I lie to cover for her. She's hiding things."

"Like what?"

I told Rook everything. How she'd been in the stable with some-body she wouldn't identify. How she quit walking to school with me. How I'd seen her smoking weed with Milo. Rook listened as I con-fessed everything I knew, everything that frightened me.

Heather had grown tired of me.

Heather wouldn't heed the warnings.

"I'm scared," I said, and I realized I was shaking. The wind wasn't so cold that I should've been trembling. "If I don't do something, she—"

"You can't do anything," Rook interrupted. "Heather has her own life."

"And if she gets herself hurt? Or worse?"

"I . . ." His attention went to the steep embankment.

I twisted around to see a flicker of red. A few rocks clicked togeth-er while rolling to the river. I jerked away from Rook and scrambled to my feet, cursing under my breath.

She'd been here. She'd seen me with him, heard everything I'd said, her secrets. I charged up to the fields in time to see her running.

A dash of curls.

A ruffle of a skirt.

A drop disappearing into the bloody hand of sunset.

Heather.

CHAPTER SEVEN

The Markle girl, the sister, it's hard to think of what she must've gone through. No one set about courtin' her, even though she was the right age. No one wanted that devil she had for a brother as their kin.

Whimsy ran at a full gallop, matching my frenzy. I had to explain what Heather had heard, why I was with Rook, and I prayed she'd believe me, because the threads holding us were already so tenuous. How simple would it be for one to snap? Then others would break, and we'd no longer be tied together.

It wasn't that I wanted everything to stay the same.

I wanted a change too. A life where I was noticed.

She'd jumped ahead without me. I'd never meant to hold her back, even if she was tethered to me.

Find the red. Find Heather.

Whimsy clomped across the earth. I had left Rook behind, telling him to go home, that I'd find him later. I gripped the leather reins and crossed the despairing lands. Spring in the Ozarks should've been vibrant, but there was no life in the fields. The trees greened while the fields remained the bare dirt of freshly dug graves, scarecrows standing by as mourners.

I was leading Whimsy along the winding curve of the river close to Promise Bridge when I saw a splash of color bolting through Potter's Field. Since I couldn't take the horse across the bridge, I dismounted, trusting my mare to graze.

"Stay, Whimsy," I murmured as I unclipped her reins. "Please stay."

Her ears pricked, dark eyes wide. Maybe she understood. As hard as it was to leave her when other animals had been killed, I had to believe she would be safe.

I made my way across the bridge's splintering boards and down the cove. My thumb snagged a blackberry vine's pricker, and I licked the wound, a smear of metal and salt spreading across my teeth. Even after drawing my thumb from my mouth, the blood rinsed across my skin, spiraling through the rings of my thumbprint.

"You're bleeding."

Heather came out from behind the blackberries and stared at the red glisten, fists clenched.

"I-I'll be fine. Look, Heather, I can explain —"

"You had no right to tell him those things."

Her eyes went to the acorn necklace lying below my throat, and she wrapped her fingers around it, squeezing as if she meant to crush it. I squirmed and pried the necklace away, tucking it inside my shirt. Heather's lips curled back as she watched me, and then she tipped her head and laughed. The sound wasn't wind chimes tinkling. It was glass shattering. She shook her head, jiggling the bells and beads braided through her hair. My eyes met hers, and her teeth were sharp and set hard.

"I t-told him 'cause we're both worried about you," I said. "You've always known how I feel about Rook, so, yeah, I talked to him. Sorry if it makes you angry that I care."

"You care, huh?" she growled. "So that's why you're suddenly all over Rook's lap? You just have to be like me. Stop it. Stop it now!"

"H-Heather." My throat was tight, my tongue dumb.

"You gotta get your own life!" she shouted. "It's like you want to *be* me. You always have. You spy on me. It's obsessed. It's sick."

"I — I — " My fish mouth opened and shut, opened and shut. The graveyard blurred. The quarried stone markers tilted sideways, and I wasn't sure if I leaned forward, falling to the ground, or if the earth somehow rolled up to meet me. "It ain't like that! You're never around anymore, and I'm scared you're runnin' away! I talked to Rook 'cause I needed to tell someone."

She crossed her arms. "No, you told him 'cause you put him over me. I see how you look at Rook. You gotta have what I have, do what I do. God, Ivy, love isn't only romance and secrets. It's blood. It's gory. It gets ugly. You want that? Are you ready to get gross with someone?"

She started through the graveyard, and I followed her past the etched stones, yelling, "Y-you know what's gross? Runnin' around the st-stable with someone at night, slutting off to the trailer p-p-park. You ain't in love. You're just lookin' to get laid and get high —"

Heather wheeled around, her hand colliding with my face, and my neck twisted hard. My knees hit the ground first, then my palms, bits of rock biting my flesh. The burn in my eyes turned watery, but

Heather radiated fury as she glared at me. "S-s-stop s-s-stuttering, Ivy." She snorted. "And stop following me everywhere."

"I follow you 'cause you're gonna get yourself killed!" I scrambled up from the ground, a heap of blue skirt, black hair, and mud. If Heather didn't think I could be ugly and gross, I could. "The signs say s-s-something terrible's gonna happen, and it's gonna happen to you, 'cause you don't watch your back. Like you're so damn special. Either someone's gonna get pissed that you're skanking around with the rollers or some roller might well do it, but you're gonna wind up dead! M-Mamie always said to watch the signs —"

"Enough! I don't want you lookin' out for me. I know what I'm doing. I don't need Mamie's warnings. They're lies, Ivy, to make us afraid of what's out *there*. You know what's out there? People who think we're freaks. You ain't stoppin' me. Now, get outta my way!"

"Heather, I —"

"Don't talk to me. You're a ghost. You're so worried about who's gonna die, who's gonna be torn up like the dogs. It's you. You're dead. To me."

My heart plummeted to my hips. The noises I made while struggling to speak were pig squeals, hideous and awkward.

Heather cupped her hands around her mouth. "Hey, Birch Markle, come and get me!"

"I — I wouldn't —"

"Of course, you wouldn't. That's the point. I'm not letting you be my shadow anymore. Get a life. You can't have mine."

Tears welled in my eyes, hotter than my flushed skin as they pooled in the corners before dribbling down my cheeks. My chest was tight. I couldn't breathe. Every harsh word Heather spoke ripped through me.

I collapsed against the brambles. Heather stalked off through Potter's Field, trailing along a path into the woods. I didn't follow. My body crumpled, the strength of my muscles gone and leaving behind my shivering bones.

I shook so hard that I felt myself break.

Night smothered the last crimson streak of sunlight. I had no lantern. At the cemetery's edge, the trees jabbed the heavens. The bats winged from their roosts in the forest, their bodies taking flight like charred bits of paper.

I didn't go home.

I spread myself flat on top of a grave, my back to the earth while the night swam. The dirt beneath me was chilled, but I scarcely felt it. I didn't want to feel anything.

There'd be no forgiveness, no mending of broken threads. Such things couldn't be restitched.

I hadn't tried taking anything from Heather, her privacy, her love, her life. I wanted none of it. I wanted my *own*. There was no explaining that. She talked too fast and too angrily. Too frantic. Some panic was in her. But I was angry. Raging. My tongue, swollen with venom, hadn't said the right things.

Slumber weighed on my eyelids. Yet a tingle of fear rooted in the base of my skull. I shouldn't have been out there. Something shuffled in the dead underbrush of the woods. I rolled to my side, half expecting to catch sight of a deer or coyote. There was nothing. Only the forest where Heather had disappeared. All at once, the time I'd lain in Potter's Field stretched and removed me from the safety of home. I scurried to my feet and faced east, away from the horizon.

"Heather?" I called.

We needed to get home. Now.

Something howled, something human *screamed* from so close I couldn't tell if it was inside the woods or elsewhere. Every hackle on my neck raised and pulled my skin taut.

I scanned the trees and graves for disturbance. All was calm. All was silent. A tense knot pulled at my gut. With dusk turning black, I couldn't see more than vague outlines. I breathed in . . . breathed out . . . breathed in —

A sweet, rotten scent hit my nose. The same odor had permeated the ground around Rook's boots, my feet, reddened under the sky. I choked on the blood stench, gagging while I clamped my hands over my nose and mouth. I staggered between the grave markers. It was all around me, and yet where? Left by Bart's remains? No, the rain had washed those away. This was *fresher.*

The dead leaves quaked, and a muffled *rustle-rustle-rustle* like dusty bones rubbing together echoed. I watched the woods and stepped back.

My spine pressed into something unmovable, something that shouldn't have been there.

I froze until the tremors came. My hand crept behind me, first through the naked air and then against something warm. Breathing. Something reeking of death.

With a scream, I darted away, but someone grabbed my arm, flinging me to the ground. Blades of grass slipped between my fingers, and I heaved myself forward, half tumbling as my feet snagged on my skirt. Fabric ripped, and again I hit the ground, falling like a baby trying to run before it could walk.

Closer and closer, a shape hulked between the graves. It held something long and snarled, a wig of some kind with stringy hair. It lifted the wig to place it on its head. Then the shape wiped its forehead. Maybe it was the tears in my eyes or moonlight that caught the shine of wetness on its hand, but the shape brought its hand to its nose and sniffed.

It licked its fingers.

Move, Ivy. If you don't move, you're dead.

Mamie's voice spurred me up from the ground. The shape growled, reached inside its cloak, and withdrew a knife, primitive, with a rusted blade.

I ran. My hands wound into my skirt, pulling the torn fabric high so I wouldn't trip. The shape would come and gut me as if I were the mutilated body of a deer after field dressing. Step by burning step, my muscles pried me up the cove to Promise Bridge. It wasn't until I was halfway across that I heard myself scream.

A lantern glimmered in the field. One lantern, then two.

"*Ivy!*" Violet yelled.

I rushed to the glowing stars, wiping tears on my cheeks and the spit collecting between my lips. "Oh, God. V-V-Violet—"

The lanterns came closer, and in the darkness, Violet's shadowed face emerged first and then her sister Dahlia's. Around Dahlia's neck was a scarf like she always wore since being jumped by rollers, but still visible snaking up her jaw were deep pockets of flesh so thin her teeth and tongue shone through her cheek. Her attackers had cornered her in the chemistry lab. Chemicals left horrible scars.

"Shhh." Dahlia wrapped her arms around me. "You're okay."

Violet slid out of her coat and nestled it around my shoulders. "Everyone's been looking for you. Heather said she couldn't find you."

"She lied!" I shouted. "S-she was with me and left! Someone was there, and it was horrible!"

I glanced back to the bridge, to the graveyard of unclaimed dead beyond.

No shape.

No blood smell.

Nothing.

Whimsy was grazing not far from the bridge. Violet walked toward the horse and tugged her mane so she'd follow. My horse nibbled at my shoulder, and, exhausted, I patted her flank.

"Come on," Dahlia murmured. She reached for my hand, stopped when she noticed the dirt under my nails. "We'll get you cleaned up."

We made our way through the field toward a path. The farther from Potter's Field I got, the more I wondered if perhaps I had imagined the shape hoisting that awful wig high, licking its fingers. With my hand in Dahlia's, the dirt ground into my skin, it was real.

Heather had left me there.

My bones hollowed. How could she? How could we be fighting like we never had before? This needed to stop, but how?

I didn't want to forgive. As terrible as it made me feel inside, my fury wanted to abandon her and see how she liked it.

A warning bell rang out across the fields. Throughout the village, old iron bells were mounted on posts. It was an archaic though effective warning system. One bell tolled, and the entire trail lined with bells followed. Violet looked back at her sister and me, the flame in the lantern dancing inside the glass.

"Something's happened," she whispered.

We were close to the horse pasture, and the warning bells chimed all around us. Across the field, hillmen ran with their lanterns. They ran to the horses.

I jerked my hand from Dahlia's and sprinted to the pasture, pushing past the dozen men surrounding the fence. A horse's scream ripped at my ears. Behind the fence, Journey lay on his side in the dirt. Patches of blood painted his blue-gray coat, and his legs scrambled to run, but he had no strength. His mane was gone. In its place was a slick, bloody track. The horse was scalped. His hooves thrashed, unable to get their bearings to hoist him, and he writhed, eyes so wide the whites shone.

The shape in Potter's Field had carried stringy, dark hair.

"Somebody shoot him!"

I didn't know who'd yelled, but others echoed the shout. I twisted round and scanned the faces. Each was a blur, a look of revulsion, and a whispered prayer. Sheriff parted the hillfolk, and I spotted Rook a few paces behind him before I blocked him.

"Thank God you're safe," he said, and held my wrists.

"Don't go any closer," I begged.

"What is it?"

I winced as Journey let out a pained whinny. Rook's jaw slackened. "No."

Gunfire silenced everything, or maybe the ringing in my ears deafened me. Some folks backed off to reveal the pasture. Journey was an unmoving mass. Sheriff stood over the still horse, rifle in hand, and stared at where I stood with Rook.

"I'm sorry, son. There wasn't anything we could do."

For a while, Rook sat with his knees tucked to his chest. He buried his face, but every few moments, he sucked in a deep breath. Someone found my father. He'd been searching for me along with Marsh. I answered Sheriff's questions while my father crossed his arms and paced.

"This is more than some pervert killing animals, Jay," my father blurted out. "My daughter was attacked. She could've been killed!"

Sheriff nodded. "I know, Timothy."

"Oh, shut it, Jay!" Marsh yelled. "We've heard Markle screamin' for years, and you ain't cared to do anything 'bout it till the dogs turned up dead."

A vein in Sheriff's forehead throbbed. "You think I like knowin' he's out there? I was the last person to see him before he ran off, and we tried catching him then. My daddy put down the old laws to keep us inside at night even when folks laughed at him. Maybe I should've kept his laws when I became sheriff. But as of now, I'm puttin' patrols on the roads and layin' down an official curfew. No one goes out after dark."

Rook sniffed and lifted his face from his knees. "I heard the stories, but I never believed he was still out there."

"You don't mess with a madman like Birch Markle," Marsh said.

Sheriff nodded his head in agreement. "I'll send more men. Before he follows his old killin' path. He started with animals, and I don't need him movin' to some pretty girl. Not with May Day a-comin'."

"No," Papa barked. "We ain't doing any May Day."

"Iris took it to council, and I can't argue it or I'm outta my job." Sheriff glanced in the direction of the woods. "Even if I ain't found Birch yet, I know what happened with him and Terra better than anybody in the Glen. You trust anybody else?"

Papa kicked a fence post. "No."

"All right, then. If keeping my head down when the council says they want a May Day is what I gotta do, so be it. May Day's happening, and we'll pray hard Birch Markle stays away."

Papa approached where I sat with Rook and offered me his hand. I waited, not wanting to go but not wanting to linger outside while the death smell worsened, and after a moment, Rook waved me off. Papa hugged me, his broad palm spread across the back of my head. "I'm takin' Ivy home," he said to Sheriff. "My daughter's not gonna be another victim, and you better do something about this before someone else gets hurt. Or worse."

Before Papa ushered me away, I stopped beside Sheriff to ask, "If you find Birch, what'll you do with him?"

His lips pursed. "We'll do what we should've done twenty-five years ago. We'll put an end to his madness."

CHAPTER EIGHT

His sister did what she had to—had Birch hauled down to the storm cellar by some of the young men. Seemed like he was gone, but we was just prayin' he'd never get out. Then he did.

Two days after Journey's death, I sat in a pew in the Glen's church. My family never sat too near the front, always by a window so Papa could look outside during Pastor Galloway's sermon. Pastor wore a troubled expression. Nothing in the church was real ornate like I'd seen in art books—just a plain table and cross on the wall. Dried wheat in some milk cans were all the decoration. Sometimes in fall, when we prayed the harvest would keep us through winter, there were cornstalks bound together, and Heather and I taught the little ones to make crosses from the husks to hang above their beds.

To have faith in the Glen was to know the old ways. Superstition and harvest rituals went back in our blood longer than the body of Christ. Mamie said any pastor preaching to us accepted that we had ways that were unwritten in the Good Book but nevertheless kept us close to God. If God created nature, then reverence for nature was reverence for God. Townies didn't get it, not with their trips to the city to attend the mega church.

Mama reached forward to the pew ahead of ours where Aunt Rue sat with Marsh.

"Where's Heather?" Mama whispered.

Aunt Rue looked over her right shoulder. "She has a stomachache and stayed home."

I didn't believe Heather was sick. At supper last night, we didn't speak, avoiding each other, but she was fine. Distracted and pacing and going between the living room and the door off the kitchen. She wanted out.

She was out now, I was certain. She could fool everyone. But not me.

I glanced across the aisle to the Meriweathers. Rook twirled his glasses around by one of the earpieces. So pale, a gauntness about his jaw, he looked as if he hadn't slept since Journey was killed. At the end of a prayer, Sheriff nudged him to remember to say "Amen."

I was transfixed by his sorrow and, guiltily, the memory of his arms around me and his lips warm on my neck. Part of me knew it was wrong to think of such a thing during church, but it was a comfort through the string of bleak days. Rook peered my way, and I couldn't deny that seeing his fingers uncurl in a gentle wave made my pulse kick higher.

We prayed for the animals. We prayed for Glen kind and folks outside. We prayed for understanding. They were words we prayed each week, yet the resonance chilled me.

Pastor Galloway stepped over to the pulpit. He was older than

Sheriff and Papa, but not nearly as old as Mamie or Rose Connelly or the other granny-women who had imprinted upon his spirit a love of land and God as a child.

"Death is part of living," he began. "What's unacceptable is killin' not for sustenance but perversion. The occurrences in recent days corrupt our land."

"So what do you suggest?" Dale Crenshaw piped up from the congregation.

A hum of voices bristled in the church as families turned to one another to ask and offer suggestions of what to do with the madman in the woods.

"I say we bring the county officers," Dale spoke again. "We need peace 'round here!"

Sheriff remained seated. His wife, Briar, moved to stand, but he stayed her and cleared his throat. "If you follow the curfew, you oughta be safe. Now, Dale, you know as well as everyone else that I've been to the woods myself, searching for Birch Markle."

Flint Denial stood and pointed at Sheriff. "But you ain't found him! You're as bad as your daddy was! Step aside and let in the county cops!"

Some clapping and affirmations went up. Papa rose from his seat and ducked out of the church. Sheriff squeezed past Rook and hurried after Papa. I bunched my hands in my skirt. Violet shot me a sympathetic look as people patted her father's shoulder.

"We can hunt down Birch ourselves! We got rifles!"

"Set out some bear traps and catch 'im that way!"

"We need a different sheriff! Jay's too weak!"

A wild energy mounted in the congregation, one ready to over-throw the order we'd always known. What would happen to Sheriff and the Meriweathers if people no longer trusted him to protect us? What would happen if we brought outsiders to the Glen?

Pastor banged on the pulpit, and the scattering voices drew to a hush. He waited until all eyes were upon him. "What's happenin' here is unnatural and must be stopped. Scripture instructs us, 'You shall not pollute the land in which you live, for blood pollutes the land, and no atonement can be made for the land for the blood that is shed in it, except by the blood of the one who shed it.'"

The dissent in the congregation remained, voices rising up to call for a hunt. I lowered my head and covered my ears to block the sound of madness.

Sunday was our night for dinner guests. I lit the oil lamps and set out dishes for my family and Heather's, along with the Meriweathers. The scent of *arroz con pollo* — chicken roasting until it nearly fell off its bones and rice seasoned with peppers dried the previous year — filled the small house. Briar brought a loaf of friendship bread, the starter for it begun in our families long before the Glen's creation, before the Templetons and Meriweathers left Appalachia, before they left their old country.

It was daunting to have so much history between our clans.

I was setting the table when a hand covered mine. I clutched the silverware tight as I looked Rook over. His eyes were tired, his hair rumpled. He must not have noticed that he'd mismatched the buttons on his shirt. Or he didn't care.

"You still ain't sleepin'," I remarked.

"I've tried," he replied. "Mama went to Granny Connelly to get some valerian root. We'll see if it helps." He motioned toward the silverware I held. "Can I help you finish?"

I divvied out half the settings. We worked with little noise other than the clinks of metal against the stoneware dishes. Even if we didn't speak, if he was tense and exhausted, I still felt an easiness being beside Rook. I didn't have to hide what I felt about him.

The cups on the table were empty. We needed to go out to the well for water. I motioned for him to come with me. Our mothers looked up from preparing a salad of early spring greens — red romaine lettuce and herbs with cheese — and shared a look as we entered the kitchen.

"I hope Jay and the others get back soon," Briar said to my mother. After the accusations at church, Sheriff had tried to show his worth by taking some dogs to the woods along with a few men and lanterns.

"I pray they find *el diablo*," Mama replied. She patted her apron pocket without withdrawing the rosary. "I've never seen the Glen worry so much."

Briar took a deep breath. "It's been worse. Before you came, Luz. I'd always hoped our children wouldn't face something like it themselves."

Her gaze went across the room to where Raven stood on a chair to mix together oil and vinegar for a salad dressing. The little girl had a patchwork fox doll next to the bowl and whispered to him. I hoped she was oblivious to the death that too frequently rattled the warning bells in the fields, silent now, though tense and poised to ring again.

"We gotta get some water," I said, and retrieved a pitcher from the counter.

"Don't be outside long," Mama ordered.

"Take Rook with you," Briar said, a tiny smile playing on her mouth as she winked at Mama.

Rook and I ducked out to the yard. Though sunset had yet to drop the Glen into darkness, torches burned along the fences, and crackles of yellow and orange soared skyward. My eyes watered from the peculiar odor of pinewood and burning fuel. Rook eased the pitcher out of my grip and pressed his palm to my back as I dabbed at my face with my apron.

"M-must be some grit or ash," I murmured.

"Here." His thumb rubbed near the corner of my eye. "That any better?"

Actually, it was.

He walked with me to the field where a water well was constructed from a cylinder of stones piled on top of one another. Several wells lay on Glen land. From the time children were small, they were taught not to play near the inviting red roofs. They weren't pretend houses but dangerous pits. It was easy to fall, easy to drown. Even with the pail and pulley, if someone fell in, getting them out before the water took them was impossible.

"I told Pastor I'm taking up with you," Rook blurted.

My feet froze to the ground. "You what?"

"I needed to get my mind off Journey. If you don't want it—"

"No," I said. "I-I'm surprised, is all."

It wasn't uncommon to go to Pastor Galloway to get his thoughts when young couples came together. For years, granny-women used to be matchmakers. They traced the bloodlines to make sure generations didn't mix too near. They knew the family histories. Sometimes they threw all that out if they saw two people truly in love.

"So now folks'll be watching us," I said.

"They already are, according to Pastor." Rook laughed. He put his arm around me and nudged me closer to his side. "He said it was 'bout time."

I stepped in front of Rook and tipped back my head to study his face. I liked the shape of his lips, the heavy frames of his glasses and how the lenses snatched all the bleeding colors of the sunset. My fingers traced his cheek, his jaw, and he gave a swift twist of his head to catch the tips with his lips. Then he took my hand and turned it over. His mouth was hot as he laid a kiss on my wrist, then another on my forearm, yet another in the crook of my elbow before he placed my arm up on his shoulder to wind it around his neck.

"S-someone might see," I said.

"So?" he asked, half his mouth spreading in a cocky grin.

He kept grinning when our mouths met. I didn't want to close my eyes. The woods weren't far off. Yet the more the kiss grew, the harder it was to keep them open. I gave in to the feeling of flying. Rook's pulse thudded with enough power that I felt it in his chest. Surely, he felt mine. My heart rose just like I did.

A sudden swirl of black wings and caws erupted from the tree line. A murder of crows rushed into the sky and perched upon the houses, the fences, wherever they could find a place to land.

Rook and I pulled apart. "Something spooked them," he said.

Somewhere within the woods, far past the youngest trees at the outer rim and deep where the oldest ones knew secrets, someone lived. I shifted from one foot to the other and wished I had Mamie's shawl to dull the gooseflesh prickling my skin.

"The water," I said.

We hurried to the well. The bucket was tied up. Age and weather had hardened the rope, and the wheel to work the pulley system was rusted. Rook gave several hard tugs to render it loose enough to turn. I stood near him, pivoting to look behind us, to the left, then the right. A crow settled on the peak of the well's roof. In the red haze of sunset, his eye was a dark gem. The edges of his sharp beak opened to reveal a pointed tongue before he gave a loud "*Caw, caw, caw!*"

Three cries from a crow. Not a good omen.

"H-hurry," I urged Rook.

"I'm trying. The rope is stiff. If I go too fast, it's gonna snap and the pail will be gone."

We were being watched.

It didn't come from one side or the other but from all around. Inescapable. It could've been the crows with their wicked eyes. Or maybe it was that dark soul lurking in the woods.

A hound bayed in the distance. Rook stopped lowering the bucket into the well. "Maybe the search party found something."

A second dog joined in the howling, then a chorus of rabid barking lifted from the trees.

Crack!

I jumped, gunfire echoing overhead. The bucket reached the water and banged against the rock walls with a clang before splashing. Rook worked the pulley faster to draw some water, but I kept my eyes on the woods, across the narrow river dividing us from whatever might come running out.

As Rook hoisted the pail from the well, he gasped.

"What is it?" I asked.

Before he answered, the smell hit my nose. Amid the sulfur and iron odor of well water, something tangy mixed in, something rank, decayed.

Inside the pail was a goat's skull with fur and flesh still clinging to its white bones.

Night fell over the Glen. That didn't stop folks from coming out of their homes to ask what Sheriff and his hillmen had uncovered, what they'd shot at in the woods. Rook showed Sheriff the goat's head from the well. Papa took some measurements, a rag tied over his mouth and nose to stop the smell from making him ill.

"What's this, Timothy?" Sheriff asked.

"That goat that'd been decapitated? We got its head," Papa answered. "Birch must've hung on to it till now."

Papa wrapped the skull in a cloth. He'd go down to the bone land to bury it soon. My stomach churned. Why was it dumped in our well? There were plenty others in the Glen. Even leave it in the woods where it'd not be found. Unless Birch wanted it found. A warning, perhaps, not to go looking for him.

"In the woods, there's some kind of camp . . ." I overheard Sheriff tell some folks gathered in the road.

"It looks like Birch has been stealing things from around the Glen and using them to make a home," Flint Denial added. "There were blankets, pillows. He'd taken all kinds of things and strung them through the trees."

"Skirts," another hushed voice caught my ear. "He's watching our girls. Wonder how long he watched Terra before . . ."

If Birch Markle came into the Glen and no one saw him, then he was closer than anyone realized. He took our things. He used them, maybe even stroked them and smelled them, treating them as souvenirs. Perhaps it was what had kept him from killing again. Or it had sated his hunger for only so long and now he was starving.

I hung back, close to my parents and where Rook perched on the slats of a horse fence. A figure with red curls in a long skirt made her way up the road. Heather walked alone, fearless, with her chin up. I navigated through the bodies crowding the path. The torches by the road shed enough light that my cousin saw me coming. She stopped and turned around.

"Wait," I called.

She halted. "What do you want?"

"You weren't in church this morning, and Mama wasn't sure you'd make it to Sunday dinner." I didn't want the conversation to go ugly. I didn't want to be accusatory. Not right away.

"I was sick."

Her cheeks were colored. She looked better than she had in a while. As if the hollowness of worry was somehow filled.

"You ain't sick." The toe of my sneaker kicked the dirt. "Did you skip church to see Milo?"

Her eyebrows drew together, and she balled her hand. Paper crinkled between her fingers. Both of us looked at the small corners of white sticking out from her fist that gave her away.

"What's that?" I asked.

"It's mine, Ivy."

"I want to make sure you're safe."

She pursed her lips. "What does it matter?"

"You're still sneaking out. Sheriff found a hiding place in the woods. It's got all kinds of stuff Birch took from the Glen."

Heather stood on her toes to look around me at the group breaking apart on the road. "Some hiding place in the woods?"

I nodded. "I know you went in there the other day. Did you see anything?"

She shook her head. "Of course not."

Heather sidestepped me and walked closer to the crowd. I ran up alongside her and grabbed her elbow. "You have to stop runnin' like this. You're gonna get hurt."

"I told you before, I don't care. Some things are worth the risk."

"You're gonna tell me some roller boy is worth chancing your life?" I demanded. "Do you know what folks here would say if they knew you'd taken up with someone like him?"

"They ain't gonna find out." She scowled. "Unless *you* say something. Which is why I can't trust you. Not with this. Not with anything. You can be worried all you want, but it changes nothing. I have my life. You have yours."

Heather walked toward the house, where we would paste on false smiles and pretend everything was fine during Sunday dinner. Rook noticed her and then me, his eyebrows above the rims of his glasses. I lowered my face. I didn't want him to see the tears stinging the corners of my eyes, and if I spoke, my voice would crack.

Papa paced near the gate separating our yard from the road. Mama came up behind him and rested her hands on his shoulders. Sheriff dismissed the last of his men and wandered toward my father. "We're gonna find this son of a bitch."

"Why wasn't this place found before?" Papa took off his glasses and squeezed the bridge of his nose. "This is the first time in twenty-five years anyone's found a place where Birch might live. I'm surprised. Nothing more."

"The screams, and every once in a while, some hunter stumbles on a deer carcass that don't look like anything a coyote would do. There's been signs he's there, Timothy," Sheriff countered. "Today we went farther than anyone's been in those woods for years. Even when folks go hunting, it ain't like we gotta go all that far to find deer or ducks. No one *wants* to go in very far. Everybody knows if you go in those woods, there's a chance you ain't coming out."

CHAPTER NINE

Terra MacAvoy was a pretty thing, sweet as strawberries, and gentle, too. Crowning her May Queen was the right thing to do.

On the first of May, mere days after the discovery of Birch's forest lair, each evening haunted by howls from the search dogs, paper cones filled with flowers were hung on all the doors in Rowan's Glen. Ribbons in pale blues, pinks, and yellows twined along the fences, unfurled in gusting wind. A spring storm was coming.

I didn't feel any celebration of life, no virtue and fertility in those bouquets or sprouting from the ground. Fear of death tainted everything. Tales of Birch Markle walked up the chimneys and crept through mouse holes in the walls.

I wore a blue dress of eyelet fabric that had once belonged to Mamie. A woven ivy crown sat upon my head.

Not a queen, a maiden.

I lined up with my parents. Papa's face was pensive, perhaps because his frustration was futile — the festivities were proceeding despite his protests. Whatever his thoughts, they remained unspoken.

Mama fussed with my hair and spread the dark locks across my shoulders while singing in Spanish. Her touch lingered on the acorn necklace. I undid the cord and placed the necklace in my pocket. I'd give it to August later.

"You and Heather still won't speak," she said.

"She's Heather. I'm Ivy," I answered flatly.

In nature, ivy and heather never grew together. They couldn't because ivy liked shade, whereas heather required sun. They did better apart because, side by side, one withered.

The beat of a bass drum, steady and hollow, began down the road and signaled the procession's start. Mama scrambled to gather some long Timothy grass and hand it to my father. She checked over the white and yellow scarves wrapped around her arms to flow behind her, light perpetual. More families in costume, everyone from Coyote Jones in an animal pelt to Iris Crenshaw with purple petals painting her face. The drum's rhythm was louder, and I bounced in place. I wanted it over.

The girls my age led the parade, the drummer behind them. They laughed and scattered flowers. The order of the procession was the maidens followed by the drummer and the youngest children. Others filtered in after, I supposed to keep any rogue children from darting off. We'd walk forward, some dancing, some skipping, all to the field where the May Queen waited.

I picked up a willow basket and sifted through lilies of the valley and ivy leaves. The flowers were fragrant, the leaves fertile green with edges so sharp they might cut. Then I fell into the parade, walking in time with the drum's beat. Close to me was Violet. Her dress was purple with a tiered skirt, and her crown mixed purple and white violets against velvety leaves. When we were little, Violet had begged to play with me. But Heather never let me give my attention to anyone but her. Violet was shy, and Heather was too much to ignore.

Violet smiled. "Of course Heather was voted May Queen."

"Was there any doubt?" I asked with a sigh. "Did you know they couldn't vote for me 'cause of my mama?"

"Stupid rules. You think it'll ever change?" She waved at a pair of young girls in bunny masks and tossed sachets to them. The girls scuttled forward to grab the flowers, giggling, excited. Maybe dreaming they'd one day be crowned May Queen. I wondered if they understood that only one of them would be chosen each year.

"It must be hard to be so close to someone like Heather," Violet mused.

"After a while, it's impossible."

I laid eyes on a little girl wearing a mask of black feathers with silver ribbons streaming through the black. Raven, Rook's younger sister. I waved to her, and my gaze roamed the assembling crowd. I saw a woman with a black eye mask and striped sleeves down her arms and another wearing the mask of a fox with a long coat. The animal faces blurred, the eyes all dark and empty, while human hands clapped. The catcalls and cheers became a barrage of yelps and howls. A ring of sweat beaded under my crown.

Then Rook appeared.

He mounted a fence post high above the road, the stormy sky behind his back. A black cape shaped like wings fluttered, and his face hid behind a dark-feathered mask that came to a pointed, gray beak.

Beside him, a figure wore a gilded mask of a summer sun — August, always at his friend's side.

My neck grew hot, and I halted, nearly tripping Violet, and she linked our arms to pull me forward. "Keep going, Ivy."

I couldn't stop. The crowd fell in place behind the maidens and the drummer. We reached a clearing, a field unused in years, but dried pumpkins littered the grounds, musty gray and riddled with bumps where they rotted. On the side nearest the woods, a man in a blue cloak and jaybird mask was posted, rifle in hand — Sheriff, guarding the tree line.

Heather waited in the field near a massive brush pile. Her red ruffled skirt billowed out around her. Pink blossoms on a fernlike crown topped her curls. Pregnant Aunt Rue beamed under the heat lightning skirting the clouds. Farther back, almost invisible, Mamie stood. So strange to see her away from her room in the attic, away from her octagon window where she watched the Glen's days pass. I hadn't expected her to come. Could it be that she'd finally speak? What would it take to break her quiet? She held a walking staff. The end was covered with knotted cloth, most likely soaked with moonshine, and burned amber flames.

The drumming ceased. Silence. I surveyed the crowd, the animal masks, and elaborate costumes.

Heather drew near and joined my aunt. Mamie handed the torch to Aunt Rue, who passed it to Heather. Applause went up, a roar that rattled my skull. Numbness deadened me from my fingers to my chest, from my toes to my hips, as I watched Heather approach the brush pile. She was so much like one with the fire while she heaved the torch onto the leaves with a *whoosh*. Plumes of smoke streamed toward the sky. The perfume of fire and smoke was so heady, I dizzied, tipping backwards until a hand caught between my shoulders.

"Breathe in through your nose, out through your mouth," my father instructed. "It'll keep you from hyperventilatin'."

I did as he said, and the brain fog lifted. My belly stayed queasy, though I wasn't convinced that was only smoke.

A sack was near Heather's feet. The harvest inside was valued more than all precious metals. It took hours of sifting through remains of last year's harvest to select the best seeds. Heather plunged her hand deep into the sack and withdrew a palm filled with these. She flung out her arm, seeds raining, some picked up by the breeze. The dirt would find the seeds and drag them into darkness. In time, they'd sprout. In time, another harvest would come. But some plants wouldn't grow, strangled by another's roots.

Heather was the May Queen. Beautiful, nurturing, simple.

That was the surface. Beneath were secrets and the desperation to keep them hidden.

The songs were old, from the mountains, and smoke muddied the blue dusk. Amid the banjo and tambourines, the cheer of hillfolk, the sun drowsied. A soft voice settled the noise, Heather's, as her fingers plucked an acoustic guitar. I leaned against a maple tree and closed my eyes. I couldn't stop hearing her.

"Down in a willow garden . . ."

My ivy crown itched, and I reached up to yank it away.

"My true love and me did meet . . ."

I ringed the crown around my forearm and spun it until some ivy split free and drifted to the grass.

"There we sat a-courtin' . . . My true love dropped off to sleep."

Empty bottles piled up. The music and dancing continued, so much dancing. Rook busied himself entertaining Raven and the little ones by being a horse for them to ride. Small girls wove ribbons around the maypole with Heather and Violet leading them, everyone prancing and laughing.

I was apart from it. Not sure where I belonged or wanted to be. I gave a halfhearted wave to Heather accepting embraces and kiss-kisses on her cheeks. Her gaze flicked my way, then a jut of her chin and a spin away. Her skirt rose and fell, the curls in her hair rose and fell, and inside, I fell.

My father stayed back from the hillfolk, and I spotted him with Sheriff at the perimeter. I slipped between the crowd where Violet twirled between August and Jasper Denial until I was away from the celebration. I crouched near a trellis that'd eventually support sugar snap peas if the dead vines wrapping it were any indication.

"They best not've made those bonfires outta peach wood," I heard my papa say.

Sheriff twisted around from his post and tipped his head. "I saw Mamie pickin' over the fire piles at dawn, throwin' out any cursed wood. She carried it to the river for cleansing."

"You see anything out there, Jay?"

"Sun ain't even full set. Woods are wide."

Papa rocked on his heels and scanned the trees, I suspected, for a shift in shadows, a crack of a twig, anything strange. "Some folks are sayin' this is foolery."

"That's the wine talkin'. They're too relaxed and lettin' down their guard," Sheriff replied. "You know, Timothy, this is my job. You try and enjoy May Day."

My father gave Sheriff a pointed look. "Ain't gonna happen."

Sheriff clapped Papa on the shoulder. Something unspoken floated between them, an ether of memory.

A bellow rose up from the woods across the river, beginning low in pitch, then rising to *yip, yip, yip.* It cackled and screamed, a madman's call. The echo chased shivers down my back and arms, my fingers gripping the trellis tighter.

The celebration silenced. The dancing stilled. Only the spit and crackle of bonfires and whipping flames broke the paralysis. Sheriff took his lantern off his post and held it up to shine across the river.

"Some loons, Jay!" someone yelled.

Another dissenter joined in. "And a turkey!"

There was laughter from some gathered, while others shifted and pulled together. It was birds, but what had sent them calling? No one knew what to believe. Who to trust. It was a bad root that spread infection beneath the earth.

"What're you doin'?"

I pivoted to find Violet breathless from dancing. In one hand, she clutched a bottle of blueberry wine, burgundy liquid rolling around inside. She pushed in against the trellis.

"Trying to find somewhere quiet," I explained.

She took a good look at Papa and Sheriff. She smelled of sweet wine. "My mama says Birch Markle is real. She remembers when he killed that girl. Now those dogs and Rook's horse . . . Someone's here."

Someone who used to be here and never quite belonged, according to the stories.

Violet brought the lip of the bottle to her mouth. When she spoke again, a sloshiness mushed her voice. "What'd he look like?"

I peeled away from the trellis, staying by the riverside. The water was reddish, as if bloody and poisoned. Violet handed me the bottle. The sound of wine lolling around the glass curves was tempting, and I drank the thick, berry liquid.

"That bad, huh?" she asked.

"Th-that bad," I answered.

My mouth sour from wine and bonfire smoke, I slumped on the steep peak of the bank, too aware of the celebration. Families roasted chickens, their skin crackling while the herbs rubbed over them burned with an odor like Mamie's medicinal pastes. Our ancestors built fires where they danced, leaped over the flames, and used smoke to send up prayers for a good harvest, prayers for protection of land, animals, and folks.

Mamie and her stories.

I wished I knew the endings.

Violet wobbled. "Dahlia didn't come. She used to be like Heather, you know, outspoken and brave. It was taken from her. Heather ought to be more careful. She don't want to end up like Dahlia."

"Heather don't wanna be told to be careful," I said.

"You girls'll be in trouble if anyone catches you down here."

I caught myself from losing my balance as I contorted to see Jasper Denial and two others from his side of the Glen. The girl was Star, and the boy was named Elm. I didn't share classes with them, and they took the same route to school as Jasper. As such, I didn't know them well.

"Look what I got!" Jasper said as he showed off a crate filled with a half dozen bottles of wine.

Violet poked him in the shoulder. "What'd you do? Sneak 'round and grab bottles from under folks' tables? All I had to do was hit my family's barn and the fermentin' barrels. We got loads of Crenshaw claret, and I didn't make myself into a thief, young Jasper Denial."

She grabbed one of Jasper's stash, tossing it to me. I coiled my hand around the bottleneck. It felt strange to be among a group that wasn't Heather, Rook, and — often enough — August. I looked between them to find Rook, but he was nowhere to be seen.

"Y'all lookin' for the madman in the woods?" Star asked, holding her lantern below her chin to cast eerie shadows across her face.

Elm laughed and elbowed her. "Anybody who says they seen him's a liar."

"You dummy," Violet said, tipping her head toward me. "Consider your company."

I jumped as Star's fingers glided over my shoulder. She stood over me, silhouetted by her gauzy dress and silver-blond hair. Her eyes were dark and sunken, wary as she looked me over. "He's comin' for you, Ivy."

I clambered to my feet and snatched up my wine with a growl. "Jackass."

I left. They laughed behind me, and despite hearing Violet scold them, I wove a path along the river. To get away. Clear my head. Every few steps brought my lips to the bottle. I walked and drank. Walked and drank. Blinking. Drinking. Swimming in my thoughts but not feeling.

Don't go out after dusk. The sky was at dusk.

Don't let yourself be alone. I was alone.

I wheeled around to see how far I'd gone from the May Day celebration. The bonfire leached into the sky behind me, an amber eye against the darkening horizon. Metal clinking against itself — *chink, chink, chink* — caught my ear. I whipped back around and faced Promise Bridge. The wood planks bobbed up and down. Someone had crossed it. Someone I didn't see.

My mouth went dry, and I backed away a step. *Go back. Find the others.*

Someone else found me first. Violet panted as she caught up to me and pressed her clammy palm to my wrist. "Ivy, I'm sorry."

The others were with her, sullen-faced in their lantern light. Jasper nodded. "Just takin' the piss outta you. No harm, right?"

I didn't answer. Promise Bridge's suspension rocked back and forth, enough that Elm noticed it.

"You messin' 'round on the bridge?" he asked.

"Not me," I answered.

Elm and Star started toward Promise Bridge, and Jasper trailed after them, leaving Violet and me on the riverbank. She called, "Where are ya goin'?"

"To find Birch Markle!" Star replied. "That's what Ivy wants us to believe she saw, right? So let's get him!"

The lanterns Elm and Star carried were ghost lights glowing across the bridge, and from within the woods, more strange calls echoed on the wind. Violet clutched my hand as we stumbled after the others. They'd picked up their speed, running now, wild as they hunted a monster. The bridge rattled beneath my feet, and I clutched the chains to steady my spinning head. No matter how fast or slow I moved, a sensation built inside my skull like I might pitch into the water below.

Violet let go of me. "We gotta hurry or we'll lose them. We can't be caught in the woods by ourselves."

I grabbed the post at the bridge's end. My mouth, dry not minutes before, was now tangy. "I'm gonna be sick."

Violet hedged as the lights veered to the woods. "C'mon, Ivy. You gotta keep movin'. We can't lose them."

I pulled myself up from hunching over, sweat above my lips. I shouldn't have drunk so much. The others still carried wine along with their lanterns, and their laughter resounded from within the woods. Violet linked her arm with mine to hurry me along. The nausea let up after a bit, and I trudged down the path where Potter's Field spread out under the wasted light of dusk.

No one wanted this land, Ivy girl, Mamie once said. *The unknowns return to dust in this here place. Tuberculosis and influenza* patients, prisoners rottin' away in cells. Folks who died alone with no one willing to claim their remains. Folks put 'em in pine boxes with only crossed arms and corpse money on their dead eyes. But the hillmen bought the land cheap, coaxed crops to grow from the clean side of the river there, and pretended it was better than the rest of the land. There ain't any doin' away with that boneyard. We don't speak of it, but everyone 'round here knows we're the undertakers of the unclaimed.

During daylight, the graveyard inspired a hollow sobriety. But at latest dusk, the feeling of Potter's Field was of tremendous loss, not of life, because all things died, but rather of the people of whom not even a memory remained.

"Violet, where are you?" Star called.

"We're comin'!" she replied so loud and close that my ear ached. Her step quickened, and I had to keep up or risk being alone in the woods.

"Someone's here!" Elm yelled.

We veered toward his shout. Crispy leaves blanketed the ground, and Violet and I ran together deep into the woods, a place where there was no trail. Running, running. We trusted the dim glow of lanterns ahead until we caught up. There, standing amid tree trunks and scrubby bushes, the others stared out from dark eyes and pasty faces. They weren't laughing now. The boys, who carried knives when working out in fields, had them drawn. Star raised her lantern, and her voice trembled. "We found him."

In the middle of the cluster was a tall shape in hooded rags with arms surrendered to the sky.

"Oh, my God." Violet broke away from me and drew closer to Jasper.

I crept along the clearing, using the bordering trees for support. My head rolled back to look above where the canopy of branches and leaves was strung with fabric, a web of paisleys and plaids, velvet and burlap, all knotted together. Skirts of Glen girls, remnant pieces from clothing loomed across the branches, haunting to see. Twine coiled around pieces of metal — spoons, gardening tools, knives — and tied around the webs to clink against each other.

It was a collection.

My eyes parched as if I'd stared too long at a fire. There was so much to see. Someone had made this place into a curious home. This was the place Sheriff and his men had found, the place where they'd set up a stakeout and never found another sign of Birch. Maybe he had other homes deeper in the woods, and God only knew what he kept there. But he was here now.

"Monster!" Star shrieked and pointed.

The shape was tall, taller than anyone else in the cluster, but he was also slender, with long, knobby digits for fingers and hanks of dirty hair creeping from his hood.

Birch Markle, the madman in the woods.

Jasper narrowed his eyes and flexed his grip on his knife. "Don't run, or when we catch you, we'll slit you in half."

Yet Birch bolted through the woods. Violet whipped back around to grab me while I struggled to hold my footing against the tidal wave of long hair and skirt and shouts of "Monster!" from her and the others.

"Vi," I hollered over the yells, "st-stop! This is insanity!"

"He's the mad one, not us," she said. "We'll catch him, cut him up to feed the pigs, and no one'll be afraid again."

There was murder in Violet's voice, a swept-upness. This chaos had to stop. Chasing him down and whatever else they had planned wouldn't change what he'd done.

I yanked my arm from Violet's hold and charged back the way I prayed I'd come into the forest. I was in so far I wasn't sure I'd know my way out during full day, let alone half night. My vision was hazy, my steps sloppy. I ran faster, then crashed against someone barreling along the path. My backside thumped the earth, and I lay motionless, everything around me spinning so I was uncertain of down from up.

"Ivy?"

Rook. He was close, but I couldn't find him to focus.

His skin was rough as he took my wrist. He held a lantern. "I was by the riverside and heard noise."

"They're chasing him," I said, breathing heavily.

"Who?"

"Birch Markle. They found him in the woods!"

Rook yanked me to my feet. "Show me where."

I waved in the direction from where I'd come. The movement left me hanging on his vest, hoping not to fall.

"You're drunk. You should go home."

"Not until we stop them," I said. "Come, quick!"

With a growl, Rook dragged me down the path. The swell of dead leaves rolled with the wind. The *ting-ting-ting* of broken glass wind chimes and old spoons swaying above broke the silence. Ahead, there was a glow.

"There," I told Rook. "Follow that light."

Birch Markle could've killed me in Potter's Field. He didn't. The others could kill him now, but I wanted him to atone for what he'd done. He couldn't be punished if dead.

The others' lanterns grew brighter until we reached a gap in the trees where a body lay on the ground, a rock near his side. His arms were wrapped around his head as if he tried to block a hit. Near the front of the cluster, Violet scrambled forth to pick up a stone.

"Stop!" Rook ordered.

Violet glared at him before her arm arced back. The stone sailed the distance to thud against the cloaked shape's hip. Jasper held his knife. Elm and Star threw what they could — rocks, empty wine bottles, sticks. Maybe because of the dark, maybe because they'd been drinking, the majority of blows missed their target.

Birch lay still on the ground.

"You can't kill him," Rook shouted.

"The hell we can't," Jasper replied. "Comin' in the Glen, killin' those animals, attackin' Ivy. We ain't afraid no more. And where were you? Some sheriff you'll make someday."

Rook shoved Jasper. "Fuck you!"

The throwing slowed as Rook put himself between the others and Birch. My skin was too tight as I stared at the hand with knuckles scraped raw that crept out from the cloak. Rook wound his fingers into the hood covering Birch's head and yanked it back to reveal dirty blond hair stained with blood.

Milo.

CHAPTER TEN

It's said there weren't no animal Terra couldn't tame. By the time Birch Markle got to her, he was more animal than human, but he wasn't one to be tamed.

Lemons and thyme scented the Meriweathers' kitchen. The lemons hung from a potted dwarf tree, and bundles of thyme and other herbs dried on a hook were suspended from the ceiling. Neither fragrance masked the antiseptic odor of iodine wafting from the room where Milo Entwhistle lay on the coffee table.

Mamie told me living rooms were once known as death rooms, back when funerals were a home matter. After mortuaries came into fashion, there was no need for keeping bodies on ice at home, and the death room was rechristened the living room.

Rook had convinced Violet and the others they were wrong about Milo. He was just a roller boy from the trailer park. We shared classes at school. Birch Markle was somewhere else, but that fear from a collective childhood nightmare nearly got Milo killed. Until the others scattered, terrified because of what they'd done, I whispered in Milo's ear to play dead.

Because I wanted to know why he'd entered the Glen.

Because I thought him many things, a roller, a dealer, maybe a killer.

Because he'd come for Heather in the woods.

I ran my thumb around my empty mug's rim, the second tea I'd guzzled to heal my wine headache. My brain clanged against my skull like driving nails through a horseshoe.

Rook joined me in the kitchen. He unclipped his suspenders before fidgeting with his shirt buttons, a swift glance my way before continuing to unbutton. He tossed aside the black fabric and his undershirt before grabbing a fresh undershirt from a wicker basket of folded clothes. I retrieved the shirts, untangling the crumpled fabric to find it wet. My fingers were red. "Were you hurt?" I asked.

He fixed his clean undershirt and replaced his suspenders. "No."

"But there's blood."

He pushed his fingers back through his hair, loosening the dark strands until a few fell across his brow. "Blood ain't unusual 'round here. I got into some when I stopped the others from beatin' that guy."

I didn't know what to say. Milo had left both our hands red.

Rook opened the wood stove and tossed in another log. The nights remained on the cool side of pleasant, and it'd be a few weeks yet before we could let the night fires turn to ash.

"You think Milo killed those dogs? Journey?" he asked.

"*They* think he did," I replied.

"That doesn't tell me what *you* think."

"What I think don't matter," I said.

"Matters to me." Rook approached me, thumbing the collar of my dress. "Where's your acorn necklace?"

"My pocket. August gave it to me last week, and I plan on giving it back to him. It ain't right to wear it if we're together."

"I made that necklace," Rook said.

"You?"

He gave me a weak smile. "You were mad at me, so August told me he'd give it to you. He was supposed to tell you." His brow knotted. "Why'd he let you think he made it?"

I shrugged. Anything I said risked making Rook mad. I didn't want any more anger.

"It wasn't right of him to let you think it was his gift," he muttered.

Maybe August would've told me the truth if I hadn't seen dead Heather with a smile slashed into her face.

"Here," I said, and fished the necklace from my skirt pocket. "You put it on me." Rook swept my hair aside, retying my necklace, and when he finished, he seemed calmer.

Then a scream echoed from the neighboring room. I jumped and darted for the door. I reached it first, only for Rook's hand to cover mine on the doorknob. Fingers warm on top, metal cold beneath. His breath was against my neck.

"Open it a crack," he whispered.

The doorknob hitched, the hinges hummed, but Sheriff and Papa were too busy to notice. Milo yowled again. He was bare but for his jeans begging to slither off his bony hips. His skin glowed under the light, purpling bruises near his left eye. A gash crusted on his lower lip. Sheriff pushed him down on the table while Papa examined

Milo's forearm, which was swollen and bluish-red where blood had flooded the tissue.

"You got a fractured ulna, boy." Papa traced his finger near Milo's wrist. "Broke right here. You also got some radial dislocation."

"You sure?" Milo thrashed against my father. "Ain't like you took any x-ray."

"Doc might work on animals, but he knows when a bone's off-kilter," Sheriff said, "so I suggest you calm your spirits and hold tight."

Milo's eyes were huge, and the one was such a mess it'd gone red to the blue of his iris.

"We got a radio and can patch in a call to your folks. There's a truck to drive you to the hospital," Papa offered.

"No parents, and my brother and sister are busy. If you're a doctor, fix it. Pop it back in and slap on a cast. I'll find a way to pay you back. Swear on it." His tongue slicked over the blood on his lip. "I'll muck stalls, plant crops, whatever you need. Just no more bills."

Papa set down Milo's arm and pulled Sheriff by where Rook and I were eavesdropping. "The boy needs help, Jay. The right thing would be to haul him to the hospital."

"It'll bring questions here, Timothy."

Papa sighed. "I'll patch him all right, but he'll get aftercare if he's smart. Just give me a hand with this and pray he doesn't throw a blood clot."

Papa started back to the coffee table, and Sheriff lagged a step behind and muttered, "Lord have mercy. This idea's dumber than a box of shit."

Milo poked his broken forearm, cocking his head with the fascination of a kid coming across roadkill.

"It's kinda gone numb," he said.

"That's shock," Papa explained. "You oughta go to the hospital."

"No. Damn. Hospitals."

Papa picked up Milo's shirt from the floor. "You want a cloth to bite? This is gonna hurt."

Sheriff cracked his knuckles and positioned himself behind Milo, hands on his shoulders. Milo studied Papa manipulating his forearm. Papa paused over a silver ring on his pinkie. He slipped it off and placed it in his veterinary bag. "Your finger's swelling. Should the ring cut off the blood, you don't care to lose your finger or that ring. What's your name?"

"I didn't say," Milo answered.

CRACK!

A groan twisted Milo's face, and blood dripped down his chin from the gash in his lip. I clutched the door frame, ripples of disgust running through me as the bones inside his body ground together.

"Hold him tight," Papa ordered. Sheriff adjusted his grip. Papa settled his fingers around Milo's wrist. "When I was eighteen, I was a missionary in Mexico. A buildin' collapsed, no doctors for miles. This one fellow's hip dislocated. It bulged, stretchin' his skin all shiny. Man alive, he was screamin'.

"Anyway, this girl — didn't speak a lick of English — begged me to help, said he was her brother. My granddaddy was what old-timers called a bonesetter, and I remember seeing him piece back together a hillman trampled by horses. So I did what he did. This fellow's hip was fixed, and the girl was so grateful she came home with me. The next day, her daddy said I'd married her."

Milo gave a good-humored laugh, then came a swift jerk of Papa's hands.

POP!

The only time I'd heard that noise before was a wet June when Heather unearthed a raccoon skull from the riverbank. It was squelched down in the muck, and once a bit of air got inside, it uncorked and flew into the air. She'd caught it in her slippery hands. She'd laughed when she'd done it, too.

Milo's face reddened, but he sniffed back what had to be mind-bending pain. He spied me and Rook playing ghost by the doorway. "I see you back there."

The door rocked open. My steps plodded against on the floor. I'd forgotten about the crown adorning my head, now stuck with dry grass and forest leaves.

"You," Milo said, "I know you."

"Know's a relative term," Rook muttered.

"How'd I guess I'd bump into the likes of you again?" Milo could've been more brazen than brains, or so hurt that adrenaline talked to Rook for him; yet he struck me as more likely putting on a show of false bravado. The wiggle of the coffee table's legs as he shook gave him away.

"You got a problem with my boy?" Sheriff asked.

"No, sir. We've just seen each other 'round."

Rook settled back in his boots, face blank, and I wasn't giving up what I knew of Milo.

"Why are you here?" Sheriff asked.

Milo's breath wheezed. "'Cause I like to party. Didn't know the inbreds would stone me half to death."

"Oh, you're plenty used to being stoned," Rook said. "Woods ain't a long walk from here. You're welcome to go back."

Milo attempted to straighten his spine, gritting his teeth. He switched his attention to me. "Why'd you help me?"

"M-m-murderin' folks is wrong. They'd have killed you."

In the woods, with the lanterns and loomed fabric above, the others would've pounded him with their stones, wine bottles, whatever they found. I thought it better to catch the monster alive than destroy it.

Yet was that monster Milo?

"Who told you there'd be a party?" Sheriff asked.

Heather.

"Around school. People talk," Milo replied. "I had to wear that getup to blend in. You know what's said 'bout y'all. I had to find out how much is true. Plenty, it seems."

I assumed he was referring to the raggedy brown cloak, now splattered with blood, that hung over the back of one of the Meriweathers' kitchen chairs.

"Hey, now," Sheriff cut in. "You've gotten some kindness from the good folks of the Glen. Don't be a peckerhead."

"Good folks of the Glen." Milo snorted and shoved off from the coffee table and not without limping or letting loose a pained moan. He lifted his shirt off the chair with his good arm and slipped it over his head with a hiss. "Don't think I haven't noticed your lawman's star. You gonna do anything about how your good folks jumped me?"

"We deal with our own kind."

With his shirt all cockeyed, Milo stared me down, his good arm roaming his pockets until he found a squashed pack of cigarettes. "You be careful out there, Ivy."

My belly gave a warning quiver. Inside, I writhed under the intensity of his watch. Somehow, I'd find out what went on between him and Heather.

"Let's get you to the clinic, get your arm in a cast," Papa intervened.

"Mind if I have a smoke?" Milo asked.

Sheriff nodded. "Stay close to the house. For safety."

Milo's gait was creaky, the walk of battered bones. There were bells rigged up by the front door, and they sang out even after the door slammed behind the boy. The lantern outside the door lit up his blondest hair while streams of smoke traveled past the window.

"You think he'll go to the county police?" I asked.

"Nah, bunch of hot air, that one," Sheriff said.

Papa closed his veterinary bag. "Don't be so sure, Jay. Folks always know more than they let on."

I headed back to the kitchen. My thoughts were a sticky web of dead dogs, dead girls, skirts loomed through trees, and Milo's bloody eye; fists clutching rocks, Heather. I felt sick and didn't want to empty my stomach on the Meriweathers' floor. I shoved open the back door to breathe air perfumed by May Day.

I smelled cigarette smoke. Milo sat with his back against the fence and his bad arm tight across his chest while his other hand brought a cigarette to his lips. Rook motioned for Milo to get up and said, "You best get that arm fixed up. You don't want to be caught here if folks are thinkin' you're that devil in the woods."

Milo stood and closed the space between himself and Rook. "Shame I ain't, huh? Then you might have a real reason to hate me."

"I don't hate you," Rook said. "Just hard to see where we have common ground."

Milo flicked some ashes to the dirt. "I know y'all think I'm shit, but I got reasons to be here."

Her name spun through my mind, a tornado of upset and hurt.

"Heather?" I asked.

Milo's mouth twitched. "No matter what you think about me, we ain't that different."

The back door of the Meriweathers' house opened, and Papa exited with his bag. He must've noticed the tension between Rook and Milo, how they stood with nothing remotely close to friendship between them, and approached to ease back Rook with a hand to his chest.

"None of that," Papa said. "I don't care what your history is, but this fellow needs a cast, and I'm giving it to him. Pastor says we look out for our neighbor, and our neighbor's more than who lives next door, Rook."

Rook bowed his head, mumbling, "Yes, Dr. Timothy."

Papa opened the gate in the Meriweathers' fence and stepped out to the road. Milo followed behind him, and I looked on for a bit as they headed off toward the clinic. As a veterinarian, Papa interacted with folks outside the Glen more than most. When I was at the clinic, I shied away from outsiders, focusing on the animals they brought for care. Listening to Milo, watching his pain and anger and resignation, I couldn't help but feel that tug in my chest, wondering why Heather was drawn to him, why she took such risks for him.

The black sky went on forever. Sounds in the distance of the May Day celebration chimed across the fields. Rook ventured over to his greenhouse that harbored fragile seedlings. A burn pile of belladonna was drying on the ground. It seemed no matter how it was torn, the weed was too resilient to die.

"We shouldn't stay out here long," Rook said, and dragged over a crate. I sat. I wished to smother away the sadness and pretend he and I were outside on the first night of May with no other fears than the strange shapes the fire from the torches cast across our faces.

The wind blew the tattered clothes of the scarecrows, shaking the bells strewn along the fences. The berm of forest rose in the distance. Something squeaked as it flapped overhead, a bat circling, once, twice, a third time.

Bats flyin' a circle thrice brings luck that ain't nice, Mamie once said.

We weren't alone. Others ran toward us.

"Rook?" I pointed. Closer and closer, a girl and a boy ran. I recognized Violet's blond hair and her purple dress. She was whimpering.

"Vi!" Rook climbed over the fence to hit the road on the other side. Violet's crying stilted with her every footfall. I ran at her, grabbed her wrists to pull her close, and held her.

August's and Rook's faces spiraled tighter, and in the center, my body pressed against Violet's shivering frame. She gripped a tattered crown of dried flowers. Heather flowers.

"P-please, Vi," I begged. "Where's Heather?"

"We don't know," she answered with a sniff. "No one can find her."

I reached for the crown. The pink blooms were all wrong, flattened and sparse, even for ones dried and used by the granny-women. Strands of red hair clung to the crown.

As if ripped from Heather's head.

CHAPTER ELEVEN

It wasn't until the mornin' after the May Day festival that folks noticed Terra ain't come home.

The hounds' baying was constant. They were the dogs we tried so hard to keep safe, sent now to track and hunt. Aunt Rue needed a sedating tea brewed of chamomile, gingerroot, and herbs that wouldn't bring on the baby a month too soon. My duty was to select items belonging to Heather to give the dogs her scent.

I'd have told the dogs my cousin smelled of lavender soap and she dabbed rosemary oil behind her ears. Dogs didn't understand those things. Their noses knew body chemistry, every miniature galaxy within our cells. They knew when someone was dead or alive.

"Choose cloth," Sheriff had instructed. "It holds the body's oils, and the dogs'll get the best of her smell. Hair's good, too."

Heather's broomstick skirts were twisted around wooden dowels and arranged in a rainbow. Her blouses and vests, each echoing some memory of her, were ordered in her bedroom closet. As I picked through the fabric, something fluttered to the floor, a paper from a crafter in the Glen. The family made stationery and journals for the farmer's market. The note was velvety, as if unfolded and refolded numerous times, and I read the date heading the page, January 4, this year:

Dear M,

    I'll never betray you. Don't you trust me? You can tell me your secrets. You know how I feel, how I think you are brave, strong, and so much more than where you live. Where you're from.

    I'm not only a Glen girl. I'm your girl.

    Why can't you believe me? Do you know what I do when I'm all alone? I think about you. I think about that cigarette on your lips I want to kiss. I think about your messy hair and your lean body. I remember the taste of you, wanting more, and I wish what I give myself was as much as what you give me.

    You can trust me. I trust you.

    Is it crazy to say I love you?

    — H

A few lines down, a different handwriting replied:

My H,

    I trust you. I trust you more than I trust anyone. I've never been closer to anyone. I can't say why. But when we're together, I want to tell you everything. It's right there. I want to give in. I'm learning to give. To you.

    — M

I refolded Heather's love letter.

She'd been seeing Milo far longer than either of them let on. But was that all they hid? How deep did their secrets run?

My thoughts were unsure of too much, and I numbed myself to find something to bring to Sheriff. I rummaged through her drawer and selected her black gauze shirt and the red curls knotted in her bone comb, but the note remained tucked inside my camisole, hidden beside my heart. I left the door to her bedroom open, sunrise poking through the patchwork curtains. She'd be back. She *had* to come back.

I stood on the bank all day while the dogs snuffled the river water, their paws splashing. They ran across fields and snooped around the stable. Promise Bridge continued to swing even after the dogs crisscrossed it and barreled over to Potter's Field. They tracked her smell to the woods, to the place where Birch had made his home of girl skirts and old spoons, but then her scent was gone. They searched for blood and came up with nothing. Heather had vanished.

I clutched the shawl around my shoulders. I watched from my vantage point on the shore, until northern winds brought a chill and the earth sparkled with mist. By dusk, an owl roosted somewhere in the trees and sang its darkening elegy.

Hoo . . . Hoo . . .

Who . . . Who . . .

"I brought you coffee," Rook said, and held out a thermos. "I added cream and honey, the way you like it."

He uncapped the thermos and poured me a steaming cup.

The heat soothed the stiffness in my joints from standing in one place for so long.

"Did you tell my pops about Heather sneaking around?" he asked.

"She's already so furious that I betrayed her," I said, setting down the coffee. "If I do it again —"

"Ivy, that don't matter if it gets her found."

"She'll never speak to me again."

Who . . . Who . . . the owl wondered of the clouds. *Her . . . Her . . .*

Rook pulled off his glasses and rubbed his eyes. His fingers nudged mine, and I loosened my hand so ours could twine together. He said softly, "She'll forgive you."

One of the hounds barked and barreled back into the river, the Sheriff's hillman barely able to hold the tether and falling face first in the water.

"P-please, Rook," I pleaded. "Don't tell Sheriff Heather's secrets."

"I can't lie to him," he protested and set down the thermos.

I grabbed his other hand and brought both of them to my cheeks so that his forefingers traced my lips. His thumbs drew a heart beginning with the crescents under my eyes and ran down to my chin.

"Help me," I pleaded.

"How?"

"Help me find her. I need to make things right. I didn't have that chance before she disappeared, and . . ."

My knees gave. Rook dropped his hands to my shoulders and tugged me against him. Keeping me from falling.

She was gone.

I'm not letting you be my shadow anymore.

She could've run away.

Get a life.

The crown was hers. She could've pulled it off.

You can't have mine.

Heather had once trusted me with everything. I didn't know why that had changed, what changed in her, in me. She kept so much to herself and scattered crumbs of half-truths.

Rook embraced me, his lips against my forehead, his nose touching the part in my hair. My fingers treaded his suspenders, along the planes of his back muscles. His shirt buttons embossed my skin. The fabric was wet where my tears had pooled between my cheek and his chest, but he held me tight, no matter how long the cries shuddered my back.

"I'll do anything to help," he promised.

I lifted my face. "Even keeping some things from your dad?"

A slow nod. "Yeah, but if we don't get anywhere, I gotta tell him."

I wasn't alone.

Knowing Rook would help, even with Heather missing and the chasm her absence created, made the hollow not seem so bottomless. It was dark and cold, but Rook was down there as well.

His lips skimmed across mine, only for a heartbeat.

A group of hillfolk, including August, were searching the field with a hound. August wore a stony expression and raised his hand in a wave. I shooed Rook over to his friend while I reached for the thermos and poured myself more coffee. The moment I unscrewed the lid, the clouds shifted, allowing the scarlet haze of sunset to bleed across the desolate land. Something metal glinted near the river.

Rook and August didn't notice how I inched down the shore to the twinging spark. The hound up near August's group howled, some odor on the wind tickling his nose. He lurched hard to the left and started down the embankment. I had only a minute to seek out the metal winking against the spoke of light before the group lumbered my way.

"What is it?" someone yelled as the dog scratched at a dirt patch fifteen yards up from me.

"Can't tell," the hound's handler called. "Get Sheriff. We got something. Boomer's digging hard."

I sifted through clods of dirt and grass until I unearthed a metal chain with a rusted nut. Folks must've trampled it into the ground.

The dog barked and whined as his claws exhumed some secret. The hillmen stood around, anticipating Boomer's find. Rook claimed a position at the base of the group, vacillating between the search and where I unstrung the chain from the mud.

"Boomer, move," August said, and eased aside the hound. He knelt and brushed the ground before holding up a thick string. A piece of red thread. "This is Heather's! I've seen her wear it!"

I bit back a slug of bile. Mama and the red threads our family wore. They were supposed to keep us safe.

I thrust the thoughts from my mind and picked harder at the earth. Rook knelt by me now and helped me wipe away dirt. Link by link, I scraped off the soil and bits of grass until I uncovered a necklace with charms and treasures made from relics people had discarded or lost. It was ugly and enchanting. Heather's necklace.

A lump swelled in my throat. "You see what I have?"

Rook's lips tucked together, his glance flicking to August. My fingers wound the chain, looping around each nut, each tarnished pendant that Heather adored. I'd counted them, was with her when she took things from the earth and made them special. Some charms were missing, mostly rocks she'd turned into jewelry, the green glass circle with her birthday. My hands quaked, the links trembling against each other with a soft jingle. *She never took it off.*

CHAPTER TWELVE

Oh, they searched for Terra. Everybody knew it was a right shame. Then she was found on the riverbed, half sunken in mud, the swamp grass ready to take her.

The next few days were a haze, that silvery part of the mind plunging me underwater. It felt like hours before surfacing. My skin was heavy, my clothes weights that made it impossible to lift my arms or move my legs. Since Heather had abandoned me in Potter's Field, I'd only remembered to breathe. I hadn't yet climbed out. Without her, I couldn't.

A metal pail hung from a willow near Milo's trailer, clattering against the tree in the wind. It didn't bang with a hollow noise. Something was inside. Probably so Milo could leave out weed and get paid. Beside the trailer was a carport housing an old truck and a chicken run. A half dozen hens pecked bits of corn, and some fluffy chicks waddled among their mothers. I reached for a chick, coddling it in my hands to enjoy its downiness.

"What the hell are you doin'?"

Milo stretched on the steps and dumped what looked like needles into the BIOHAZARD bin by the door. On his hand without a cast, he wore a latex glove, which he snapped off and placed in the bin.

"Pettin' a chick," I said.

He half smiled. "Ivy, hey. Thought you were this hippie broad who tries to free our chickens, tells them to 'Fly away, pretty birds,' and I'm like, 'They don't fly!'"

He withdrew a tin of lip oil from his pocket, one of the products Aunt Rue sold in the market.

"Heather gave that to you," I remarked.

He nodded. "She said this'd help. People ain't usually so nice to us."

I set down the chick, shamed. Judgments came so fast. I lived that, yet had made assumptions about him.

Milo held up his arm with the cast, which had grown dingy over the past few days. "Your daddy's the vet who patched up my arm. He's got my ring, which I'd like back. Your family's got good folks."

"We try."

Milo drew a cigarette from a pack in his shirt pocket, and put one to his lips. With his good hand, he lit it, taking a long draw. Something was off about him. His body didn't hang with his usual jingle-jangle, and his face was drawn, more so with the fading bruises on his cheek.

I set the chick into its run and unclipped Heather's necklace. "You know what this is. Some charms are gone. Where are they?"

He reached for the necklace, but I yanked it back before he grabbed hold. His fingers brushed mine and he laughed. "You're adorable."

I looked over my shoulder at the gate in the fencing surrounding the trailer park. Rook waited there, plucking at some green vines.

"Touch me again, and you'll learn whether what you've heard about the Glen is true," I said.

Milo hoisted up his jeans to his waist instead of letting them fall so low that any farther would've been indecent. "All right. Let's have ourselves a talk. Go inside. Him, too. I ain't havin' you weirdoes hanging outside my door."

I entered Milo's trailer with Rook close behind. The front room was claustrophobic, with an air mattress on the floor. The blankets were neat and pulled tight, pillows fluffed. There were two baskets of folded clothing, one with some items I recognized as Milo's, and the other I guessed was his sister's, given the black lace bra on top. The floor was waxed, and the spartan furniture was dust-free.

A girl a few inches shy of Milo's height and waif-thin, maybe a year or two older, swaggered into the front room. I barely remembered her from school before she dropped out. Her pants were leather and her shirt a halter under black fishnet. A blue star tattoo marked her thumb. Save for heaps of mascara and matte red lipstick, her pale eyes and pouty mouth matched Milo's.

"What are they doing here?" she asked, her tone not at all friendly.

"Came to talk about Heather, I reckon," Milo said.

She wandered to an antique rolltop desk and stuffed some bags of green herbs into a shoulder bag. She snorted. "So, Ivy, what'd Heather tell you 'bout us?"

"N-nothing," I blurted. "How'd you know my name?"

"Heather talked about you, told us lots of things." She maneuvered around me in the small room and stopped, taking hold of Heather's necklace. Her brow furrowed. "Why are *you* wearing this?"

"Heather's gone," Rook said.

Milo raised his head from his pillow on the air mattress. "Gone?"

"She's been missing since May Day," I explained. I hadn't been in school to tell him, but he must have noticed her absence. "I know Milo's . . . close to her, so if anybody knows where she's at, I figure it's him."

The girl dropped the necklace. "My brother don't know where she went."

"What about you?" Rook asked.

"There ain't anything 'bout me." She tucked her bright orange hair with its dark roots behind her ear and bent over to pick up some barn boots, one with a scuffed toe. The boots I'd seen in the stable when everything with Heather changed. No wonder I'd been mistaken — they were the same kind as Rook's boots.

"Milo, I'm borrowing your shoes," the girl said. "I gotta sell some bags to pay for last night." She pushed open the screen door and pointed at her brother. "Don't do anything dumb."

She headed outside, boots clomping loudly, and went to feed the chickens.

Milo's gaze shifted from his sister to Rook and me, studying the gap between our bodies, how it narrowed, the way Rook's hand rested on my shoulder. "Ah, so you're a thing."

"What about you and Heather?" I asked. "Your sister's gone, if that's what's holdin' you back."

Milo's hand covered his mouth. I wondered if he thought about kissing Heather.

"Emmie knows all about Heather. She came here a lot." His face took a sad shadow. "Heather needed a place she felt safe."

His words stung. Even with Birch Markle's screams and the animals dying, I still considered the Glen safe. Though I planned to attend college, maybe be a veterinarian like Papa or study art, I'd never leave, not forever. I needed the fields and horses, the harvests and quiet, because the Glen was my *home*. To Heather, it was a trap.

"Why were you in the woods on May Day?" Rook asked.

"Heather wanted to meet me there." Milo ran a finger along his cast's edge. "She wanted out."

My brow knotted. "What do you mean, 'out'?"

"She was gonna run away, Ivy." He shook his head. "Maybe that's what she did."

But where'd she go if not with Milo? She bared her soul to him, shared secrets with him. I went to Rook when I was troubled. It stood to reason Heather did the same if she was in love with this scarecrow-bodied boy.

"So is she here?" Rook asked. "Are you hidin' her?"

He moved toward the hallway and glanced at the other rooms. If a door creaked, a foot fell daintily against the floor, all this would be over. If Heather came out from wherever she was.

Milo pushed back his shaggy hair. "You heard Emmie. I don't know anything. I figured Heather's plans went out the window when I got attacked. Guess she ran while she could. I hope she turns up. But she's scared."

"Of what?" I asked. Heather, who seemed so fearless, was frightened?

"She couldn't tell—" Milo cut himself.

I followed his gaze to the screen door where Emmie stood scowling, her jaw set hard. Who knew how long she'd been listening?

"I'll be back," Milo said, and got up to join his sister.

From the window, I watched Emmie pull him out of earshot. Rook walked over to a bookcase and scanned the titles, which left me to nose around for a bathroom. After I finished, I noted the closed doors in the hallway. My knuckles gave a soft rap against one.

"Heather? You in there?" I asked hopefully.

From within the room, someone coughed. I tested the knob to find the door unlocked and eased it open. The room was dark, but a smell of antiseptic and sickness hit my nose so hard I covered my nose. If Heather was in here, she was either sick or—I switched on a dim light.

A skeletal body lay on a hospital-style bed. My back went rigid. She'd not been gone long, but what if she'd been attacked, forced to stay here? How long could she be held hostage before her body gave out? She'd written of secrets in her letter. How far would Milo go to keep those secrets hidden?

I inched closer. An arm colored decomposing yellow and webbed with bruises stuck out from the sheets. An IV pole was beside the bed. I rounded the edge, and all the breath left my lungs.

Not Heather.

A young man, one who was obviously ill, stared with open, vacant eyes. Gaze fixed on a picture of trees on the wall, he didn't realize I was beside him. A medical chart hung off the foot of the bed, and I bent down to read. Mark Entwhistle. He was only twenty-four.

The human shell on the bed choked on phlegm. I bolted upright and knocked my head on the IV stand, making a racket so great Rook poked in his head.

"I was looking for Heather," I explained, rubbing my head.

"You shouldn't be here," he whispered.

"No, you shouldn't," Milo said from behind me. He squeezed past Rook. "My brother's sick, and the last thing he needs is some busybody snooping 'round for things that ain't there."

"I-I'm sorry," I said as I staggered into the hall.

Milo shut the door and pressed his back to the wood. "He had a bad night, needs his rest. Emmie's gotta sell some weed to pay for last night's nurse."

I could understand not wanting us to disturb his brother, but something about the sick man in that room didn't seem like the kind of secret Milo had talked about in his letter to Heather. It was unfortunate, yes, yet not something that'd change what Heather thought of him.

The front door swung open, boots loud in the trailer. Emmie thrust her pointer finger toward the door. "Y'all need to leave. There ain't anything here for you, but I can tell you that even if Heather was here, she wouldn't go back to that hellhole."

Rook had to pull on my wrist to unfreeze my feet from the floor. I shuffled toward the front room and glanced back to Milo, but he wouldn't look my way. There was nothing more I'd learn about Heather right then, but my questions mounted.

Outside, I didn't want Rook to see my simmering frustration. I rested my head against his chest and glowered at the closed door.

I wished Heather had told me about Milo instead of crushing her spirit by hiding him. I didn't understand her attraction, but I knew about wanting someone, to hear his voice and have time where it was only the two of you. Yes, I'd have done everything to keep her in the Glen. Because I was selfish. Yet maybe if she'd told me what she planned, I'd have understood.

"Are you gonna talk to my pops about all this?" Rook asked. "I know you don't wanna get Heather in trouble, but something ain't right."

"I'll tell him."

But as I walked away from the trailer, from Milo and drugs and his sister, I knew I wouldn't talk to Sheriff until I found out what the Entwhistles were hiding.

Instead of stopping by the clinic upon returning to the Glen, I had Rook take me to Whimsy's new pasture. Papa had moved her and the other horses after Journey's slaughter. He said the horses remembered and would spook.

Sheriff had tracked down a new stallion for Rook, but I'd not seen him yet. As we drew near the pasture, Rook pointed out an Andalusian grazing near Whimsy. Beautiful charcoal-gray tail flicking flies from his white coat. Rook propped up his foot on the horse fence. "His name's Veil. He was a jumping horse for show, but when he was injured, his life got real bad. Pops got him from a good rescue."

I smiled. "You ride him yet?"

"A couple of times, made sure he wouldn't buck me off."

The two horses loped around each other. I liked the rhythm of their hooves, the points of their ears, and even the spray from their noses as they huffed.

"Let's go riding, Ivy."

"It ain't safe," I protested. "I'll be in trouble if my parents find out."

"You won't be alone. I'll be with you."

He had a point. Veil nickered at me, eager to nuzzle my hair and skirt no matter how Rook shooed him, as we pulled out our reins from the tack room. I clipped Whimsy's reins to her halter. Her head bowed. She knew things were different. Not just with Journey. With me. That I missed a piece of me. A tide of sadness swept inward on me, and I propped myself up against my horse, my hands on her withers, my face in my forearms. She was strong and wouldn't let me sink no matter how great the weight.

"The first time I rode Veil, it was almost impossible to make myself get on," Rook said. "I kept thinkin' 'bout Journey and how you and I rode off together that last time. I'd convinced myself the same thing would happen to any horse I rode, but it hasn't happened yet. I tell myself it won't happen again."

I needed to hear that.

We rode through the fields. Clouds rolled in from the southwest, and Rook tipped his head back as if expecting rain. There'd be none. The leaves didn't flip over.

I knew what Rook wanted to do. He was taking me riding because he knew how much I loved being out with Whimsy, and I hadn't ridden her in far too long. Sitting on my horse's back, feeling her move beneath me, her body and mine as one, I needed that freedom, that forgetting.

Rook sped up Veil's pace to match Whimsy's until we rode beside each other. He was so at ease with his horse. It was the simple things — the flex of his thighs, the tightness of his stomach, things I couldn't see in myself — that I enjoyed watching in him.

He halted Veil and watched Whimsy and me trot, every part of me bouncing. "View's nice here, Ivy."

"Oh, shut up."

"You're doin' it on purpose," he said, and kicked Veil to catch up with Whimsy. We both laughed. Riding with him felt good, and —

Heather was gone.

How dare I feel good and enjoy that moment when I had no idea where she was?

"Ivy," Rook called. "Hey! Did you hear me?"

I saw him again. "I'm sorry. What?"

"We should water the horses," he said. "Denial Mill's up ahead. We can stop there."

We guided the horses to the water. The mill groaned as the wheel turned, a constant whirring against the liquid babble spilling over rocks. The river was shallow, the lack of rain during April and a dry winter speeding the shores dry. Only the middle had any depth. Shoals submerged in rainier seasons formed a rocky bridge across the banks. I unclipped Whimsy's reins before she lowered her head to drink while I stooped to admire a tan snail shell in the dirt. Lavender wisps and a hint of green spun over the shell.

Rook was holding Veil's reins when he joined me. "You're not really here, are you?"

"What do you mean?" I asked.

"Most of the time, you seem far away. I don't know if it's 'cause you always watch people or you're thinkin'. Sometimes it's like watching a ghost haunt the same place the same way day after day. You hold back, and it makes me wonder if you're ever really in the moment."

I lived a guarded life. There was trust in the shadows.

"I don't know how to be me right now," I admitted. "Heather always pushes me when I pull back."

Rook's hand rested on the sway in my back. I pressed my body against his — legs to legs, his front to mine, arms wrapping around me. His forehead touched mine, and his glasses slipped down his nose so my eyelashes blinked against the lenses. "Sometimes when you hold back, what you hang on to winds up hurting you."

I closed my eyes, shivered while Rook's fingers traveled to my hips. I didn't want to hold back with him. I wanted to know what it was to sweep away all fetters restraining me. The scruff on his chin scratched my forehead. Warm air swirled above us while cool water misted my ankles and, higher up, beneath my skirt.

All of it was real. Right then. That second.

I circled my arms around him hard, because the harder I hugged, the looser the knot in my throat grew. How could I like how he held me when half of me was hollow?

"Rook?" I choked on his name.

"What?"

"I don't want this to stop. This moment."

He scrunched my skirt at my hips. The urge to cry out — in sorrow, in confusion, in craving him — ballooned in my chest. It came out instead as a gasp when he lowered his face into the curve of my neck. As if awaiting my cue, he didn't kiss me, and I didn't know if I wanted him to or if I wanted something else.

I missed Heather.

I missed the way things were before.

Don't stop.

I listened to Rook's breathing, the trickle of water washing the river stones. I listened to the creak of the mill's wheel as it turned.

Down in the river's valley, we became entangled and reclined on a piece of limestone. I brought my mouth to his. His tongue flicked mine, his hands on my back and then lower. I traced along his shoulders, the muscles from working fields, and yet there was softness to him. That softness didn't stay the longer we kissed. He pulled back and looked around.

"What is it?" I asked.

"Making sure we're alone," he said.

"And what would you do if someone saw us?"

He smiled. "Pretend I was saving you from drowning."

"I'd like it if you gave me mouth-to-mouth."

His laugh was hushed but cut short because I seized him, knocking his glasses askew as I kissed him. I didn't care how wet or messy it became. I didn't care if our teeth knocked together. I wanted him to take everything that hurt, to lick it from me, and replace it with *something* else. I paused over the buttons of his gray shirt, popping each one open, one by one, until I came to the lowest button. He inhaled.

"If you don't want to do this, it's okay."

But I did. My intention held firm. "I want this, Rook."

He lost the shirt I'd unbuttoned and spread it out on the rock as a makeshift blanket. I lay back and invited him to climb on top of me. My fingers ran along his arms to his shoulders damp with sweat, and his mouth wandered from my lips to my neck. His trousers hardened against my skirt, enough to take away my breath. It brought out a curiosity in me, and when I reached down to unbutton his pants and touch him there, he moved against my hand for more.

I wanted him. He wanted me.

That way.

His lips dressed my neck with gentle kisses until he came to the collar of my dress, and it was a new kind of thrill as he eased the top off my shoulder to kiss me there, too. I could lie under the sun for hours with him kissing me like that, just enough pressure, lips so warm that I shivered when the air cooled where he'd been.

I understood why Heather wouldn't tell me who she was with in the stable.

Sharing it ruined the delicacy of the two of you.

Rook's fingers slid up the inside of my thigh, higher yet. I held my breath, shuddering because he scared me. And amazed me. How I'd known him my entire life but never in this way. I could never go back to knowing him before this.

I slipped down the top of my dress so it draped at my waist, pulling back my hair for him to see everything. Though I liked my shape, I wondered what Rook thought of it. I also liked his smile, his dimpled cheeks, especially as he looked at my body. Heather's necklace of found things slid between my breasts. His hands moved across the soft part of my abdomen before inching upward.

I studied him kissing my tummy. It'd make a good drawing, him pushing up my skirt, his lips treading along my thighs. I tipped back my head, feeling all the ways he kissed me, listening. So much sound, so much shifting around inside me. His mouth stayed gentle as I lowered my head against his shirt covering the rock. With white sunlight in my eyes, I rode higher with each kiss.

The elation cracked my heart.

Yet I smothered sobs, covering my grimaced mouth. I had to hide it from him, not because I didn't like what he did—I did, I wanted it—but rather the void in me ripped open, fresh and endless.

I reached down to touch his hair, my voice crackling to whisper, "Stop."

Rook raised up from my skirt. He stared at me with spooked eyes, pants hanging open. "Ivy? Are you okay?"

He hoisted me up to sitting and lifted my dress's top to cover me again. Then I must've seemed too prickly to touch. Nothing would help me except to cry, and Rook gave me that. He buttoned up his pants, slid into his shirt, and focused on the water spinning past us.

After a bit, he said, "Anytime you say no, I'll listen. If it's too fast, I'll back off. I'm . . . sorry."

My eyes stung, hot, grainy, and liquid.

"It's n-n-not you," I croaked. "Why? Why right now? Why does everything lead me b-back to feeling so lost and ruined?"

Worry, sadness, anger, everything wailed from my throat. My face was hot, my hair tangled, and I hated how the wind dried the tears pooling beneath my eyes.

Rook's thumb brushed my cheek. "Let's get you outta here."

Too tired to move, I shut my eyes, but that only made all the sounds louder.

Pulse pounding. Rook shushing me. A crow squawked three times.

I breathed. More noise. The rustle of my skirt falling back over my legs. Water traveling over pebbles. Tree frogs peeping in the woods.

The mill was silent.

"It's not turning," I said.

"The mill?" Rook asked. "Maybe the water's too low."

"No, I heard it when we came here."

I wiped my face and shook off everything surging out of me, locked it back in my cells. The wooden wheel had halted. The top of the wheel pitched back and forth as if trying to turn, but something was caught on the bottom.

I hopped from one rock on the shoal to next, lifting my skirt out of the water, and Rook jumped behind me until we reached the opposite shore. Together, we trekked along the bank where the absent water left a scooped-out hollow plagued by roots and algae-covered rocks. Too dark with shadow and thick with mud, something had wedged itself beneath the wheel. I remained on the shore as he wound his long legs around the wheel's scaffolding, slopping through the water until he was higher than knee-deep.

"You see anything?" I asked.

He bent over, shielding his glasses from the sun. "I'm not sure. There's something stuck in the mud, I think."

I glanced back to the horses, still drinking and oblivious. My tongue slicked over my lips before I gave up and followed Rook out into the water. Cold welled around my legs, and my skirt became heavier before billowing around me like a giant lily pad. I pushed it behind me to stop it from becoming hooked on the wheel.

"Be careful," I reminded Rook. "If the wheel spins while you're messing with it, you'll get crushed."

With a nod, he hung on to the scaffold, and I could see now where he poked at a mass bobbing beneath the wheel with the driftwood. He slipped his glasses into his pocket and with a splash, disappeared into the water. I glanced up at the riverbank, the steep cove, and counted. *One, two, three, four . . .*

My arms wrapped around my chest. My teeth chattered. Veil neighed, the worried bellow horses give when something unsettles them. A leaf swam by on the river's surface.

If he became snagged on something. If his lungs ran out of air. If he was swept downstream by the current.

If, if, if.

I slapped at the water, whipping around, looking for any sign of him. He'd been underwater for too long.

"Rook?"

All was hushed. I was wading closer to the wheel when hands grasped my wrists.

I yelped at the same time Rook broke through the river's surface. He sputtered on the water and choked, panicking.

"There you are!" I cried. "What happened?"

He spun me away from Denial Mill, holding the sides of my head so I couldn't peek. Rivulets of water streamed down from my temples to my cheeks where he held me. Each breath was ragged, a fight not to scream.

"Don't look. Ivy, whatever you do, don't look!"

"What's wrong?" I demanded. He coughed up more water and

tried rushing me to the shore, but I dug my heels into the silty river bottom. "Rook, c'mon! What is it?"

"Go!" he finally managed. "Take Whimsy, and get my pops! Go now!"

"W-what'd you see? You're scarin' me!"

"Ivy, no!"

The cold water around me met a growing cold inside me, beginning in my gut and spreading down my veins. I peeled away from Rook and waded a half circle back to the water wheel.

"Please don't," he begged, and again sloshed with me through the water. "You don't wanna see that."

But I had to see. I had to know.

I eased through the water until what appeared to be wavy, reddish-brown marsh grass floated on the surface. My bones hard and muscles harder, I slipped my fingers between the grasses, except it wasn't grass. It was wet hair. Wet curls. Soggy and discolored from sitting in the water for days. Hair clinging to my skin. Her May Day skirt wrapped around one of the wheel's paddles. Down beneath the water, I felt her. The eyes open and fringed by lashes, the straight nose, and hard pearls of her teeth. Her lips were gone. All of her beneath the water, out of sight.

The mill wheel groaned. Heather's body loosened and submerged further, yet I was stuck in the middle of the spinning water wheel. Rook shouted, but I couldn't understand him. One arm fished through the wheel's scaffold, then a leg. I held my wet skirt close against me to keep it from snarling on the wheel. Almost free.

My head jerked, my hair knotted and pulled behind me. My head rolled back on my neck and faced the glare of the sun overhead before I fell, my back splashing the water where there was only cold and darkness.

Chapter Thirteen

Terra's fingers were all black and chewed up, and no one was all that sure if the vultures got her or if it was that damn Birch Markle. The devil had that boy crouchin' over her dead body and lickin' the girl's blood off his knife.

Ice water flooded my nose, my mouth. My hair clouded around my head and over my face. Giving in to the lull of the current seemed much easier than propelling myself to the surface. The water flowed around me until my soaked hair and skirt no longer weighed me down — rather, I became weightless.

It was fitting in a way. To lose Heather, find her, and then lose myself.

I could stay with her.

My fingers stretched, and I turned my head. Eyes opening to take in the murky river water. There was grit and mud and grass, but there was also Heather's fish-white face and constellations of freckles. Her dead head creaked on its neck, swiveling to face me, lipless mouth forming words. Since she had no breath, no bubbles escaped as she spoke.

Find it.

"Find what?"

Her eyes were open, the green gone from them. Her teeth clacked in blue-black gums.

Find it, Ivy.

My fingers bumped against hers. They felt like stumpy logs of clay, and shreds of her skin flaked against mine.

I took hold anyway. Cousins. Almost sisters.

Together again.

"Help! Somebody, help me!"

The voice. It sounded like Rook, but not. He was molasses and black earth, and this voice was jagged, full of rocks and twigs.

My cheek chilled as wind licked off water droplets. A hand cupped my head while an arm wrapped behind my knees. "Ivy, wake up. Please, God, no. I love you. Wake up . . . *Somebody fucking help me!*"

No. Don't take me away.

I liked it in the water. In the dark. With Heather.

Cattails rustled while a horse gave an impatient stomp. My back pressed against the shore. The underwater weightlessness vanished. My arms, my legs, all my body was heavy, so much that if the shore wished to open and swallow me, it could. My mind was loosely aware of buzzing.

"I gotta see my daughter!"

A hand stroked the hair drying across my forehead. A trail of sludge wound down from my lips around my jaw and neck to pool behind my ear. My eyelids crusted with sediment. Somehow, I wiped my face enough to blink.

Sun so blinding. I flinched.

"Thank God," Rook said, and sat beside me. I suspected he'd been crying. I tried to speak, but a clot of river water forced up my throat to spill from my mouth. Rook hoisted me up and smacked my back to dislodge more. As the coughs settled, I rubbed my nose to blot the water reeking of dirt from my face.

Horses. Denial Mill. I recalled going there with Rook and wading in the river because the water wheel had stopped turning. Some hill-men were examining the wheel with Flint and Jasper Denial. Near the top of the riverside, my father rushed up to Sheriff, his cheeks whitened. "Jay, they said Ivy's down here. Is she —"

"We had a bad scare, but my boy got her breathin' again. Promise kept, Timothy. I wish I'd done better."

Papa's shoulders drooped. "Done better?"

I looked away from the men, from Rook, and on the shore lay Heather. Not screaming, not crying out, I crawled over to the gray girl in the red ruffled skirt. The ruffles were tinged dingy brown, like her curls. Dark water beaded in her nostrils. Two silver coins covered her eyes. I knelt over her, my hands in my lap, then on her forearm.

"Ivy?" Papa asked from behind me.

Heather's mouth was too open, too wide without her lips. Such a ghastly smile without any blood or color, so I ripped off my sleeve and placed it over her face. Her shirt was stained with dark smears of blood. She was stiff, so waxy, and chilled.

There was nothing of her magic and light. She was a muted husk of what was once radiant. I squeezed my eyes, burying my face against Heather's shoulder. Tears stung my skin as they slipped down my cheeks. My chest and throat distended with a horrible pain. The finality of sorrow. Its wail shoved out of me to echo above the river, and I held her closer. All the softness went out of her.

Heather was murdered.

But I'd I returned from nearly dead. To find out who did this to her.

CHAPTER FOURTEEN

Oh, folks ran after Birch. Jackdaw Meriweather, his boy Jay, all them with their hounds and rifles took off after him into the woods. Thing is, Birch always liked the woods. He knew them. He was the woods.

My mother's feet formed twin shadows beneath my doorway. I recognized their shape, the thickness molding her calves. Sturdy legs held up my world that had been obliterated two days prior.

Mamie's blanket snuggled around my shoulders, and no matter the heat outside, I couldn't warm up. "Death-touched," Mamie would've said.

When I was small, a boy from the Glen called Jet Winslow became death-touched. He was riding his bicycle near the highway when a dairy truck collided with him. The damage to his head was bad enough his hair from then on came in white where it should've been brown. Jet's folks called Mamie to pray over him with Pastor Galloway. Doctoring with iodine and bandages did their part, but Mamie had charms and herbs and a handful of tonics. She laid snakes on him so his cold blood went into the serpent, but that boy never got warm again.

Later, he suffocated in a silo of livestock feed, but that was an accident.

In my room, I waited for Heather's fingers to rap the window. Dead Heather or living Heather, I'd take either. My pencil shaded her neck, her thin lips and the freckle on her nose, her reckless hair and willowy frame. I sketched for hours. Days. Until my eyes were bleary. Until my paper was blotted with tears.

If only I could wish her back. Even if she were so angry she slapped me, I'd do it. Just to have her.

Each night, I blew out the candle at my bedside, smelling beeswax and smoke drift to the ceiling to raise with it my prayer that the next morning Heather'd stumble down the dirt path and laugh.

She wasn't coming back.

"*Bonita?*" Mama called through the door.

I crossed the room, still dressed in the blanket and nightdress. In my mirror's face, my skin was ashen, gray, as if someone had spilled water on me and sopped away half my color. Mama waited with a cup of steaming root tea. Mamie had written down the recipe — Sleep-Away-Sorrow. Mama brought the tea to me around the clock to numb my mind and stop the nightmares. If she missed a dose, my screams shook the windows.

"Rook's here," Mama said, passing me the cup.

I sipped. The tea was cold. It turned cold the second the mug entered my grip.

Mama followed me to the bed. "See him, Ivy."

I swallowed the rest of the tea in loud gulps. The herbs laid their dumbing potion over me. Mama chose a cornflower-blue dress with lacing up the front, then eased Mamie's blanket off my shoulders, untied my nightdress, and fluffed the blue dress over my head. She said nothing about the two necklaces I wore, Rook's acorn token and Heather's chain of found things.

After winding my hair in a loose braid, I found Rook in the kitchen. He stood on a stepladder affixing a potted strawberry vine by the window. Pale berries poked out between glossy leaves.

"You only gotta water it," he said as he descended the ladder.

I pulled out a chair from the table and flopped down on it. My muscles were sand-heavy. No rain in days, and the house was dry. Every surface — tabletop, counters, floors, pails — layered with dust. A picnic basket covered by a checkered cloth rested on the table. At first, I guessed food from Briar, but the buttery smell of Mama's empanadas wafted out.

"You gonna talk?" Rook asked.

I eyed the back door. Rook stretched out his hand. His skin was warm and toughened, and I stopped from crying out because he felt so good and alive. I'd forgotten not all skin felt like river mud.

"How much do you remember?" he asked once outside in the yard.

"E-everything," I replied.

"*Everything?*"

"What you said." I studied my feet, too long and skinny for my body. "W-when you wanted me to wake up. I heard you."

"The thought of losin' you scares the hell outta me."

His fingers traced my arm when my mother opened the door. He hopped back a step, ramming into a crate of ale bottles with his boot. Mama raised an eyebrow as she brought me the picnic basket from the kitchen table.

"Take this to your *tía*'s house," she instructed.

"You comin'?" I asked.

"Ivy, I'm tired," Mama said, and started back to the door. "I've been in *la cocina* making food for days. Just do this for Mama. Rook can go with you, *sí*? Don't wander."

Mama went back inside, and I lifted the edge of the basket's cloth where she'd stacked a dozen flaky golden empanadas. With the basket slung into my elbow's crook, I reached inside my dress and withdrew Heather's necklace, running the charms between my thumb and forefinger before stuffing the chain inside my collar, where its metal dangled over my heart.

"What are you thinking?" Rook asked.

"Not much. I'm drugged. I can't believe she's making me do this."

Rook opened the gated fence, allowing me to go before him. We took a few steps down the road, and he shoved his hands into his pockets, pausing at a scarecrow. Its head was a pumpkin from last autumn, only now soured with rot and slime.

"She's just trying to help out your aunt," Rook said, nudging the picnic basket with his knee. "Your mama's a good person."

"She says she still feels like she don't fit in here," I replied. "I mean, look at us. There ain't any other Mexicans in the Glen, and the ones at school—I don't relate to them 'cause I've always lived here."

"I think you're beautiful." I blushed but Rook turned my chin. "I like how sometimes you speak and there's some of your mama's accent in there. You don't gotta be anyone but you, Ivy."

"Heather said I was tryin' to be her. If we weren't fightin', I'd have been with her. She wouldn't have died."

He shook his head. "Or you'd both be dead."

We walked down the path under the sun. Sweat beaded along my hairline, and wide cracks mapped the ground where the earth split from drought. All the grass, even the oat grass so tolerant of Ozark heat, bleached white. We needed rain, and soon, if there was to be any hope for a decent crop.

As we passed the posts, I noticed some new signs tacked to the wood, decrees from Sheriff.

DON'T GO OUTSIDE ALONE.

STAY ON KNOWN ROADS.

Hillfolk took posts along the trails, shotguns in hand and eyes narrowed in the unforgiving sun. Watching.

When we reached Heather's home, her bed sheets were hanging on a line in front of the house. Laundry usually sun-dried behind a house, but when a family was in mourning, they put their loved one's sheets in front to announce a passing.

Other hillfolk had visited my aunt's house, evidenced by baskets of fresh bread, eggs, and even a wheel of the Lemays' best cheese on the porch. Rook helped me gather the food. I turned the doorknob to let us inside. When I found it locked, I lifted the doormat to look for the spare key, but it was gone.

Because now it was *after*.

I took off Heather's necklace and pieced through the bits of rusted history until I came to a time-darkened skeleton key. On a hunch, I slipped it into the lock and listened to the pop of the lock yielding.

"Lucky," Rook muttered.

We walked through the living room. A white veil was draped over the mirror above the fireplace. Our footfalls fell hollow on the warped floor. I sped up my step as unease slithered up my spine and knotted around my shoulders, strangling me. A house in mourning, a house that had no life in it. We went into the kitchen, where I showed Rook how my aunt liked her necessities packed in the icebox.

"Aunt Rue, I'm in the kitchen," I called out. My voice returned with a tinny echo. "Mama sent over food."

No thumps of movement, no murmured voices. Rook shrugged. "Maybe they went for a walk."

A family in mourning didn't go for walks. I wasn't sure where Marsh was, probably at Papa's clinic if he couldn't bear to be home. I instructed Rook to tidy up the kitchen and living room, giving him a bucket of hot water and oil soap. I bumped against a Mason jar on the counter. Initially, I thought the jar was filled with coffee beans, but these were larger.

"Pawpaw seeds," I remarked. "When I was little, some townie showed up when Heather and I were outside playin' ring-around-the-rosie. This woman was grieving hard, and she asked for Mamie. She gave Mamie money and begged her to bring pawpaw seeds to town for a burial, said they needed them thrown on a casket to find out who killed this woman's father."

"Did Mamie go?"

"She did."

"Did they find out who killed the man?" he asked.

I didn't know and drew my fingers back from the Mason jar. "They're gonna throw them on Heather's grave tomorrow."

Rook lifted the bucket of soapy water and then took the rag to wash down the floor. Too much heat in the past couple days, too much dust blowing through open windows, and I was sure they left the windows open as much as possible to make sure Heather's spirit wasn't trapped.

While Rook cleaned, I sneaked down the hall, past my aunt and Marsh's bedroom. Aunt Rue lay asleep, her strawberry-blond hair haloed on her pillow. Sunlight poured in and glinted off the sharpened blade of the ax under the bed. Mamie had put it there to ease the labor pains once the baby came.

The door to Heather's room was open as I left it. Pieces of quartz dangled from the ceiling to catch light, and I glanced to her dresser. Heather decorated the top with a jewelry box and another collection of found things too large to string on her chain — glass bottles with labels for things like "gargling oil" and "viper drops," animal bones she'd washed and bleached in sunlight. Everything was a treasure to Heather. She'd been a treasure to me.

My throat closed, my heart rising because it wanted to fall out among her things.

I smelled her.

I *smelled* her in this room.

I expected to turn around and find her behind me with her tilted grin. She wouldn't be there. She was in a barn over ice. By law, for any death unattended by the Glen's doctor, Sheriff had to call the county police to send their medical examiner. They went to Papa's clinic, the most sterile site on the Glen's land, and pulled open the dead, dug around their insides for clues to what killed them, and stitched them up. All of it recorded with notes and cameras. There was no affection in their cuts and examination. It was science. A crime in Heather's case. The Glen's granny-women would've stood by to make sure traditions were kept and wrapped her in rags soaked in wahoo tea before placing her in a pine box so we could say farewell with Pastor Galloway reading Scripture and . . .

I wasn't here for this.

Every drawer went opened in search of something. Mindful of Aunt Rue's sleep, I rapped quietly on floorboards, wondering if a loose one would spring up and uncover some mystery. Tapping in her closet, even with her dresses brushing against my face like her fingers pushing back a wild tangle of my hair. I pulled out a chair and picked around her ceiling, where I sneezed away cobwebs.

All that was left on her stripped bed were bare pillows, the mattress, and frame. I poked around in hopes of finding something she'd hidden. Down on my hands and knees, I scooted underneath the bed. Heather was too good at hiding things.

There was nothing for me to find, and I reluctantly pulled myself up before giving the room a last look. I spun on my heels, intending to help Rook with cleaning, but I pivoted right into Mamie. "Oof!"

My grandmother held my face. Her mouth twitched, yet all I received was the comfort of her hands, so worn that her fingerprints seemed eroded by age. Her hands dropped to Heather's necklace peeking out from my collar. She inched across the charms and pendants, lingering on the gaps of the missing ones.

"I know, Mamie," I said. "I w-wish I could find them. I want them back. I want her back."

Can't have her back, girl, her eyes seemed to say. *Don't mess with tryin' to conjure the dead to talk after they're gone. Nothing good comes of raisin' a tormented soul.*

If Heather's soul was in torment because of the mystery of how she died, I had to uncover every truth about her, even the ones she wanted me to never know. Was it going against her wishes? I didn't know. I wanted—no, needed—her to rest in peace.

I needed to find peace in her death.

But how could I live without her?

Mamie shuffled past me in the doorway to enter Heather's room. Like me, she felt along the dresser and bed frame, old pill bottles and animal bones, before stopping on the jewelry box on the dresser. I knew the hinged top, the carving of budded plants easy to mistake for wheat. It was heather. I supposed this was where Heather stored her necklace at night. If I were to take it, I'd have one more of Heather's belongings to claim as my own. Except having her things wasn't the same as having her.

"I don't want it, Mamie," I said.

My grandmother looked over her shoulder at me with her keen eye. She drummed on the box's lid before pressing it into my hands. Her thumbs over mine, she made me trace the box's corners.

Ivy, look.

Okay, Mamie, I'll look.

My breath held tight, I flipped open the silver hinge on the front. The odor of cedar oil to keep away moths whiffed out, and then Heather's soapy, lavender smell. It was empty.

I almost expected something to be inside.

"Why, Mamie?" I asked in a hoarse whisper.

She touched the red thread bracelet on my wrist, then backed out of the room.

Alone, I knelt on Heather's floor with her box in my lap and smacked the lid. *Damn it, Heather, there should be something here, something to tell who you really were.*

Whap! I hit the box again, then again.

My hand throbbed with the blows to the front, the top. I didn't care. I hurt.

Another hit. *Thud!*

I cocked my head. That sounded different. Hollow.

Tapping along the box, I searched for the empty spot. It rattled. I bit my lip and tugged. A false bottom fell away, revealing a gap, and scrap after scrap of folded paper fluttered into my lap. All in the same stationery as Heather's note.

M,

I don't want to hide anymore, but I can't tell anyone about us. They wouldn't understand. Especially not Ivy. She keeps asking questions. She knows too much, and she's obsessed. What

am I supposed to tell her? Nothing is what she thinks it is. Birch
Markle isn't all there is to be afraid of. I'm ready to leave it all
behind. Even her.
　　—H

H,
　Soon, I promise.
　Soon you'll be free. Just hang on.
　—*M*

M,
　Meet me in the woods.
　You know the place. We can't leave anything behind.
　—*H*

I crushed the notes and shoved them in my skirt's pockets. I
couldn't read them right now. My thoughts were too scattered yet
intent on one thing.

Ivy is obsessed.

OBSESSED.

I stood and left Heather's room. Rook's *scritch-scratch* while he
scrubbed echoed from the kitchen. In the hall outside Aunt Rue's
room, the air was stifling. She needed a breeze, and I crept around
the bed to open the window in hope the humidity would dissipate
outside. I turned to my aunt to whisper goodbye, but the word withered.

Aunt Rue sat up in bed.

Her legs dangled over the edge. Spidery veins crossed her calves, which were milky, as was her face. The purplish cast under her eyes revealed she mustn't have slept much. The bloodshot whites rimming her irises were visible.

"You gotta rest, Auntie," I said.

She stared blankly. The wind fluffed the curtains and her mussed hair. Her toes didn't reach the floor from the bed, but between her feet, the ax head was visible.

"He comes for girls with secrets, you know," she said in a brittle rasp, and the sound raised every hair on my arms. "Terra MacAvoy had them. My girl did too. And you."

"Wh-what about me?" I asked.

She didn't blink. Her arm lifted as if raised by invisible marionette's strings. She pointed at me.

"Nothing can stop him."

Chapter Fifteen

We weren't havin' another May Queen after that. The grief of losin' Terra, such a pretty, spirited thing, was way too much of a cross for the good people of Rowan's Glen to bear.

By dawn's light, Mama held my hand as we walked the Glen's northern end. Lush willows near a pond formed an alcove for eternal respite from life. Gramps was buried in the cemetery, as were his parents and theirs. Mamie's side of the family as well. Stone markers rose from overgrown grass, untouched but for moss clinging to storm-worn dates.

Pastor Galloway would lay my cousin to rest. Papa went ahead with Marsh. I didn't tell anyone of Aunt Rue's warning, never told Rook, despite my trembling. I fibbed that being in Heather's home had brought too much sorrow, instead of showing him that I'd found more notes. I didn't know if Aunt Rue was well enough to bury her daughter. God help me, I didn't want to see her again anytime soon.

When Mama and I neared the graveyard, I heard Papa yelling.

"Who the hell did this? Where's Leaf Clement? He knows better than to dig a grave the day before burial!"

"Timothy, he might've done it at sunrise," Pastor declared.

Mama's hand tensed over mine. We joined a cluster of Papa, Sheriff, Marsh, and Pastor. Mama tugged me past the pine box near the open grave. Heather was inside that box. Forever.

Papa knelt to examine the graveyard dirt. "Soil's dry. This ain't done this mornin'. We ain't buryin' my niece in this hole. Leaf's gotta dig a new one."

Pastor stepped forward, Bible in hand. "Timothy, be rational —"

Papa threw Pastor a dark look. "You know what the old-timers say. We bury a body in a grave dug the day before burial, then death comes for the kin."

The cemetery fell into silence, but not the liquid hush of birds skimming the pond's surface. It was the silence of anger. Pastor pulled my father aside. Half of me felt the prickle to measure the grave's depth. The other half sought to run far away.

Nothing seemed more terrifying than lying in a box while dirt piled on top. Eventually, the dirt would become heavier, thinning the air, and I'd strain to take a breath. I'd feel the weight and—

I wouldn't be buried alive.

Graves were for the dead, for the Heathers.

Mama worked her rosary in prayer. *"Padre nuestro, que estás in los cielos, santificado sea tu nombre . . ."*

I took a Spanish class once in seventh grade. Didn't matter that

I spoke some at home, the teacher said I was too slangy. Other students, mostly rollers fluent from growing up in immigrant families, called me *pocha* because I didn't act Mexican like them. I stopped speaking my mother's tongue. I wondered how Mama felt giving up all but her language to come with Papa.

"I want to bury my stepdaughter," Marsh said to Sheriff. "Her mama's a wreck, and last thing we need is y'all makin' a scene."

Sheriff frowned. "I'm sorry this happened."

Marsh glared, his nostrils wide. I half expected him to yell at Sheriff to get out, that he'd done nothing to keep that girl safe. While he'd helped Papa patch up a boy some drunk kids had thought was Birch Markle, the real one had killed Heather and thrown her in the river. Meanwhile, Birch was still in the woods, still night-screaming.

Mama let go of my hand and met Papa, embracing him. His hands rested on her hips. I couldn't hear what they murmured, but I noticed the way her fingers slid through his hair, how she brought his forehead to meet hers. She loved him. She loved him with all her heart and wanted to take away some hurt.

Some loss.

After promising things would be done proper, Sheriff made his way to me. "Your cousin was spotted goin' off alone in the days before her murder," he said. "You know anything 'bout that?"

The truth was, I didn't know enough to give him an answer. Not really. She met Milo. There were drugs, sex, but what did telling any of that matter now except to disgrace her?

"She mention runnin' into Birch Markle?" he asked.

I shook my head.

"Ivy, girl, if you know anything that might've caused your cousin trouble, you gotta tell me."

Not until I knew what those things meant first.

Our families' closest friends gathered after the funeral. It wasn't open to anyone to come and pay their respects — that'd come in church when Marsh or Aunt Rue attended next, and seeing as Aunt Rue was bedbound, that would be some time. I suspected they didn't want visitors.

Marsh poured himself some ale and offered more to Sheriff and Papa, who both declined. Drinking was for a celebration, but Marsh perhaps wanted to drown the misery of the day. I didn't want to be close to the grief. It was better to numb myself in the kitchen by cutting wedges of cheese or slicing bread, setting out cream churned to butter and pinch bowls filled with mixed salt and herbs. Busyness kept away reality.

"You shouldn't cut yourself off," Rook remarked, leaning against the doorway separating the kitchen from the guests filtering in and out.

"I — I can't talk to anyone," I said, voice broken.

I wiped my eye with the heel of my hand and took up the knife to cut another loaf of bread.

Rook wrapped his arms around me from behind while his chin

rested on my shoulder. I longed to crumble, to break my knees and never run again. The sobs building in my throat caught in a web of stammers. A soft sniffle behind my ear, and I turned my head enough to see Rook's eyes damp behind his glasses. He loved me, but he grieved Heather's loss, too. She always *was*. Now she'd never be again.

I laid the knife on the cutting board. We held each other in mutual sadness, in changes that came too fast. Love and sorrow were similar, in that both ripped you wide open and left you without skin.

"I hate this," I whispered into his shirt. My lip rubbed against a button. "I hate feeling so tangled inside."

He held the back of my head, lowering his mouth to kiss the top of me.

The bell by the front door rang to announce the arrival of another guest. I composed myself and took out a fresh bread plate. Papa opened the door to Dale and Violet Crenshaw. Violet carried a pie and gave me a wan smile. Sheriff pivoted from talking with Pastor and marched over to Dale.

"You ain't welcome here, Crenshaw."

"What're you talkin' 'bout, Jay? I've been friends with Marsh for nearly forty years. We're payin' our respects," Dale argued.

"No, you ain't."

Papa stepped between the men. "What's going on here? This is a time for condolences."

"Fine," Sheriff huffed. "I'm taking you to the station, Dale."

Mama hurried Violet to me. "Help Ivy in *la cocina, sí?*"

Violet's feet skidded. The pie shifted in her hands, and I grabbed it to keep it from splatting on the floor. No one dared leave the room until we knew why Sheriff and his deputy were squaring off in a house of mourning.

"I was gonna wait until I had a word with Marsh and Rue," Sheriff said, shaking his head. "Heather's autopsy report came this morning."

My breath hitched.

"What's this gotta do with Dale?" Marsh asked.

"Heather was poisoned. By Crenshaw wine. The medical examiner confirmed what the granny-women already thought — there was belladonna mixed with her drink. That girl never had a chance."

Dale balked. "Jay, are you insane? I'd never go after another person."

"You can't go 'round accusin' people of things!" Violet yelped. "Besides, ain't we said it was Birch Markle who killed her?"

"How the hell is Birch gonna have a bottle of wine?" Marsh shouted back.

Tension brewed thick and thunderous. Violet stood by her father. Marsh near Sheriff, Papa between both sides. There was no escaping the anger.

"You got something on me, Jay? Come to my winery. Show everyone what you find," Dale snapped.

"I'll do just that. Right now," Sheriff replied.

The front door swung open. Dale muttered a curse. Mama and Briar stayed behind to care for my aunt and Mamie, but I had to go. If this was how Heather had died, I had to bear witness. *Find it,* she'd told me. Maybe this was it. She'd chosen me to see that she had justice.

As the last to leave, I pulled the door shut. My mind poked at the idea of Dale Crenshaw poisoning my cousin, how the father of a friend might be responsible for such cruelty. I only had a vague sense of Rook at my side, matching my stride despite his much longer legs, and keeping me from wandering lost. I knew the Glen. I loved the Glen. The Glen was home, yet without Heather, it was another hollow.

When we reached the Crenshaws' fermentation barn where they stored barrels of aging wine, a crowd gathered. A crate was filled with cobalt-blue glass bottles. Sheriff piled bottles in the crate before he grabbed another empty box to collect more.

"Keep at it, Jay," Dale growled. "You're takin' my livelihood for no good reason. I ain't done anything!"

Violet was a statue huddled against Dahlia and their mother, Iris. So much work in the field. So much time pressing the grapes. Those bottles represented the maintenance of fickle vines to produce Crenshaw wine generation after generation.

Sheriff found an open bottle with the cork shoved in it. He swished around the wine, popped the cork, and sniffed. "This is goin' for testing, and if it's poisoned, Dale, you're a murderer. Somebody gave it to that poor girl and left her half-dead on the riverside for Birch Markle to finish her off."

Or maybe Markle snuck into the festival and poisoned it himself. He could slip in undetected. He'd done it before. Yet I didn't see Heather taking a bottle from a man covered in animal skins. Someone she trusted gave it to her.

"Did you see what was left of her, Crenshaw?" Sheriff hollered, disgust twisting his features. "She was *mutilated!*"

A wave of nausea gripped me. I'd seen Heather's corpse. Her living ghost had warned me.

Death seemed close, so cold, so real that if I reached into the fog, I'd find its fingers and lock hands.

CHAPTER SIXTEEN

Wanting to forget that terrible things happened don't change the past. The past makes you. It'll break you if you let it, and Lord have mercy on broken souls.

The lantern on my desk guttered as I sketched Heather's arm, arced from her body as she choked a bouquet of dandelions gone to puff. I hadn't left room to draw her face. Only her arm, her ribby side, bony hip, and skirt. Her curls. All of it red, red, red. I wanted to remember her in color, not the gray shell on the shore.

That Dale Crenshaw could've killed her didn't sit well with me. It seemed off, badly so. There had to be more.

I tapped my pencil against my lips and glanced to Heather's jewelry box that I'd taken from her home. What if Heather found out the secret Milo mentioned in the note? His sister didn't want him talking to us. To what extent would the Entwhistles go to keep Heather silent? Birch Markle may have had his way with Heather's remains, but someone she trusted put her in his sight.

Down the hall, my parents' movements weren't the usual post-dinner sounds of washing dishes and murmurs meant for each other, sometimes punctuated by Mama's trickling laughter. This night's noises were feverish with too many thumps, and when I opened my door, I caught sight of Mama standing face-to-face with Papa.

"Don't go, Timoteo," she begged.

He lifted her hand and kissed her fingers. "Luz, I gotta. It's about—"

Mama jerked back. Some anger shook her, yet her voice was a whisper I strained to hear. "Say it. Say her name."

Papa lowered his head. I crouched on the floor, my lantern's flame altering the shadows. Altering the way I saw my father's face.

"Say her name," Mama ordered.

I held my breath, waiting, and when Papa finally spoke, his voice was hoarse.

"Terra."

The girl Birch Markle killed.

Mama retreated from Papa and pointed toward the front door. "Go. Get out."

I didn't know what I had witnessed between my parents. They bickered from time to time, but this was a vein burrowing deeper than a mismatching of minds. Something bitter nudged Mama's words, and from the resignation in his tone, Papa sounded as if he knew he deserved whatever hell she unleashed.

He reached for her, but she swatted at him, and he left her standing in the hall. A moment later, I heard the back door latch as he exited. Still not moving from my spying place, I narrowed my eyes while Mama leaned against the wall to cross herself and slumped on the floor. Her brown hands with their strong joints gripped her forehead, then her shoulders quaked. My door creaked on its hinges, and my feet padded along the floor.

"Mama?" I called.

She didn't move. I scooted in beside her and curled my arms around her. She was beautiful, even as she cried, even with gray glittering at the front of her forehead. I liked the shape of her wide lips, the same as mine.

"Where'd Papa go?" I asked.

"His friends," she answered. Then she scoffed, a sour half laugh. "They've always been *his* friends."

"What do you mean? They like you."

Mama's gaze slid to mine. "Other than your papa, the only person in this family who ever really liked me is Mamie. She and Timoteo taught me the language. She taught me how to do things the Glen way so I wouldn't be such an outcast."

My chest ached hearing Mama's bluntness. I knew a wall existed between her and others in the Glen. Heather had loved my mother. She'd never treated Mama as different, but maybe there were things I never saw.

I followed Mama to the kitchen, where she drew out a kettle and filled it with water. I placed it on the wood stove. She chose some glass jars from a cabinet, a mortar and pestle, and ground herbs for a tea. The blend to calm my nightmares, I guessed by the smell. As she mixed, I noticed my father's veterinary bag under the table. I slipped past Mama and sat in a chair, lifting the bag with my foot.

"Do you miss La Pintada?" I asked, and eased open the bag.

"Sometimes," Mama admitted. "The village was small, far from any cities. I sold fruit, whatever was in season. Your father came with a church to build houses, and I noticed him because he spoke my language better than most of his group. I gave him extra fruit."

I smiled at the thought of my parents being close to the age I was now.

My fingers dipped inside Papa's bag, and I raked the bottom in search of Milo's ring. The tubing of the stethoscope was sleek, the glass thermometer cool, and I tripped over packets of needles and catgut sutures. Then I found a buttoned pocket inside the bag and pulled open the snap, hoping Mama hadn't heard the sound.

"Papa said he helped your brother after he was hurt," I said.

Mama's back remained to me, and she opened a metal tea ball to dump the herbs and roots inside, fastening it with a small, hinged lock. "He did. I miss my brother."

I remembered the letter Mama received a few years ago from the Mexican government, how her hands shook and she screamed in such horror that Papa came running. A landslide in La Pintada. Everyone was gone, her parents, her brothers and sister, their children. Friends she had while growing up. They had all died in the mud, and no one had told her until after their bodies were buried. Even if she wanted family outside the Glen, it didn't exist anymore.

"Do you wish you could visit their graves?" I asked.

"What good would it do, Ivy? There's nothing of them there, only ghosts."

"Mama . . ."

She held up a hand, unwilling to talk more, and went back to readying tea for when my nightmares rose. I hurried my search around the pocket until my finger looped through a metal band, and I buttoned the pocket, returned Papa's bag to the floor, and held Milo's ring inside my palm. The light under the table was scant, but the hammered silver ring glimmered with an engraved crest: bare branches surrounding an *M*. It was old, an heirloom, probably. He'd want it back. I'd offer it to him in exchange for information about Heather and what secrets she kept. What secrets helped kill her.

Mama dumped the tea ball into the kettle on the stove. "I love your father. I wouldn't be alive without him, but I didn't know everything about him when I married him, how complicated it'd be."

"If you'd known then what you know now, would you have come?" I asked.

She set those char-black eyes on me. "*Sí.* You don't stop loving a person because they have secrets. You make their secrets your own."

I couldn't think about attending school, though Rook brought me assignments from the days I missed. How could I walk the hallways knowing she wasn't in another class? All I wanted was to sleep. To go into the black hollow.

Rook wouldn't let me.

One of Heather's notes was tucked in my pocket. I reached inside to touch the paper, as if touching it would let me tap into what she had been thinking. Connect me to her once again.

Meet me in the woods, she'd written. *You know the place.*

Milo was in the woods on May Day. They'd planned it that way, and Heather had made him swear he'd not leave anything behind. Maybe they had.

Strolling through Potter's Field, I rested my head against Rook's arm. He had come over and read books aloud when my head ached. When I'd awakened, I'd found an odd portrait of me in ink in my sketchpad. I worked in pencil. Rook had stayed, even when I slept. He stayed in the living room with a thin blanket Mama had brought from her village to block the draft.

He stayed because he was Rook.

"Are you sure you're up to coming out to the woods like this?" he asked. "The funeral was yesterday, and I'm worried you ain't thinkin' right."

I shrugged. "I have to know, Rook. Milo told her he was gonna meet her out here. She was gonna run away from the Glen, but why?"

"Does it matter?" Rook asked.

"Yes," I snapped. Rook jerked at the sharpness of my reply. I took a steadying breath and closed my eyes.

Rook stepped under the shadow of the trees. "I don't know, Ivy. All the shit Heather was hiding, about anything could've happened to her that night."

The hunting rifle strapped to his back smacked his hip. If we traveled too deep in the woods, if we heard twigs cracking and flocks of roosting birds upset the sky, I had a mind to yell into the woods, then wait for Birch to slink out of his secret spot, all so Rook could put a bullet between his eyes.

"If we're found out here, we're gonna catch hell," he said. "God, the things you drag me into."

I grinned. "Ain't like you didn't come willingly. You've only known me my entire life."

My *entire* life.

Rook was born just over five months before me in September, on the proper side of the fall equinox. There wasn't a day I breathed that he didn't breathe with me. In spite of the chaos, knowing that brought some comfort.

"After school tomorrow, I can't stay with you," he said.

"You're needed at home with your mama and Raven. I understand."

His jaw contracted while he checked his rifle. I fought back the urge to warn him. Gramps didn't die of brain fever or cancer. He had been cleaning his rifle, and the rifle cleaned off his head. The bang from the bullet had reverberated to where I was playing outside with Papa's shepherd dog, Elsinore. As had Mamie's screams. It was months before they stopped picking bone and broken teeth from the walls.

"I ain't needed at home," Rook said. "Pops has me on watch."

"What?" I crossed my arms. "You ain't goin' out there like bait."

The idea of Rook standing patrol, even with a rifle, made my gut tremble as if I'd eaten bad berries and swallowed mustard tea to make the bad come back up.

"I'm doin' this, Ivy." He replaced his rifle on his shoulder. "I'll be sheriff someday, but nobody thinks I can do it. Even my pops says I got no mettle. What kind of guy knows more about plants than how to disarm someone?"

"One who'll help his people through a bad winter," I said.

"One who can't stop a murderer."

I gave a snort. "Your daddy ain't stopped Birch either. Papa said Dale Crenshaw's wine came up clean. So we still got a murderer runnin' 'round."

Rook scowled. I'd pushed too far. He didn't have to prove himself. Not to me.

His nostrils flared with frustration. "We got people comin' to our house asking when the Glen will be safe. Birch Markle is a curse on my family. When Grandpa Jackdaw died, he begged Pops to find that bastard. I don't want Pops beggin' the same of me."

He took a few steps and gave a bitter laugh while I held still behind him. "I'm awful at hunting. The sight of blood makes me yellow-bellied. But if Birch comes for you, I'll drop that monster dead."

I joined Rook's side and maneuvered my arm around his. How I wished we were on a simple walk in spring. Nothing was so simple. I was tied up in unraveling the strings my cousin had loomed. She'd walked along those threads, hoping not to fall between the gaps. She fell, and the strings were left behind. It was my fault I'd gotten tangled in them.

Ahead, I recognized the fabric remnants forming a tent among the trees. So many colors, like woven rainbows. Sunlight pierced the seams to catch on the dangling prisms of quartz and spoons.

We weren't the only ones there.

Milo was perched on a rock with his head bowed and hand against his forehead while Emmie fingered a gauzy scarf draped over a branch. My eyes darted around the dreamlike place, and I realized now — in daylight instead of the drunken light of Star's and Elm's lanterns — these weren't Birch Markle's totems. Everything spoke of Heather, discarded velvet pillows hidden under ferns, bottles made into charms only she'd use as a decoration. On a tree trunk, the bark peeled to reveal cuttings of initials. H + M.

I should've known before . . . but she'd denied it. She'd lied to my face. To protect Milo.

"What are you doing here?" Rook asked.

"Just saying goodbye. Since we weren't welcome at the funeral, we came here." Milo's sister gave a bitter smile. "It's a Glen rule, ain't it? Bury the dead after three days, or at least three days after a body's found?"

I narrowed my eyes. Glen kind didn't talk about our ways with outsiders, not the intimate traditions. We might sell our goods, help out with a secret charm bag or two for a price, but we didn't share our lore.

"How do you so much about Glen folk?" I asked.

Milo wistfully looked into treetops. "Even after you've left Rowan's Glen, it stays in your soul."

My mouth fell open. "What?"

"Our mama was Glen born," he admitted.

Was this what Emmie had warned him not to tell us? It could be only the beginning of secrets the Entwhistles carried in their hearts.

I moved along the boundary, stopping to study each tree. My chest felt caved in, a rumble that began with my heart fracturing, grief renewed.

Emmie added, "Mama left after the last May Queen, Terra MacAvoy, was killed. You can't stay after evil's touched your blood."

Your blood.

My blood.

How much were they like me, like Heather and Rook? Did they know how to make firefly lanterns or predict a bad winter by when the sycamore shed its bark? Maybe their mama tried to breed it out of them by giving her children an outsider daddy. She could've gone anywhere, and yet she raised them close to the Glen.

"Mama always said not to go back 'cause all you'd find in Rowan's Glen were lies and death. Not far off, was she?" Emmie remarked.

"So you heard of Birch Markle?" I asked.

Milo nodded. "Our mama told us the story. But someone like Heather comes 'round maybe once or twice in your life. You don't turn that away, no matter if you're scared."

Heather had mentioned being scared. Not of Milo. Of something in the Glen? He was her sanctuary. They'd even built a haven in the woods where they thought no one'd find it. As mystical this place was, a hollowness crept through me. She was reckless. She turned her back on Mamie's stories. The omens had warned her. She'd ignored them.

She didn't want to believe.

She didn't want to be part of the Glen.

"We're gonna catch him," I said.

Emmie crossed her arms. She looked so much like her brother in the face, in the swagger of her gait — her skirt wanting to shimmy down her plank-straight hips. All she needed was a cigarette glued to her lips.

She scoffed. "Catching him don't bring back Heather. Can't bring back Terra MacAvoy. She's bones by now."

Milo put his arm around his sister. They edged away to leave the clearing, but Rook hopped up and called to them.

"Hey, before you go, just curious what your mama's name was," he said.

Milo glanced back. "Laurel."

He turned away, and together, he and Emmie retreated from Heather's hideaway to cut through the trees, not bothering to stick to a path. They were twin cryptids, creatures of no classification, visible for only a few steps before the underbrush folded around them.

I picked up one of the jewel-colored pillows and sat. Once I was home, I'd bundle up under Mamie's blanket and drink her tea. Praying my nightmares about teeth and knives and bloody skin would stop for a few hours.

Rook took a spot beside me with his knees tucked up. The woods were muted, no crackles of unseen squirrels or deer moving between trees. Even the birds hushed. Perhaps in mourning for the girl who used to dance here.

I laid my head on Rook's shoulder. "What'd you think of what Milo and Emmie said?"

"That they know too much about the old May Queen," Rook answered.

"What if—" Bringing the words to sound meant unleashing an idea, a terrible idea. "The MacAvoys ain't in the Glen anymore. Do you think they're Terra MacAvoy's kin?"

Rook gave it a moment of consideration. "If they are, they'd have a hell of a grudge against the Glen."

My eyelids twitched. The acridity of smoke burned my nose, and I sat up, looking first for a house fire, then to my lamp, where a smoke plume danced from the wick. The oil had burned dry after I'd carried my drawings to bed to page through and fallen asleep. The papers were scattered across my blanket, and every place I glanced, Heather stared back.

Poisoned wine. Terra. Milo.

Heather's necklace draped across the front of my nightgown. I felt along the metal links until I came to Milo's ring, which I'd strung on the chain.

Why was Heather by that river?

To find me.

"She didn't care," my sleep-muzzy mouth fumbled.

She did. What if she came to apologize?

If I kept thinking these thoughts, I'd scream and wake the house. I groped around my nightstand, searching for my mug in hope maybe some scant tea drops remained to dull my brain. My fingers caught the mug's curved handle, and with an awkward spin, the cup crashed against the floor. I waited for Mama's feet to bombard the hall.

Silence.

With Mamie's blanket on my shoulders, I climbed out of bed, past my window, white with condensation. Heather used to write messages on the glass, made me figure out the backwards spelling. Our code. I wiped down the pane, removing the fog. Something lay on the windowsill outside.

I cranked open my window and picked up a piece of agate wrapped in wire. I'd been with Heather when she unearthed it. She polished it and made it a charm for her necklace. I'd noticed it was missing, but here it was. Smudged with dried blood.

I dropped the stone charm. It landed on the floor and rolled a few inches before coming to rest against the wall.

Heather's blood.

I tried to scream, though my tongue seemed too large. Someone was standing in the field.

"D-d-dreaming," I told myself. "Or a scarecrow."

I didn't want to touch anything, but I urged myself — sliding down the window to shut it. But then I couldn't see where the figure was, if it neared. My palm flattened against the glass and slashed up to down, like a gash through the fog.

"No!" I choked on the word.

The shape in the field loomed tall, shrouded with moonlight around the cape of animal pelts. The torch fires' gory red glow, the neigh of a horse ridden by a guard somewhere far off. Despite the closed window, I smelled decay and heard the flies buzzing.

Birch Markle stared at me.

I plummeted to the floor, with my knees tucked against my breasts, and I didn't move until the robins began their morning song.

CHAPTER SEVENTEEN

Just 'cause a fellow's mad don't mean he can't know the land and how to live off it. Birch's been out there all these years. Only a few times anybody's caught a glimpse of him in his animal skins, living off wild honey, bugs, and blood like some kinda demented John the Baptist.

Copper circles like pennies dried on the field. Some creature died last night, and its blood fed the Glen's soil.

As soon as I awakened, I'd braided a garland of basil and clover. The stems twisted in my fingers, each movement in time with the memory of Mamie's tales. *Clover keeps the bad away, and where there's basil, no evil can a-enter.*

I hung it over my window.

I didn't want to go back to school. Classes were insignificant now. What was there to learn? All the teaching couldn't prepare you for death. Once, I'd been a good student, wanted passing grades, but now it was a routine I didn't care about. I'd been away since Heather first disappeared, and the only reason I went back was because Papa said I must.

No one was around when I left for school with Rook. Mama was at Mamie's house, helping after Marsh banged on our door in the middle of the night. He had a limp from where Aunt Rue hit him.

"Woman trouble," he called it. Not the baby kind, either. Aunt Rue was in the field, naked under the moon, and hollering for Birch to take her.

I tried sleeping again, even covering my ears and drinking more tea, but the screams found me.

During class, I felt the stares, heard the whispers. As much as we liked to pretend the Glen was an enclave unto itself, it wasn't true. The inside and outside mingled, not much but enough that neither could be unaware of the ripples running through their individual streams.

The dead girl, someone whispered.

She's one of them, another voice stroked my neck.

I was a dead girl. I'd joined the ranks of Terra and Heather, felt the chill settle and turn to peace before Rook ripped me away. To walk between the worlds was my fate. How could I explain that I wasn't who I once was but something haunted?

I wanted to live.

I wanted to be Ivy. I hadn't been ready before, but without Heather, the shade where I dwelled grounded me in a way I had never been when she pulled me toward the light.

I missed her, though.

The whispers were too loud, and I raised my hand to be excused to the bathroom. My literature teacher dismissed me. Milo lifted his head from playing with his cell phone. The classroom was too small and tight, the whispers too hot in my ears, and my throat constricted around itself until I couldn't breathe. I hurried down the hallway to a drinking fountain, gulping, gulping, gulping water until the fever went out of my cheeks.

I rifled through my pockets for a paper. Heather's words were the last things of hers I had, even if they were to Milo and spoke of their promises, the nakedness of their fears.

H,

You say you don't want to hurt me. Then come with me. I'll help you get out of this middle-of-nowhere hellhole. Where we go, who we are won't matter. On May Day, after sunset, I prom-ise I'll wait for you in our place in the woods. That's when we'll leave. All those secrets, you won't have to worry about anyone finding out. Not your family. Not Ivy. No one. It'll be just you and me.

Trust me.

— M

M,

I'm scared.

— H

H,

Don't be scared.

I'll be with you. We got this.

— M

I crushed the paper and shut my eyes. No more crying.

Footsteps shuffled down the hall. Even with my closed eyes, I sensed Milo's tallness looming over me. He smelled of smoke and medicine. I'd feared him at times, but now, this second, he was gentle as he took the paper from me.

I waited a minute before opening my eyes and asking, "Did you mean it? All those things you said to Heather?"

He swallowed and covered his full lips. His skin was scruffy with light brown stubble. He mimicked my posture with my back to the lockers and then slid down the metal, slumped with legs splayed out.

"Fucking Heather." His nose reddened. "It ain't supposed to be this way."

I sat beside him. My hand hovered above his back, and when I dared touch his shoulder, he was bonier than expected, quivering with each breath. This roller boy hid his face and muffled the sounds of his crying. He could be hard and mouthy, but how much was a reaction to life being hard and mouthy to him?

From what Heather had told me that foggy morning, I believed she'd loved him. I never considered he actually loved her with the same depth. No one loved like Heather.

Hesitant, afraid, I wrapped my arms around him, and as we hugged, warm teardrops fell from his face to soak my shirt collar.

He sniffed. "People like Heather, they're so bright they burn out too fast."

Except Heather didn't burn out. She was extinguished.

At the end of the school day, Rook and I walked along the road toward the Glen in a slow, thoughtful stride. My brain dizzied with Milo's grief, the love letter I once again scrunched in my hand.

Rook eyed the scrap of paper. "You're being quiet."

"I have too many questions," I answered.

"Start with asking one."

"What if Milo promised to run away with Heather and never intended to follow through? Or what if they were gonna go but Emmie stopped them?" I grabbed my head. "What if we're just wrong about everything?"

"Hold up. I said to ask one question, not all of them." Rook forced a smile. "I don't trust Milo, but he was in the woods waiting for her. His sister, though . . ."

We neared the trailer park and walked along the chainlink fence. Heather was a ghost here, a memory of a laugh, a sudden stream of red curls. I'd walked beside her for years. Her footsteps carried a certain weight that I always knew when she was close by.

We were near the gate of the trailer park. Milo's trailer was visible with a heavily rusted truck sticking out of the carport.

"Why the hell would they meet in the woods, of all places?" I asked Rook. "Heather knew it was off-limits. She liked danger, but he must've done some convincing or — Rook?"

He was distracted by the fence, examining the vine weaving the metal grid. His fingers nudged some dried blue-black berries from last fall still clinging to the vine. The fence was a wall of green as far as I could see.

"What's this?" I asked.

"Belladonna," he replied, looking up. "An awful lot of it."

I held the kitten on the exam table in the clinic while Papa changed the cotton around her paw. I'd found the green-eyed ginger kitten on the doorstep after school yesterday. At first, Mama tried to stop me from checking on the sound of meowing, convinced it was a devil's trick. The sky was blood, shadows unpredictable and filled with story. It'd be a sin to leave her outside, Papa had told Mama as he lay on the floor with the kitten and dangled a string for her paws to bat.

We named her Wednesday.

Papa put away his stethoscope. "You still drinking Mamie's tea?"

"Mama won't let me miss a dose," I replied. My hands rubbed the kitten's back, letting her tail circle my wrist. She was so pretty, so red and affectionate.

"Sleep-Away-Sorrow works right well. Mamie only brews it up when your head's better off sedated while working out what hell it's seen." Papa scrunched his nose. "Too much anise for my taste."

"You've drunk that tea?"

"Indeed."

"When Gramps died?"

"Long time before that," he said.

I placed Wednesday in the nest I'd made behind the counter where Heather used to sit so many days after school.

My fingers drummed the counter. "Wh-why's Sheriff promised to keep me safe?"

Papa dropped a cleaning cloth in a bucket of vinegar water. "'Cause he's a lawman, and that's what they do."

"He says he owes you. What happened? What made you go on that missionary trip? Nobody else 'round here does them, and it ain't like you're that prayerful a man."

"Ivy!"

"Y-you can't tell me you left only to go to vet school. That's at Mizzou — but you went to Mexico. Why? If you hated being here in the Glen, why'd you come back?"

His mouth tightened, eyes steely behind his glasses. "I left 'cause the future I planned wasn't gonna happen. I came back 'cause I forgave. Sometimes all you can do is forgive and hope folks learn from the past."

"Did they?" I asked.

"Your cousin's dead, so no, they didn't."

For the next hour, Papa remained in his office. I was alone but not. It was impossible not to feel Heather. I reached for the thermos under the counter and poured more tea. My mind was overaware, and I didn't want that. I wanted Sleep-Away-Sorrow's warm-bath sensation, of sliding down into a pool of nothingness. *Drink it fast, make it hit harder.* No memories of Heather's lipless grin and her neck bones cracking. No more recollection of her teeth clacking together to shape words.

Find it, Ivy.

I swallowed the last dregs and withdrew my sketchbook. The drawings weren't mine anymore. I couldn't recall penning the images: torn dresses with darkness leaking from wounds, horses without manes, and boy hands on curved hips. If anyone saw what resided in my book, they'd think I'd gone mad.

I felt closer to death than life.

I reached under the counter to retrieve my pencil sharpener. My thumb snagged on a hole inside, one that opened up through the underside of the countertop. I shouldn't have thought much of it — carpenter ants, mice — any pesky critter could've chewed through the wood. Yet I was half asleep, and the hole was magical. I stuck my finger inside.

A folded paper fluttered out.

It was marked with uneven lines in my cousin's writing. Words like *mounds, shrubs, marsh, river.* It was a rudimentary map of someplace deep in the woods. Where it led, I had no idea, but wherever it was, Heather had kept it secret, with a cryptic sentence amid her description of the grounds.

Be afraid of what's right in front of you.

I'd been afraid. I was still afraid. Except I didn't know what to fear anymore.

My head lay on the desk, paper against my cheek. The pencil rolled and poked me in the lip while my eyelids became curtains to blacken my world. My pencil traced my profile, and some part of me knew when I slipped off the page my hand kept working, though I didn't dare see what hauntings in my head came out . . .

Teeth. Human and animal mixed together in the same mouth. The mouth hovered close to my forehead, breath reeking of honey, boy sweat, and coagulated blood. Vultures would come soon. The stench would draw them.

I pushed back the shape, but I had no hands, only stumps where glossy, scarlet pools thumped against the dog heads tied together on the shape's chest. There was no place to run, too many trees behind me, and from somewhere else, water trickled close by. I prayed it was water.

"Shhh," the shape said, and pressed fingers to my lips.

The skin was cold.

Because it was mine.

The shape held my dead hand.

"Shhh," Birch Markle repeated. "All secrets you keep are someone else's lies."

Shrieks tore from me until my vocal cords bled in my throat, then I kept screaming . . .

"Ivy!" Papa shook me. His hands enveloped my cheeks. "Ivy, wake up!"

One more scream jerked from my mouth, and Papa tugged me against his shoulder. I flexed my fingers. They were stiff and frigid, but they bent and moved. Alive.

"The nightmares will stop," Papa promised, still hugging me.

"How are you so sure?" I asked.

"Mine did."

Dark was coming.

Already the torches were lit when we left the clinic at dusk. I held Wednesday close to me and glanced westward to the sunset. The last vestiges of violet dissolved in the sky.

We stayed in the middle of the road, avoiding the ruts from wagon wheels. My hair fell over my face, the only sounds the *swish-swish* of my skirt and muffled steps of Papa's boots.

"You asked why I drank Mamie's tea," he said. "I lost someone."

I hesitated. The risk was worth knowing.

"Terra?"

Papa's mouth flexed.

"I heard you and Mama," I said.

He stopped along the fence. Nothing around us except dried fields and the bowing heads of scarecrows. His fingers traced the aged wood, tapping it. "Terra and I grew up together. Her family, the MacAvoys, grew pumpkins. Scores of 'em, like you had a pocketful of orange marbles that you decided to toss in the field one day. Terra was gonna become a vet. My God, she loved animals. Cats, dogs, birds, every critter came to her. Jay's daddy, Jackdaw, was sheriff and got after her for keepin' so many animals."

The smile on Papa's face—the same look he gave to Mama—was one of tenderness and thought. Then his smile faded. Sorrow recognized itself, I believed, and my sorrow saw itself in my father. I joined him by the fence, enveloped by the torches' glow.

"You loved her," I declared.

My father lowered his head and walked on. I joined him, waiting for him to admit what he'd hidden my entire life. He murmured with grief so thick I could wring it from the air. "On May Day twenty-five years ago, Terra was May Queen. After her crownin', we were gonna meet in our secret place to figure out how to tell Pastor she was pregnant and ask him to marry us. Instead, Marsh and Jay, we were all messin' 'round, and I passed out drunk. Terra waited for me. Nobody heard her scream after Birch Markle got outta his family's cellar. She wasn't found until a few days later, when Jay was tending some horses. He heard some cackling by Promise Bridge and found Birch poking a stick at what he'd done."

The May Queen.

Why Papa hated May Day so very much.

"The county police investigated," Papa went on. "They didn't believe that Birch killed her, said I'd done it, that I didn't want the baby. The thing was, I couldn't remember what had happened that night, and the police took me to their station in town and questioned me for two days. We didn't know any lawyers, and Mamie and my daddy didn't have the money to hire one. Jackdaw brought Jay and Marsh, handed the police eyewitnesses, but they said my friends were coverin' for me."

"Is that why Sheriff hasn't brought in the county police?" I asked.

"Can't trust 'em." Papa rubbed his forehead. "It wasn't until Birch's sister told the police she knew her brother did it . . . He'd killed some animals before . . ."

I held Wednesday tight under my arm. Suddenly, it seemed too easy for her to escape. To meet some horrible end. I caught up to

Papa. He put his arm around me and kissed my forehead. If this awful history had never been, I wouldn't exist. I swallowed the sickness of that thought and said, "You left the Glen."

"I never intended to return, but guilt brought me back. I couldn't leave Mamie and Rue. Maybe I thought I could stop Birch from killin' animals if I took care of them. The Glen, for good and bad, is home."

Papa paused near the gate of our home's fence. His eyes were heartbroken. Telling me about his past had restored his grief. "It was easier to let myself think Birch was dead, but I knew better. I saw him once in the field, when you were a baby. He was covered in rotting skins and watching the house. I ran for my rifle, but he was gone. He's been in the woods since. Folks said he began screaming after I first left. He ain't stopped."

CHAPTER EIGHTEEN

No one seen Birch much, but no one wants to. The screams are bad enough. Those who've caught sight of him know him by the smell. You don't forget the death stench. Makes your blood run right cold, it does.

"You gotta warm up, Ivy. You're too cold." Violet spread out the blanket in the field for a late picnic. "Your fingernails'll turn blue."

I drew Mamie's blanket around my shoulders. Beads of condensation rolled down the glass of sweet tea resting on a crate she had overturned for a table. She slathered bread with strawberry marmalade made from last year's crop and nudged it toward me.

"You won't eat?" August asked from his perch on another crate. "Ants'll get it."

Beneath my blanket, I crushed the folded drawing of the map within my palm. I'd slept with it tucked under my pillow the night before.

"Have it." I offered the bread to August, content to pet Wednesday, who was nipping my fingers.

He swiped the slice of bread. "I ain't one to turn down food."

I smiled. Being among friends felt good, not hiding away inside my room with its shadows and cobwebs. They came over after school, time I once spent with Heather. Time I now didn't know what to do with myself.

Violet tipped back her head and twirled under the sun's marigold rays. Her hair floated around her, some braids held with beads. She was barefoot and oblivious to the dirt covering her toes, happy under the sun's spires. This was day's sharpest light, when it became piercing and fought the encroaching dusk.

"I gotta run," August said. "I've gotta get home."

"Why don't you patrol with Rook?" I asked. It was a blunt question, rude maybe. He was Rook's best friend. If Rook wasn't with Heather and me, he was with August. That boy should've gone out with him.

August lowered his head. "Don't think I ain't out there by choice. My old man has a bad ticker. Even foxglove won't help, according to Granny Connelly. I gotta be here for my mama. You understand, right?"

I bristled and looked away. Understanding was one thing. Liking it was another.

"You comin'?" he asked Violet.

Violet shook her head. "I want to stay with Ivy."

"Well, make sure you leave before sunset. Sheriff might drag you to the station for not obeying his law." August rolled his eyes.

"Sheriff's an idiot. That wine he took from my daddy wasn't even tainted. He came to our house with his hat in his hands, trying to apologize, but Daddy ain't having it. Says he hopes Birch Markle causes Sheriff so much grief he'll be run right outta the Glen."

I cringed. Anger was an easy emotion, forgiveness much harder, and I had to suppose that in her upset, Violet didn't realize she was talking about Rook's father and wishing him gone.

She flopped down beside me and put her arm around my shoulder. "We won't talk anymore of Birch Markle. Talking about him makes him come after you."

August waved goodbye and jogged off, all lumbering limbs and flopping hair. He had a knife in a sheath on his hip. Even Violet set her rifle against the fence while we picnicked. Everyone armed themselves against the madman from the woods.

I was next.

Violet blushed. She sat on the edge of the picnic blanket. I knew that grin, the way her fingers fumbled in her lap as she racked her mind for words.

"Can I talk to you about somethin'?" she wondered. She scooted close to me and tucked her knees against her chest. "I gotta tell you. I want you to be happy for me."

The cherry-pink in her cheeks bloomed brighter. The air around her lightened.

"You seein' someone?" I asked.

"August. I was supposed to meet him last night. I know it ain't safe to go off, but . . . you know what it's like when he looks at you. When he touches you. All you can think of is bein' alone with him again."

I did know.

"I didn't mean for it to happen," Violet went on, still smiling. "With everyone so scared, folks dyin' and the dogs, but being with August feels so good. I wasn't sure when to tell you 'bout it."

"What do you mean?" I asked.

"You've had such a curse on you."

"You didn't want it to spread."

She reached forward to pat my leg. "I'd never think being your friend would hurt me, but you're a bit of a black cat. I also knew I'd get in trouble if we were caught sneaking 'round."

"It ain't worth it," I blurted out. "Stay safe, Violet. You and August gotta find a way to be together that doesn't get you roamin' at night."

She gave an understanding nod. Maybe Violet would listen, not give in to recklessness.

"You're shivering," she remarked.

"Birch is gonna kill me," I said.

"He won't." She pushed my hair behind my ear. "Rook's hunting him."

Rook was a terrible hunter.

The span of woods seemed endless, and the hillmen tried to cover as much of the Glen as possible. Rook could wind up patrolling alone. He could be pulled into the river or bloodied in a field. His bones could be stripped, his skin worn as leather. I shut my eyes, but the half dream punched through with a sun-bleached spine and glasses with cracked lenses.

My eyelids were heavy as bags of grain. Wednesday curled up near my feet.

"How do you think it happens?" I wondered.

Violet's forehead crinkled. "How what happens?"

"Birch Markle would've been about our age the first time he killed. I don't get how someone can cut open a dog and play with what's inside. How does that idea get in someone's head?"

"His mind wasn't like anybody else's, and I guess nobody 'round here knew what to do with a mind like that." Violet stretched her legs and stroked my cheek. "You need more sun, get some color."

"I'm not worried about my damn color." The tremble began in my lower lip and squiggled down my chin. I had to take my time, or I'd trip all over my words. "Birch Markle took away Heather. We were havin' the worst fight of our lives, and I never got to say I was sorry. I never got to forgive her. I never got forgiven. I don't know how to live with that."

Violet angled her head, her voice soft. "You're doing it right now." She pulled a few pieces of my hair loose and twisted them around in knots. "I know I ain't the same, but we've always been friends."

We had. The only thing stopping us from being closer had been Heather.

"I feel like what happened to Heather's my fault," she said. "You were with me when . . . Maybe it's like people say. She should've been more careful."

Down the road, a girl walked toward us. The wind blew her light hair and ruffled the scarf around her neck. Unlike many hillfolk, Dahlia didn't arm herself against a sudden attack.

"Time for you to come home, Vi," she said upon reaching the field.

Violet brushed off her skirt and packed the crates and picnic basket. Dahlia's arms were folded across her chest, and her expression was stern, though it was impossible to tell what shape her mouth made. Her scars were savage things. Only at rare times did she venture from the Crenshaw grape fields. There were stories she went with the granny-women when there were farming accidents, that she tended wounds with herbs and tonics. These were the women on the Glen's fringe. They dabbled in plants, poisons, and prayers, and welcomed Dahlia in their shroud.

Violet finished returning the crates to my yard. She and Dahlia met each other, face-to-face, similar in their sisterhood but for the twisting roots scarring the older girl's neck and cheek, and then they walked away, taking identical steps, hair blowing out in moon-white tangles.

I missed having someone walk beside me.

I missed my Heather.

My parents split a bottle of peach wine after dinner. Papa read aloud to us from a book he'd found at a thrift store. Mama curled in close to him, her head on his shoulder. I noticed his hand moving up her back before unpinning her hair to loose the dark waves. I was glad to see my parents at peace again, but I couldn't concentrate on the story; I kept thinking of Rook out there, patrolling in the dark.

Wednesday tiptoed along the mopboards and leaped onto the mantel, green eyes catching the oil lamps' light. Most cats we'd kept stayed outside, but Wednesday had reason to come indoors. She'd already brought Mama a dead mouse, which Papa reminded her meant the kitten liked her. But now she stared at the window, back arched and tail straight.

I interrupted my father's reading and pointed to the kitten. "Papa?"

He followed the cat's gaze and shut the book. The warning bells outside chimed. My parents and I held still. The bells on our back door jingled.

Papa stood. Wednesday paced along the door and hissed. I peered through the filmy curtain over the window. All seemed asleep in Rowan's Glen. The floor creaked. The cat clawed at the door. The bells swinging and ringing against so much quiet inched trepidation up my spine. Papa removed his rifle from a closet, felt around the shelf, and pulled down a pair of bullets, which he sank into the rifle's chamber. Suddenly, a blast of gunfire resounded across the Glen. We waited with breath held.

BANG!

A second shot echoed in the night. Papa's finger eased back the curtain. He opened the door, motioning for Mama and me to stay back.

A rumble caught my ear. It started muffled, rhythmic, but it was a sound I recognized.

Hoofbeats.

Louder and louder, faster and faster, a horse sped at full gallop. I angled closer to the door to peer past my father. The torches' light revealed a charcoal-maned white stallion jumping fences, reins loose. Riderless.

I shoved Papa aside and bolted down the steps.

"Ivy, no!" he shouted.

"That's Veil!" I yelled. Where was Rook?

I tracked back from where Veil fled, where the shots came from, and my stomach pushed past my heart and lodged in my throat. My legs couldn't carry me fast enough, but I forged ahead with my feet stomping the hard earth. He had to be close. He had to be alive. He had to —

Rook was sprawled on the ground. I ran to him and slid aside his rifle. The gun's barrel was warm and wispy with smoke.

"Rook!" I shouted. "W-wake up!"

His eyes remained closed, blood seeping from a gash in his forehead.

I placed my hands on his shoulders and shook him. "Wake up! C'mon, you gotta get up!"

No matter how I yelled for him to open his eyes, he wouldn't.

Water splashed, then the tart odor of apple cider vinegar and witch hazel skimmed my nose. Amber glass bottles set upon the counter clinked together as Mama reached for one to pull a cork. More trickling liquid. More splashing. A rag soaked in a bowl of the healing solution.

Then Mama poured steaming water from a kettle into three mugs. The perfume of the tea, of comfort and old stories, chased away worry and fear. I stirred honey in my cup, the chime of the spoon hitting the side too loud in the wordless kitchen.

Mama prepared a fourth cup and squeezed Briar Meriweather's

shoulder, Briar's hand reaching up to cover my mother's. After, she carried the tea and healing cloth down the hall to Rook's room.

"Did he say what happened?" I asked.

"Birch Markle," Briar replied. She cupped her mug for warmth or comfort, maybe both. "I begged Jay not to send him out."

The anger as she spoke was tempered by fear, by relief her boy had made it home. "I sent Raven to my sister's house when Jay said Rook was hurt, should think about pickin' her up soon."

The door down the hall clicked. Papa and Sheriff entered the kitchen. Sheriff rubbed his face, drawing his expression haggard.

"He could've been hurt worse," Papa said. "The horse bucked him after he got off a couple of shots."

"But he's okay?" I asked anxiously.

Sheriff nodded. "Luckily. He's restin' now, said he might've hit Markle with a bullet, that he went running off holding his arm. Timothy, I need you to help me round up some men for a search."

Papa and Sheriff headed outside. Briar stood and drew a shawl around her shoulders, picking up a rifle from beside the kitchen door. "Luz, come along while I pick up Raven? I don't wanna go alone."

Mama nodded, and she and Briar walked out the door, the lock loud behind them. I sat alone in the kitchen with my tea. In its surface, my eyes disappeared in the tannin-dark color and left my mirror image skeletal.

Go see that boy, lay your hands on him. Get the fret outta your head. Fret only gets you dead.

The chair scraped against the floor. My fingers reached out to touch the cool walls of the hallway, and I walked deeper into the shadows. I wasn't afraid in darkness, not here. Not when a shaft of a cinnamon-colored light leached out through the cracked door of Rook's room. I nudged the door open enough to step inside, shut it behind me, lock clicking.

Rook lay on his bed, shirtless, with his eyes closed and only a pair of drawers to cover the middle of him. The rag of vinegar and witch hazel covered a comfrey poultice on the left side of his forehead. A red tendril from the gash poked out from the edge. His glasses rested on his nightstand at a precarious angle, and my steps were muted as I crossed the floor to fix his glasses so he wouldn't knock them off by accident. As I folded the frames, I watched his chest rise and fall. His breath. His life.

He could've died.

One wrong move, and Birch could have slit him from ear to ear.

One more burial in the Glen's cemetery. How would anyone tell Raven what had happened to the older brother who adored her so? How old would she be before she forgot the sound of his voice? When Gramps died, I was older than she was now. I couldn't remember how he sounded.

Not enough memories, too much death.

Too damn much death in our land by the woods.

A sob struggled up my throat, and I clamped down best I could, didn't want to disturb Rook, but a murmur sneaked out. I pressed my fingers to my mouth to stop the next one, except I hiccupped, and then my eyes went wet and my knees jellied. My skirt puddled around me as I dropped by his bedside and bit the heel of my palm to silence myself.

"Are you cryin'?"

Rook's voice was a rich heat that sank through my hair and coiled around me. I gasped, wiped my tears, but he'd seen me wrecked before. I twisted around to face him with my cheek against his mattress.

"Y-you scared me tonight," I said.

He reached for his glasses and sat up to remove the rag from his forehead. "I'm okay."

"If y-y-you died—"

Rook's hands slid beneath my arms and eased me onto his bed, in his lap, shushing me with his forefinger. I grasped onto him and closed my eyes. He was *real*. The smell of plants from his green-house was trapped in the room; the vapor of chamomile and clove tea clung to his hair. His finger against my mouth, roughness and heat and softness all merging as one. I kissed his skin, the side of his finger, the tip. I turned over his hand and laid my lips on each of his knuckles because I wanted to never regret not kissing each part of him.

Once I finished with his hand, I swiveled around in his lap to straddle him, my fingers treading up his arm to his shoulder. I'd seen him naked before when we were little and swimming in Meyer's Pond. Once I realized that I thought him handsome, sometimes I watched while he worked in his family's field, shirtless and sweaty enough to warm my face. I ran the edges of my nails, down his abdomen to his waist, spreading my chills to him. His lanky muscles were defined, and yet I liked his softness.

"Shouldn't you be home?" he asked.

"I had to come," I said.

"Where's everyone else?"

"Our fathers are roundin' up men for a search, and my mama went with yours to pick up Raven from your aunt's." I drew my hand along his face, and he pressed the hard part of his jaw into my palm. "I kept worryin', what if you were hurt, how bad it'd be. I just buried Heather. Please don't make me bury you."

His eyes focused on mine, so intensely green. Without any rain, they might well be the greenest thing in the Glen. "I was afraid you died in the water, Ivy. I was so damn mad at you for leaving me and scared and sick. When you were drowning and I pulled you outta that river, I had the feeling you didn't wanna come out. Did you?"

"No," I said. His lips parted in a stricken look. I rushed to finish, "I could've stayed under, but you didn't let me. Every breath I have is because you put it in me. I'd be a fool not to know what a gift that is."

I traced the smooth line of Rook's collarbone and lowered my mouth to kiss him there. The catch of his breath, the tickle of his touch as he moved my hair behind my ear so he could see my face — my mouth, the shift of his legs and scratch of the hair on his legs rubbing against my thighs beneath my skirt. He unbuttoned the back of my dress and slid it down my shoulders until it pooled at my waist.

I suspected he knew why I was cold now, and he used his hands as best he could to warm me, used his mouth on mine and lower to find some heat. I reached down to ease off his drawers while his hand disappeared under my dress. His drawers hit the floor first, and my dress landed on top in a crumpled heap. Every movement with Rook was instinctual but also a lesson. If I liked it, I asked him to do it again, and he responded in kind. I kissed from his neck to his chest, the muscles of his stomach. Lower. I came up, his tongue teased mine, and I opened to his mouth, ran my hands up through his hair to grab hold as I kissed him back harder.

"You're sure?" he asked. "If you need to wait—"

"I'm ready." And I was. He glanced to his door, and I tilted my head, running my finger across his wrist. "Are you?"

"It's just . . . You know, but yeah." He opened a drawer on his nightstand to retrieve a condom, and tore open the foil packet. How Heather had giggled through the condom-over-the-banana demonstration in health class, but right then, with Rook, it didn't seem so funny.

The darkness in the room thickened, bathing us in the amber of his oil lamp. Steadily, I moved on top of him while his hands guided my hips. My body ached—with grief, with sex, with secrets shared and unshared. From withholding myself from myself for too long.

Everything hurt. Sex with Rook, no matter how good it felt once the initial pain faded, didn't remove loss. I didn't seek to fill that hollowness. It was there. It was part of me now, and it would be for however long to come.

Yet giving this part of my body to Rook, him giving his to me, didn't feel like empty desperation. This moment with him would've happened no matter the sadness and chaos. I'd thought about him for so long, thought about kissing him, touching him. Being kissed. Being touched. Wanting to know what it was like, and I liked it. I watched his head on the pillow as it shifted in hope of not hitting the headboard against the wall, of him liking the way I felt against him. His eyes met mine, and his smile eased when he realized I was staring at him. He shuddered and held me closer. Every day of my life, I'd known this boy. He'd been my friend. He was so much more. I hadn't recognized the shift when it occurred, but I'd gained someone other than Heather with whom I could be so bare.

When it was over, both of us sweating and breathing hard, we took our time redressing, opening the window to let in the night air. Rook fixed the buttons on the back of my dress and placed his mouth on my neck before sweeping aside my hair. The sound of approaching voices outside hurried our last few kisses, and then I backed away toward his bedroom door, smiling.

"Your hair's a mess. I like it." He turned on his side and rolled his fingers in a gentle wave goodbye.

I was in the kitchen with now-cold tea when Briar and Mama re-entered the house. Mama motioned for me to come with her, and I got up with a hushed "Good night" as I passed by Briar, who held Raven sound asleep on her shoulder. She opened the door, ready to lock it behind me, but she lingered, watching while I joined my mother beside the greenhouse.

"Stay safe on the road. He could be anywhere out there."

The hounds' howls kept me awake past midnight.

When I slept, it was fitful, dreams of mouths and gentle hands, horses' hooves pounding the land, and throwing myself underwater, drowning until all went gray. My father came home long after the torches had burned themselves black.

No one found Birch Markle.

I rubbed my eyes. Remembering, wishing. Mourning a red curl.

I went to the kitchen, still in my nightdress, and cuddled inside Mamie's blanket, where Wednesday wrapped her body around my ankles. I missed sitting on the back step and waiting for Heather to find me before school, before Rook joined us. I missed those mornings of giggles as she wiped the rim of fresh milk from above her lip, of timid smiles when Rook handed off the basket of eggs and my heart jumped because my fingertips had skimmed his.

One deep breath, a second, a scream built inside my belly. Tea. I needed some tea to halt the clatter in my mind.

My hands fumbled with a pitcher of water, spilling as I poured it into the kettle, which I set on the heat. A glass jar of herbs and flower buds was on the counter. A piece of twine held a card to the top, and Mamie's handwriting read *Sleep-Away-Sorrow Tea. Peppermint, valerian, hyssop, lavender, St. John's wort, and others known only to me.* I smirked. Of course, Mamie wouldn't give away all her knowledge.

I rummaged through the drawer in search of a tea ball and

noticed it sitting in the sink's basin. I moved aside the vines of Rook's strawberry plant. Sunrise had always been my favorite time of day. I awakened before my parents, and there was magic in the fog covering the field. Now I liked sunrise because it meant the night terrors left, at least for a while.

My gaze settled on the field across from my house. Some white cloth huddled in the middle of the dirt, a bed linen yanked off the line and carried by wind.

Bed linens didn't have blond hair.

I rushed to the door, ready to pull it open and dash outside, but I halted. He could still be out there. Blade in hand. Stink of death surrounding him.

That body could still be alive.

I grabbed Papa's rifle from the closet. It was loaded. Good. The door opened without sound, not even a squeaky hinge, as I crept outside. Scattered pieces of clover and basil lay on the ground and withered. The garland of protection over my window was ripped apart as if it were weeds torn from the ground. I was staggering down the remaining stairs when I stepped on something round, cold, and smooth. A green glass circle marked March 27. It'd broken in half when I stepped on it.

Birch Markle had been here. At my house.

"M-M-Mama!" I shouted. "Papa!"

I needed to hear their frantic footfalls. I whipped my head, scanning the dirt road. It was empty. The morning quietude was undisturbed except for the scattered herbs and the body in the field, out of place and unreal. I picked up the halves of the glass circle. The glass was cool and damp with dew, but it didn't warm against me and instead felt like a cold lump against my skin. A tear of grief and horror spun through my gut until I managed to scream again.

"Mama!"

Thumps and bangs from within the house. I tried crying out again, but my voice deteriorated into only a high-pitched whistle every time I breathed. Mama reached the doorway first and covered her mouth as she saw the broken garland and then the glass in my outstretched hand.

"I-it w-was Heather's." I choked on the words, tears running down my cheeks. "B-Birch was here!"

Papa came up behind Mama, still groggy with sleep, but he held her shoulders as she wept. *"Dios mío."*

"What are you doin' out here alone? Have you lost your mind?" he demanded.

"The field," I said. "There's a body."

Papa paled and slipped on his boots. He nudged me to go back inside, yet I stayed locked in place. If I moved, I'd know for sure this wasn't some nightmare.

Papa took the rifle from me and eased open the gate before approaching the fence separating the field from the road. A hoarse utterance caught my ear. "Oh, God."

The heap of a white dress and bluing skin lying in the field seemed like an illusion in the fog. I broke out of my stupor and went through the gate. My feet were dirty. So were the feet of the girl in the field.

Her hands, too. The rest of her so white like milk — until I came to her neck. Her face was turned from mine; there was a gaping hole where the front of her throat used to be. Had she been *fed* upon?

I crept along the body of the girl. Dried blood speckled her chin. Her lips were the same plum shade as the emerging sunrise, while her eyes were open, irises blue and pupils fixed.

Violet Crenshaw was dead.

CHAPTER NINETEEN

We've always been afraid he'd be drawn back to take one of our girls. He'd take her into the woods and make her his bride. We even wondered if we should give him one, just to make him go away for good. But of course, we couldn't. That'd be murder.

I did the coward's thing and hid inside when the Crenshaws came with Sheriff, somber-faced and holding his hat to his heart. Dahlia knelt beside the sheet covering her sister's body. She clasped Violet's dirt-smudged fingers, her head lowered, back quaking with violent jerks. She didn't sob loudly, only held Violet's hand until her parents enfolded her, and the three of them made the long walk home.

Rook met me outside my bedroom window an hour later. He put his hands on my hips, his lips against my head. How I wanted to collapse against him. My middle ached from being with him the night before. I expected strangeness between us, but there was no tender moment to speak of what we'd done. Instead, I had a bucket of hot water and rags and scrubbed wood. The garland had left greenish stains around the window. It hadn't mattered. The bad wasn't thwarted.

"I g-gotta get rid of it," I said.

"The sun'll bleach it out," he offered.

"Not good enough."

I kicked over the bucket. The barren earth sucked the hot water into its cracks as quickly as it spilled, no mud forming. It was all dust and decay, rot.

Violet had been so pale, drained. I still smelled the metallic and musky-sweet tinge of death.

Rook folded his arms across his chest as I thrust open the door of the small work shed where my parents kept tools, some equipment from the clinic Papa swore he'd fix but never got around to. Through the clouds of dust and forgotten things, I dragged out a wooden plank and rifled around until I found a hammer and nails.

"What the hell are you doin'?" Rook asked.

"Boarding up my room," I said. "I ain't lettin' Birch Markle even think he can get to me."

I balanced the plank across the window, holding the nail in place, and swung the hammer as hard as I could. The nail drove halfway in. Again, I banged the hammer on the nail head, but this time, I hit so hard, the wood cracked. I made my way to the other side of the plank and reared back the hammer to drive in another nail, nearly whacking Rook behind me.

"Jesus, Ivy, you're gonna kill yourself," he griped. "Or me."

He reached for the hammer, but I held it back from him.

"Let me do this." I wheeled around, swinging the hammer against the wood and nails. "She didn't deserve to die. She wanted to make things better, and he went and k-killed her anyway!"

"I know," he said in a near whisper. "I wish I could make it better."

"M-m-make it better?" My throat was ragged with crying and screams. "He killed her outside my house! Do you think that was a c-coincidence? Haven't you heard what folks say, Rook? Birch is comin' for me next!"

"I don't believe them," he said.

Crack! The hammer hit the wood. Rook flinched. I wrapped my fingers around the top edge of the plank and tugged. It didn't take away the stains from the garland, but it would make a hell of an obstacle if someone one wanted in my window. I beat nails into another wood plank until the edges split.

I wasn't going to die. Not by Birch Markle's hands.

The hammer felt good in my palm. Weighted, heavy. I could pound that particular evil if he came up behind me. Returning to the work shed, I came back with some twine I belted at my waist, the long ends dangling by my thigh. I secured the hammer with the twine. A knife might slip. A gun could misfire. But this hammer, I liked it.

"We go now," I said.

"Go where? Ivy, get a grip," Rook argued.

"I'm g-going to the woods, and I'm gonna find Birch Markle. I'll crack open h-h-his skull so I don't have to see another Dahlia weepin' over her dead sister or another Aunt Rue half mad with grief over Heather. *I* don't want to die."

My shoulder brushed past his arm, and he grabbed for me. "C'mon, Ivy. This is insanity talkin'."

"I'm following the map Heather made. I'm going with you or without."

Rook slapped the side of the house and shoved his hand through his hair.

Too much death, too much sorrow. I had to find where this madman hid in the woods, and I'd bring out Birch, dead or alive. Once I'd thought it better to make him face justice for what he'd done. I'd thought it wrong to get swept along in the mob mentality of killing him while the killing was good. A mob wasn't personal.

What I wanted was.

Rook took a hunting knife, some water, and cheese, and gathered our horses. We rode to the fields. The carefree galloping of the past was gone. Veil swung his head from side to side, ears pert and twitching. Rook's hand slid from the reins to rub his steed's neck while he murmured a soft, "Easy." Yet the horse stalled. I circled Whimsy around him to drive him on by the mare's lead.

"He remembers last night," Rook said.

"You never told me what you remember."

I angled Whimsy close to Veil and stretched my leg to nudge the stallion's rear flank. With a grunt, Veil lurched forward.

"We were patrolling." Rook looked so tired, with dark shields under his eyes. The cut on his forehead scabbed. "This *thing* comes hulkin' from the field."

"What'd it look like?"

"Enormous. Tall. When it came closer, I realized it wore animal skins. The smell was awful. Like shit. I was trying so hard not to get sick, and I fired at him."

I'd heard those shots. I remembered Rook so frightened and lost when we rode to the river, when we first kissed. He wasn't that boy anymore. He was worn down. Birch had thinned us both so that his fingers could poke right through our flesh.

Rook continued, "Veil spooked when Birch ran toward us, and after the second shot, he threw me off. I thought I'd hit Birch because he held his arm."

"The hounds didn't find any blood," I said.

Something felt off about Rook's story. He'd been hurt — there was no doubt. Still, a peculiar niggle pecked at the worry seeding in my mind.

"You think I'm lying?"

"No!" I answered too fast. "I know dogs' sense of smell, though. They should've caught something."

As we came up the field, we saw that two hillmen were stationed near Promise Bridge. They were saucer-eyed and held rifles, watching, intent on anything coming from the across the water. They'd never let us cross. We'd go south near where the animals were buried. The river wasn't so wide there, and the water level was low. I kicked Whimsy's sides and steered her southbound. Having Rook ride behind me pulled my skin tight, as if I wanted to tear out my seams and a bloody mess of me could run away wild.

"What's wrong?" he asked.

"N-nothing," I said.

"I know you. Something's up." He hurried his horse to walk alongside mine. "You can't stop yourself from stammering when you're upset."

"You sure you hit him, that it was Birch?" I felt sick even asking.

"He was big. It was dark, and he came after me. Ain't that enough?"

We were close to the bone land. If we went much nearer, we'd get the smell and the flies biting at the bare parts of our skin. I dismounted from Whimsy, unclipping her reins to leave her to graze. Leaving her wasn't a choice I made lightly. Birch might come, and I prayed she would flee. But she could go no farther. Rook climbed off Veil and angled his body by mine. His hands cupped my face, then touched the acorn necklace double strung with Heather's necklace of found things.

"Mamie said acorns are for protection," I said.

"When I made it, I didn't know what danger was in the Glen." He ran his thumb over the brown nut. "Maybe it's why you're still here."

We trundled down the bank to the river. The water was shallow, and rocky shoals and parched earth stuck up along the shores. Still, there was a chance we could step off the shoal into three feet of water or be sucked down thirty feet. The river was dangerous and unpredictable.

"Are you sure about this?" Rook asked.

"I can swim," I replied.

He deflected the lead to me to cross the river. It was scarcely deep enough to wet the hem of my skirt. I held my shoes and socks to keep them dry. We made it to the other side and dragged ourselves to the outer band of the tree line. As long as we stayed near the river and watched the sun, we'd go in the right direction. Rook trusted my instincts, and I released a tentative breath once we reached Potter's Field. No one from the Glen was stationed here. They were probably watching the fields or farther north by Denial Mill.

Yet I knew that opening in the trees and squashed undergrowth where Heather had gone into the woods. Maybe she'd come too close to Birch. Maybe he'd seen girl skin, smelled her, and was drawn back from where he'd come.

According to Heather's directions on the map, which were crude at best, we were at the end. But shouldn't there be something more? There was nothing here. What was I missing? The cover of the trees was denser, trunks like posts for watchmen. The interplay of dark and light, sun and shadow, blurred the leaves above with shrubs below. In a large oak, a tree surely two centuries old, the trunk was partially cleaved and moss unraveled down the side and spread out in a grayish-green berm on the ground.

Rook knelt, running his hand over the raised hump in the soil. "It's cushion moss. The only other place it grows in any amount 'round here is Potter's Field."

"Is that strange?" I asked.

"It makes me wonder what's underground."

The way the moss spread in strange heaps, it didn't follow the oak tree's roots, as if someone formed the ground's swell in time long past and the earth did as it always did — reclaimed what was its own. These were the mounds on Heather's map, I had to believe. I wandered along the length of the berm, pushing back the undergrowth with my toe. Chunks of lichen-coated stone sank into the ground every so often.

"Rook? Look at this." I pointed to the stones. "They're too exact to be natural, right?"

"Shit." He wiped his mouth and measured out a few more rocks. "They're graves."

I wrapped my hammer within my fist. "I don't get it. I expected to find something — a shack or something — but not a cemetery. If you lived out in the woods, where would you go?"

"A cave," Rook replied. "You'd stay dry, maybe build a fire. The river's to our east, but Pops had some old maps that showed it wound back in these woods. There are bluffs. Odds are there's a cave or two near those. Are you sure this is where Heather's map ends?"

I retraced the moss along the ground. Something crushed under my foot, something that didn't snap with the crispness of a twig. My skirt hem lifted.

A shard of white.

A scattering of pointed, pale stones.

Teeth.

"R-R-Rook." Suddenly, my back pressed against something hard. Unyielding, the same way Birch Markle's body felt behind me the night in Potter's Field. Whipping around, hammer in fist, I buried the hammer's claws into the old oak's trunk. And immediately felt foolish.

"You okay?" Rook asked, jogging toward me.

"Look down."

He nudged aside a fern and wrinkled his nose at the bare bones and teeth. "What animal's that?"

"Maybe a skunk." I grabbed for my hammer, tried to yank it from the tree, but it wouldn't budge. The claws were too embedded in the bark.

Rook braced his foot against the trunk, near the deep fissure at the oak's base, and curled both his hands around my hammer. The bark was so lush with moss his footing slid before he gave a decent jerk. The tree yielded.

Instead of only my hammer sliding out from its hold, the fissure in the oak opened, and a burlap bag tipped out, landing on the undergrowth.

"What the hell's that?" Rook asked.

I examined the bag. It'd been wedged inside the tree for ages, the fabric patchy with stains. A length of rope tied it closed. Rook handed me his hunting knife, and I cut at the rope. My fingers were numb as I opened the burlap.

Something dead was in the sack.

Something that had died long ago.

Rook wheeled away, his stomach revolting, and stooped over behind another tree. My gag reflex kicking in my throat, I lifted the bag — no heavier than a thirty-pound dog — and dumped it out. The clunks like small logs hitting each other shook my teeth, and I opened my eyes to the pile of bones.

Ribs. The spiny worm of vertebrae.

A human skull with a hole fracturing the forehead.

Rook wiped his mouth. "That's a bullet hole."

Amid the bones there were trinkets. Animal claws strung on a necklace. Tufts of fur. This was a body that'd been murdered.

Long before Heather and Violet.

"We gotta get my pops," he said, and hooked his hand under my arm to pull me from the skeleton.

Find it.

I rolled away the skull and used a stick to poke through the remnants of clothing until I saw a hand. The bones were dark from decomposition, fingernails protruding from the bone's tips. Something glinted even in the forest light. It was metal but so tarnished I might've overlooked it if the sun didn't eke through when the trees swayed in the breeze. Amid the bones, a ring was slid halfway down one of the skeletal fingers. I lifted the dead hand into mine and took the ring into my palm, turning it over.

"Did Milo tell you his mother's last name?" I asked.

"I assumed it was MacAvoy and she changed it to Entwhistle when she married his father. He said his mama's name was Laurel, which—"

"It doesn't go with Terra," I finished. "Terra's a land name. Laurel's a tree."

I held up the ring for him to see and fumbled for another ring I had strung on Heather's necklace of found things: Milo's. They were similar but not totally the same.

Rook took the rings and looked them over before handing them back to me. "Milo's has laurel leaves. But this one, they're birch branches."

"You sure?" I asked. "That means someone's pretending to be Birch Markle." That metal tang in my mouth, the tightening of every cord in my neck and throat. "Wh-who would do such a thing?"

Why Heather didn't want me to know who she was seeing. It hadn't been an *M* for MacAvoy in the family crest carved on the ring.

It was an *M* for Markle.

CHAPTER TWENTY

You can't know the kind of evil that runs in folks' souls, but you also can't know the good that lies there until you look hard enough.

Legs scissoring over fallen branches and divots in the ground, I ran as fast as I could out through the woods. Rook kept pace with me, urged me, "Keep running. Keep going." My chest heaved, and no matter the humidity in the air and mosquitoes buzzing near, the sweat layering my skin was cool. I batted away the branches sticking out to tear at my sleeves, snatch at my cheeks, and snag my hair.

Two figures came into view.

Milo had a crate filled with pillows and shrouds, crystals and pieces of metal. Emmie's arms held discarded silver cups weathered by tarnish.

They're taking Heather's things.

I clamped my hands over my mouth to keep from shouting at them while they sifted through Heather's treasures as if collecting them might command her spirit to laugh one more time, tell one more secret, all to taunt her soul.

I tapped Rook's shoulder and pointed. How could they raid Heather's things? To destroy evidence against them? A hurt stewed inside me so furious my mind throbbed.

Rook crept closer, waiting, lips moving in a silent count, before he broke into a run and smashed hard into Milo's back. They fell in a heap and sprawled on the forest floor.

"Motherfucker, get off him!" Emmie shouted and attempted to haul Rook off her brother. Milo kicked out from under him, but Rook was too fast and got on top of him, holding him down again.

"What's wrong with you?" Milo hollered.

I caught up to Rook and the Entwhistles. I tugged Emmie away from Rook, then knelt beside Milo.

"We know," I said.

Milo drew his eyebrows together. "What are you talkin' 'bout?"

"They say things run in families." I locked on those pale blue eyes. "So does murder run in yours? We thought you were MacAvoys at first, a Glen mama who left after a family tragedy, but you're Markles, ain't you?"

Milo's nostrils flared. "You know damn well where I was when Heather died."

"You were gonna run off with her, but she" — I whipped around and pointed at his sister — "never would've let you go. Or maybe the two of you decided to work together and take some revenge for your family's disgrace."

"Y'all are sick!" Milo shoved Rook back so that both boys were spread on the ground.

"Not as sick as someone goin' 'round and dressin' up like a murderer!" I yelled. "We found your kin's bones in the woods. Heather found where they were hidden, too. She had a map that led to 'em, even if she never got to show them to Sheriff. So did she tell you what she knew? I deserve to fucking know what you've been hiding! She was my best friend! She was my blood, and I hate you for what you did to her, how you changed her! You took her from me! And the only reason *I'm* not dead is that I want to know what happened!"

My voice was frayed. The tears tasting salty on my lips did nothing to quench the fire burning through me. Rook stood and put his arms around me, burying my head against him. The leaves above swayed, but the four of us were ghostly in the empty woods.

A muffled sob that wasn't my own caught my ear.

Milo's sister sat on the ground and pulled her knees to her chest, hiding her face. Milo crawled over to her and held her in a close hug. "Shhh, Em."

"I can't," she croaked. "I promised Heather."

"I know," Milo replied. His eyes closed and wiped her cheek. "It's okay."

I broke away from Rook and knelt beside Milo and his sister. "What did you promise Heather?"

"You don't have to answer that," Milo interrupted.

Emmie's head slumped forward, and the sobs she attempted to quiet racked her body. I crouched in front of her. The well for my own tears was drained, but this girl ached in a way I knew too well.

Heather, before she was angry with me, had loved me, and when she loved you, it was impossible not to love her in return.

She reached into her pocket and withdrew the stationery I recognized as Heather's. "You gotta read this."

My hand quaked as she slipped the letter between my fingers.

M,

    I'm so scared. Something bad's happening in the Glen. I think I have it all figured out. I need to tell Sheriff, but I don't know if he'll believe me. It means admitting that I've been meeting you in the woods.

    Please don't hate me. I'm not ready for anyone else to know except Milo.

    I might not be able to run away with you on May Day. Not yet. I know you're worried about me. I am too. But I'm also scared for Ivy. Even if I go, she'll live in the Glen. I can't go until I know she's safe. That she's happy.

    If anything happens to me, make sure she's okay. Tell her I love her and that I'm sorry.

    I love you.

    —H

I looked from brother to sister, confused.

Milo's sister sniffed. "My name's Mary Jane. I've just always hated it."

"*You know you can't get enough of Mary Jane.*" The echo of

Milo teasing Heather outside the trailer park scrolled through my memory.

Mary. Emmie. Em.

M.

My lips parted. All the intimate things I knew about my cousin. All the secrets. The words blurred with grief renewed. Rook took the letter, and when he was finished, he refolded it to hand back to Emmie, then took off his glasses.

"All those letters to M . . . it's you," I said to her.

Heather had been in love, but not with Milo. With Emmie.

I didn't know what kind of path love was supposed to be—it seemed like it could be anything. Stumbling, tripping over your own feet, hoping that the hand you reach out is caught by someone who stops you from falling. Someone who got you. Wasn't that what mattered? Weren't these things Heather and I could've talked about, shared with whispers and giggles and tears? She didn't have to cut me off. And her being gone cut too deep.

"Why was Milo meeting her in the woods on May Day?" I asked. "Why didn't you come?"

"That was what Heather decided. I told her I'd be there, but she said it'd be easier to get out with him than me, especially if she ran into trouble. I was supposed to be waiting at home for her. She didn't show up, and then Milo had a broken arm . . ."

She shivered again and sniffed.

"Why did you let me think Heather was sneaking off to see you?" I asked Milo.

He shook the hair from his eyes. Ever defiant and yet he seemed to pull the last threads of fight within him. "You can walk around with your hand in his" — he gestured to Rook — "and no one blinks a goddamn eye. Heather couldn't do that, and believe me, it tore her up inside. So when you came to me, who was I to spill her secrets?"

He was her friend. He'd protected her.

I thought I'd done the same.

I felt regretful that she didn't trust me enough. I'd have been there for her. Didn't she know that? But she didn't. She was too afraid. All I thought was what a loss that was.

"You have Heather's necklace?" Emmie asked.

"Yes," I replied. I showed it to her, and her fingers hesitated on the two halves of the broken glass circle I'd restrung on the chain.

"I found this," she said. "It was near the trailer. Heather thought it was cool."

I took the glass pieces off the chain and placed them in Emmie's palm. Then I reached into my pocket and gave Milo his ring. "I know this means a lot to you."

He squeezed it within his hand. "My mama said her daddy was a metalworker and made a couple of rings when she and her brother were born. She gave one to our brother Mark, but he gave it to me when he got sick. Thank you for givin' it back."

Rook climbed off the ground and took off his glasses, rubbing the heel of his palm against his forehead. I didn't know what to say to Milo or Emmie. No apology sufficed for accusing them of murdering Heather, of the other death and harm. All Mamie's tales of Birch Markle, all the forced promises to come back in after dark, the screams from the woods, they were lies. Lies the Glen believed. Lies someone had made sure seemed like truth, and not even Mamie knew what was real.

"What's going on out here? The woods are off-limits!"

We looked to the path. The hillmen from the bridge — Coyote Jones and Ash Fitzgerald, I saw now — came into view with their rifles up. As the men realized it was Rook and me, they lowered their weapons.

"Who are you?" Coyote asked the Entwhistles.

"We were friends of Heather's," Milo replied.

Coyote helped Milo to his feet. "Y'all need to get outta here. These woods are dangerous. You shouldn't be out here."

"We found a body," Rook blurted out. "We think it's Birch Markle."

The hillmen looked at each other, all disbelief and surprise. Coyote tightened his grip on his rifle and warned, "You best not be foolin' with us, or your daddy's gonna have a word with you."

"He's not," I added. I pointed from where we'd come. "It's back there."

Ash paled. "I think they're serious."

"We'll check out it," Coyote said. "Y'all drop everything and head back to the Glen."

Ash reached for Emmie's box. She held tight until he wrestled it away, saying, "We might need this for evidence."

Emmie cast a forlorn look and took a few steps toward me. "But I need what's in there."

Rook put his hand on her shoulder and spoke so softly I could scarcely hear him, despite being right beside her. "I'll come back for it later. Once we show my dad the real Birch Markle, they won't need this stuff. Ivy and I'll get it up to the road and leave the box. Come by after dark. It'll be there."

Emmie let out a deep breath. Coyote grabbed Rook around the arm and pulled him down the path leading back to Potter's Field. I trailed behind, leaving Milo and Emmie to take their own path out of the woods while I struggled to keep up. The hillmen rushed through the graves. Graves kept secrets. The woods kept secrets. Finding the truth meant digging deeper and in the least obvious of places.

"Where are you takin' him?" I asked Coyote, who still held Rook's arm as we crossed Promise Bridge, jingling chains and crackling wood.

"To see his daddy," the man answered. "Sheriff needs to hear what's goin' on."

As we charged up the hill to the road, the clang of the warning bells resounded over the field.

"Something's happened," I murmured.

Rook looked back to me. "It'll be okay, Ivy."

My gut didn't agree, though. It was an exhausting trek to Sheriff's station. The bells continued to ring, and curious folks peeked out from their homes or looked up from the fields as Rook and I were marched down the dirt road with two strangers. Yet when we reached the station, Sheriff was gone.

Coyote called to a farmer working out in his field, "Where's Jay?"

"You ain't heard?" the farmer asked. "Violet Crenshaw's body is missin'."

The mad jingle of warning bells stirred my thoughts.

The news was sickening. They couldn't leave Violet's body out in the field for the scavengers and beetles that morning, not with the afternoon warmth folks expected. So off to Papa's clinic her remains were taken while waiting for the county folks to do her autopsy tomorrow. The clinic was close enough to the highway that few Glen kind ventured there unless going to town. No one saw anything, heard anything, except for the hillman who'd noticed the door was broken off its hinges as if rage had torn it away.

Sheriff was gone rounding up his men for a door-to-door search. Not an inch of Glen land would go unexplored. With the hillmen joining Sheriff, Rook and I were alone on the station's steps. Speaking seemed so wrong. Words might break the stupor falling over us.

Dead girls, black bones inside a tree, and a letter that revealed a secret.

Sheriff approached from the road, winded from searching the Glen. "Rook Michael Meriweather, what in God's good name is goin' on? What's this about a body in the woods?"

The story came out at once, the Entwhistles, Birch Markle's skeleton, someone faking Birch's existence.

Sheriff opened up his station and motioned Rook and me inside. "You need to sit."

I shook my head. "I'm fine."

"Ivy, darlin', when you're told to sit, it's 'cause someone's got news you don't take standing."

I didn't sit. My body was fatigued, and I feared I wouldn't get up. My mind spiraled in too many directions. I wanted outside in the clear air. I wanted to breathe. Except I couldn't; what had happened to Heather was still a mystery.

Sheriff took off his hat. "I made an arrest. Some of my men are bringing him in now. Marsh Freeman killed Heather."

CHAPTER TWENTY-ONE

Folks can endure many hardships. You gotta live with your history. You may not need to talk 'bout it. But you gotta live with it. It's the only way to stop wickedness from happening twice.

When I came home, the house looked strange with the boards I'd nailed across my window. I'd gone half mad trying to save myself. Sheriff leaned against the counter. The slice of fruit bread my mother had cut when he arrived was untouched, but he took some coffee.

Papa stood beside the oil lamp, a lit match in his hand. The flame singed his fingers before he seemed to remember the match was burning, and he waved it in a hurry with a muttered curse. Mama took the matches, lit the lamp, and tucked the pack inside her apron. He stared at the lamp's glow, not moving, until she ushered him to a chair.

"I knew Timothy'd take it hard." Sheriff frowned. "Having the past dragged up ain't easy."

I showed him the map of the woods that led to Birch's body. His forefinger tapped on one word: *marsh*. "There ain't marshes back in those woods."

"She must have written it down because she knew what he did," I said.

Sheriff pursed his lips in thought. "I never suspected anything. All those years ago, your daddy loved Terra MacAvoy. The way Marsh told it, when your daddy didn't meet Terra, he did. Told her she'd do better setting up house with him. Terra didn't want him and ran off. He gave her chase down to the river. She slipped and went in the water. By the time Marsh got her out, Terra had drowned. He was scared and left her on the bank.

"Birch Markle really was mad. He belonged in an institution, and when he got loose and was found beside Terra's body, you'd make the assumptions other folks did 'bout him killin' her."

Something haunted Sheriff's face, maybe years of tracking Birch Markle, maybe how wrong not only he but everyone was. "By the looks of that skeleton, I'd say it wasn't long after Birch disappeared that Marsh found him and put an iron ball in his brain. He helped create that Markle story by screaming and making sure folks caught enough of a glimpse over the years. Until Heather must've found out what he'd done."

Killed Terra. Murdered his wife's daughter. Murdered Violet.

Marsh would've murdered me.

Sheriff sat at the table and spun the tarnished Markle ring I'd given him. "That poor girl. The things folks'll do to keep secrets hidden. I went over to Marsh's house earlier to see how Rue's baby is coming along. He was bandaging his arm and made out like he'd hurt himself, but when I suggested having a doctor check on it, he got all skittish. He tried telling me it was a scrape. Raised my hackles, 'cause I know a bullet wound when I see one. My boy shot him. Hopefully, he'll tell us where he hid the Crenshaw girl's body, and that's one more charge against him."

"Did you realize Milo was a Markle when you and Papa fixed his arm?" I asked.

Sheriff gave a slow nod. "Your daddy did. Marsh had told us he thought Heather was running 'round with some boy. He must've realized who she was with and killed her to stop her from telling what really happened to Birch Markle."

Not a boy, a girl. Who loved her. Who she couldn't tell anyone about because of blood, because of fear. Maybe Emmie and Milo told her their mother's side of the madman's legend. Who was to say whether Heather'd still be alive if she'd told everyone in the Glen what she knew? Would anyone have believed her?

Sheriff wandered to the living room, where he stood before my father. I didn't listen to their murmured voices. Finding out what had happened in the past, how far Marsh had strayed to hide an accident and how it so devastated the present, there was no resolution. Only a hollow sense it could've been avoided.

I tugged off Heather's necklace and flicked through each collected item that had brought her joy. Things others buried, she uncovered with delight, dusted them off, and strung on her chain. No matter how we covered up the good and bad of what we'd done, of who we were, there'd always be some Heather to stumble upon it and find it remarkable.

Rook set the box of Heather's belongings beside the highway for Emmie, the high beams of a truck reflecting off his glasses. I wrapped her necklace within a red scarf and tucked it down amid the other things she'd shared with Emmie. Mary Jane.

As we made our way back to the Glen, Rook's hand eased into mine. Unspeakable things weighed on my tongue, yet the silence between us wasn't full of pressure. It was simple, wind sneaking between oat grass. Heather was right. Love was gory, ugly. She was also right that when you opened up enough, you had someone else's heart.

"This is different," Rook mused.

"What?" I asked.

"Being out after dark. Not being afraid."

My lips spread. No, I wasn't afraid. Not of the dark.

He lowered his face, and I rose on my toes to meet him. His mouth was tender and warm. I was still cold, maybe not as cold as before. A death-touch didn't wear off. That didn't mean I had to feel half dead. My fingers combed through Rook's hair. He cupped my shoulders and kissed me deeper, kissed me in a way I'd remember, even if that prickle in my lips numbed right then. That kiss would linger.

"What do you think it'll be like?" I asked once the kiss was over.

"When people find out there was never anything in the woods? What'll they say when they find out Birch Markle was a big lie?"

Rook surveyed the empty fields, the scarecrows with no crops to oversee. Only torches to light the way and innumerable stars glittering overhead. "It'll be strange. Relieved, I guess. We've never believed anything else."

"The way Papa's talked about it before, families facing scandal leave the Glen."

He pushed my hair behind my ear and kissed me there. "Do you wanna go?"

"No."

"Then don't."

I hoped it'd be so simple. Hillfolk had a way of remembering the blood spilled by your name, but there needed to be someone who'd get the story right. Who'd get all the stories right and not let them turn into outlandish legends.

August's home lay off the dirt road close to this side of the Glen. The Donaghys used the barn for dyeing clothing, which August mostly handled since his father had taken ill. The clapboard house needed some upkeep, especially for the summer storm season when the hail might come, and it always came.

"We should tell him," I said. "Have you seen him since . . . this morning?"

"He wouldn't talk," Rook replied. "He was heading to the barn and ignored me when I called for him, so I came to see you."

Telling August that his girlfriend's killer had been arrested, that her body would be found soon, was delicate. I didn't want him to hear it from anyone but me. Few folks knew the gravity of the loss he'd endured. He'd been there, a comfort and friend when I needed one. My hope was he wouldn't turn me away once he learned it was my kin who'd killed Violet. I couldn't yet explain my grief for her. The friendship was never quite all it could've been.

So much loss.

Rowan's Glen needed a good year. All the hopes that'd been pinned to Heather's crowning as May Queen.

The glow of a lantern filtered between the planks of the barn. Rook eased open the door, the hinges whining in need of oil. The light in the barn was poor, but a clothesline was hung with a rainbow of drying shirts. The dyes' bitter odor was strong and burned my nose, as if the Donaghys had added some chemical. Giant glass jugs were filled with dark, reddish-black dye and lined up near the wall. The corks were slimy with whatever boiled plant extracts, perhaps overcooked red cabbage, created that shade.

"August?" Rook called. "We've got some news."

A thud echoed from deep within the barn, then footsteps on the stone floor. August's hand slithered between two dyed skirts. The rims of his eyes were swollen and reddened, maybe from crying, maybe from the fumes.

"Marsh Freeman was arrested," I stated, trying to get out the words. "He pretended to be Birch Markle. He killed Heather. And Violet. I'm so sorry."

August shuffled back to wherever he'd been working. Rook's forehead creased. "Ain't you gonna say something?"

Nothing. No reply.

Every step we took brought more of the barn's back room into view. On shelves built into the wall were dozens of bleached skulls, all with pointed fangs and hollowed eyes, boiled clean to remove the meat. There was an old anatomical drawing framed in my father's clinic with the same type of skull. *Canis lupus familiaris.* The domestic dog. Every size skull from the smallest breed to massive working hounds was present, every face on the LOST DOG signs on Papa's clinic window.

"A-A-August?"

I rounded a stall where a horse had once resided. In the pass-through was a long harvester table.

On which Violet's body lay.

The same red-black color sludge as in the jugs congealed in the wounds on her throat. *It's blood. Oh, God.*

August ran his finger along her cheek. "I swore I'd do whatever she wanted. She promised she'd never tell. But she lied. She was gonna tell Sheriff, said things had gone too far." He glanced to a jar holding a grayish-red hunk of meat and touched his thumb to her lips. "Not like she can talk now."

"What the hell have you done?" Rook asked.

August tapped a dog's skull beside her head. "You know, Violet liked what I do. I once promised if anything happened, I'd keep her skull. Those police folk from the county, they would have sliced her up. It was wrong. She wouldn't want anyone but me taking care of her that way. So I took her from the clinic, wrapped her in blankets, put her in a wagon, and brought her here. She knew I was different. I wasn't some dumb hunter or farmer. After seeing Heather get away with so much, the kinds of things Dahlia used to do, it wasn't fair. Heather never let Violet join in."

The light in the barn slanted, and the stone floor seemed to drop out beneath me. I could fall into the black earth below and never be heard again, no matter how loud I screamed. The heel of my palm pressed between my eyes and steadied me.

"Y-you killed Heather," I said.

August smiled. "She should've let you be friends with Violet, but it was always about what Heather wanted, nobody else. Violet took a bottle of her family's wine. We got the belladonna from Rook's greenhouse. We had it all figured out. On May Day, Vi got you as far from your cousin as she could, and that gave me a chance to dance with Heather, tell her I wanted to talk to her by the river. I gave her the bad wine. I did all I could to stay true to the Birch Markle story. I felt kinda bad and left you some presents from her necklace. Did you get them?"

I gulped, everything tilting.

His face took on a sour expression. "How was I to know Mr. Freeman was pretending to be Birch Markle all these years? Damn May Queens. I didn't know that he'd go after you. Getting rid of Heather was supposed to make it better for my Vi, but then she went and said she was gonna tell Sheriff what we'd done. I couldn't let her." He picked up two withered strips like leather. "Heather's smile was real pretty, wasn't it?"

My mind emptied, focused on the wilted flesh.

"Run," Rook shouted, shoving me. "Get my father."

I grabbed his wrist, but instead of running with me, he slammed

August against the table with such force that it knocked Violet's arm off the edge. August's knees hit the ground, yet he pried himself up to kick out his leg and catch Rook in the hip. Rook tumbled backwards, crashed into me, and we landed on the stone floor in a heap of awkward limbs, a tangle of my hair and skirt.

I lay still, my arm coiled beneath me. Already the pulsing in my forehead from a growing lump made my eyelids heavy.

"Get up, Ivy," Rook urged and wrenched me up under my arms. "C'mon. I ain't leavin' you here, and we gotta get help."

"I'm up," I said, but my voice was mushy. I blinked and tried to make sense of where I was in the barn — where was the door, where was August? The lantern guttered, dark then light.

A loud *ting*, metal singing, broke the silence. Behind Rook, a silhouette rose in the half-light. Tall, cloaked, smelling of old blood and buzzing with flies. August raised his arm. He clutched the handle of a harvesting sickle, the curved blade arching high and ending in a vicious point.

"Move!" Rook shouted.

He pushed me forward before the sickle pierced and tore down his back. A scream that vibrated off the stone floor quivered up my legs. He slumped over. His arms sought to grip a post that held up the hayloft but snatched only air. His chest hit one of the massive jugs of blood. It rolled with his weight, glass grinding against stone. Then Rook came to a rest. August yanked out the blade, the force of dislodging metal from meat spattering my face with liquid heat.

"What part of him do you like best?" August wondered and drew the sickle's curve behind Rook's ear. "He's a good listener, ain't he?"

The blade cut down. Something pink and fleshy plopped on the floor. Blood poured from the side of Rook's head. A moan escaped his mouth, but it was impossible to make out any words, red gushing down his cheek and bubbling over his lips.

I glanced to the old horse stall. It was hard to make out, but inside, a pole rested near the stall's door. A shovel? A pitchfork? Hay from God only knew when was scattered on the floor. I edged back from August, who knelt and picked up the outer shell of Rook's ear, flicking it so it wobbled before he sniffed it. Rook struggled to force himself up, but August slashed the blade across his back again.

Blood splashed on the ground. Rook's blood. My throat closed; I was no longer able to scream, cry, wheeze as I breathed. Keeping one eye on August, I stretched my arm around the stall door extending until a cramp seized my shoulder, but still I strained to grasp the pole.

August smeared his hands in the bloody pool leaking from Rook's wounds. A weird smile cocked his mouth, then he moved a pail beneath Rook's head. *Plink, plink, plink.* He must've drained the blood from the dogs and funneled it in to the jugs. As he bent over, entranced by Rook's redness, I made a grab for the pole.

"*Nnnugh.*" I groaned and hoisted up not the piercing tines of a pitchfork or flat edge of a shovel. Just a muck rake for cleaning horse shit. Yet two dozen metal tines of the rake scraped the floor to leave pale claw marks. They were sharp. I carried the muck rake as if ready to heave wasted bedding into a bucket, my hold firm and teeth clenched. I had one chance.

Don't hold back.

Run him through.

The tines on the muck rake didn't stab flesh. August's build was too solid, and the rake tore his shirt and gouged his back above his waist. Force meeting a barrier, the halt jarred me and I bounced back, the muck rake dislodged from my hold. He yowled, dropping to one knee before staggering away from Rook's body. Not allowing him to gather his wits, I reached for the rake and smacked his head. More tearing, this time the tender skin of his face, and blood swam down his cheek and chin.

Again, I hit him, the rake cutting close to his eye. He fell again and lay still.

One hand on the rake, I dashed to Rook and hoisted him up. My feet slipped on the blood-slick floor.

"C-come on! Move!"

My right foot flew out from beneath me, and I landed on my knees in warm liquid. Thick down my skirt, wetting my legs, I stood again and lifted up under his arms. He was limp.

Dead weight.

His muscles had no tone, his face was slack.

The cold in my head raced to my fingers and toes, a sizzling sensation but caused by ice instead of heat. His shirt was sticky and dark, like a beet with its outer layer peeled off to reveal shining crimson beneath.

"Rook, you gotta get up." I shook him, searching his neck for any twitch of his pulse. "Get up!"

A bristle of his eyelashes. His feet tried to stand only to go dumb. From between blood-drenched lips, he uttered, "Can't."

No. Tears drained down my cheeks. He couldn't give up. Not when he'd showed me how strong I'd been.

"You're with me," I said. "Take one step."

His head lolled. I didn't think he'd listen, but his foot shuffled forward.

"Take another step."

He walked again. So much blood covered us both. I didn't dare guess how much he'd lost, but a trail of sloppy, red footsteps followed us from the barn into the road. Outside with the torches, I laid Rook beside a horse fence and stripped off his shirt. A gash down his shoulder blade flayed his skin, a scarlet line along a white sliver. Bone.

The daze of panic crawled over my brain, but I took his head in my lap and looked at the opaque cartilage left from his ear before tearing my sleeve to bandage him. I prayed the pressure would stop the hemorrhaging. Blood painted the lenses of his glasses. We needed help, more help than anyone in the Glen could give. There were few vehicles on the land, but even if someone brought a horse . . .

I was reaching for the bells strung on the fence when a sickle reared in the air and ripped downward, clipping the alarm bells. I rolled onto my backside and screamed as August stood over me. Journey's mane on his head stank of rot; the furs knitted together on his back were worse.

August stepped closer. "All those stories about a madman and his girl goin' off in the woods? We can live them. You like stories. I never hurt you 'cause Violet said not to. But she's gone." He glanced to Rook on the ground. "He'll be dead within the hour."

I crab-walked back until my elbows gave. August advanced, sickle in one bloodied hand and the other stretched to me.

Was this it? If I took hold, what happened then? Would he kill me? Would he force me into the woods? I'd never stay with him. He'd have to kill me. There was no other choice in joining him.

My fingers were hesitant in meeting his. Taking August's hand was accepting my death. I could pray he'd kill me quickly, but there would be pain. He would see to that.

Rook's dried blood was embedded in the ridges of our fingerprints. Blood made the Glen go mad. The hillfolk locked themselves away after dark, and now it was August and me and the wet breathing behind me. I walked with him past the torches. I walked with him past the field where the scarecrows watched.

I didn't want to be a story.

I wanted to be me.

An owl circled overhead. I looked up. August did as well.

I had a chance. My hold broke from August's, but he grabbed me again, biting hard to tear off my fingernail. I shrieked from pain, at the surge of fire in my nerves, but my scream stunted as he swallowed the fingernail. I peered past him to Rook's too-still body. My legs shook with rage, and I wheeled my other arm around to stick my thumb into August's eye. It was wet and marble-like. I kept pressing until I felt it yield. August gave a yell, and I ran. He ran after me. *Get him away from Rook. Get him away from hurting anybody else.* I ran toward the outside.

The highway.

I breached the Glen's boundary, and the country highway stretched long past hayfields and cornrows. Pellets of gravel flew around me. The *whup-whup-whup* of his boots closing in spurred me on, but I kept going over the hill until the glare of headlights drilled into my eyes. I ran at them, cringing, tears glistening so the lights grew spikes and shone like stars. I looked over my shoulder. August rounded the hilltop. He was so close.

"Ivy! Stop!" he screamed.

The truck's lights blinded me. All I saw was white and dark blue dots. My muscles tightened in anticipation of collision, closer and closer. *Five, four, three . . .*

I leaped to the left.

Brakes screeched, and a thud pounded the road, a crunch of bone or metal, I didn't care, except that the sound made me smile.

My elbow hit the road's shoulder, and I rolled until a wire cable stopped me from winding up in the ditch. Ringing filled my ears. Grit clung to my lip and crunched against my teeth while I lay still. Blood dried into the red thread circling my wrist.

The truck's engine hissed. A man shot out to the front of his truck and screamed.

My body resisted standing, but the cable fence made good leverage. I crept along the fence and staggered toward the crinkled truck. Fissures spread across the windshield. August was a busted heap on the ground, his head twisted backwards on his neck, blood oozing from his mouth.

A second truck drove up. My body fought any movement. A cry deepened in my throat and pushed past my lips, growing louder. Someone ran toward me, seizing my shoulders, and I screamed and batted my hands to get away.

"Ivy, it's Milo. Stop! What happened?"

Milo's blue eyes grounded me, forced me to realize I had survived.

He gawked at the blood on me, and then he noticed August dead in the road. He tightened his hold on my arm, gently squeezing.

The headlights beat back the night's shadows, and I fell against Milo, bloody and exhausted.

CHAPTER TWENTY-TWO

I lie awake at night, wonderin' if the Glen did right by Birch Markle. If someone had spoken up, even helped him, maybe Terra'd still be here. Lives would be different. But askin' for help means inviting others in, and there's a right good fear of letting in too much. When you let people in, something in you gets let out.

The truck rambled down the road and halted near the Donaghys' barn. Rook hadn't moved from where I'd left him. The story of what happened haunted the truck's cab. Emmie sat on one side of me at the wheel, while Milo rode beside in the passenger seat. Air from the vents blasted my face. Some part of me understood it was cold, but I didn't feel it. The cold within me iced every layer of my skin.

Milo wrenched open the door and climbed out to offer me a hand. I took it and let go, approaching Rook's body with muted sorrow tightening my chest.

"He's dead," I said.

"I'm sorry." Milo looked down.

I dropped to my knees. Rook's eyes were closed, and I slipped off his glasses to better see his face. His jaw had relaxed, and his mouth had fallen open. My fingers combed through his hair, black as fertile earth. I drew his head into my lap and traced his eyebrows and the refined angle of his nose, the curves of his lips I'd memorized for years and had only felt against mine recently. Not nearly time enough.

I held him and smiled. I smiled because I'd known love with him.

"I'll send my sister to find his daddy," Milo said.

I handed over Rook's glasses for safekeeping. "Please. Sheriff was at my house."

Milo went back to the truck. A moment later, the truck's wheels ground against the dusty road. He found a water trough and brought back a bucket. Then he tore a strip from the bottom of his shirt and doused it in the water. I took the rag and wiped away blood from Rook's cheeks. My head slumped forward, mine to his.

I couldn't hold back.

Cries poured out of me, and my body convulsed as I couldn't breathe fast enough to let loose the anguish inside. "H-he's still warm."

I hadn't expected him to have some heat left. I didn't know how long it took a body to go cold. He died so suddenly, maybe his body didn't know it. My lips touched his forehead. He smelled too much of blood and not enough of the boy I knew.

Milo took the cloth away from me and dipped it in the water. He wiped the rag across Rook's mouth, his wet fingers hovering under Rook's nose. His brow furrowed. "Shit. Ivy." He jostled my shoulder. "Put your hand over his mouth."

Milo took my wrist. A puff of air so faint I should've missed it pushed against my skin.

"He's breathing." I sniffed. "We need help."

Milo pulled out his cell phone, only to toss it down in disgust. "Goddamn middle of nowhere."

We waited. Both of us monitoring Rook's breath, his pulse, his color. He was graying. *He'll be dead within the hour.*

No. It wouldn't be fair to find him alive and let him run out of time.

The truck bumbled down the pitted road. Milo scrambled to his feet and motioned for Emmie to speed up, jumping up and down. "Hurry the hell up! C'mon!"

The truck came to a stop.

Sheriff darted from the passenger side and rushed over to Rook. His eyes were wide, and he fell to his knees, holding Rook's bleeding head in his bare hands. "No! My boy!" His shouts to God to be merciful echoed across the field.

"H-hospital," I blurted. "He's alive."

Sheriff's mouth fell open. His gaze was unfocused, confused, until it rested on my face. "But that girl said he was gone."

"He will be if we don't get him to the hospital," Milo said. He glanced at me. "There was a wreck on the road. Someone was hit. There's gotta be an ambulance up there."

"Get him. Take him." Sheriff hustled to his feet and picked up Rook beneath his limp arms. "Please. You got a car. Take him!"

Rushing and barely speaking, Milo and Sheriff hauled Rook to the truck. Never minding the blood soaking through Rook's clothing and his own, Milo shoved Rook into the passenger seat, leaving Emmie to adjust him, and turned back to me with streaks of red on his clothing. "One of you should come."

"Just take him," Sheriff ordered. "We'll be there shortly. Drive as fast as you can."

Milo climbed in and slammed the door, and Emmie gripped the steering wheel tight. With clouds of dust billowing around the tires, the truck turned around and bounded down the road. My hands clasped together in prayer, dirty air sprinkling my face and drying my eyes and all the red and wet on my body. They were on their way.

"Where's the Glen's truck?" I asked.

"By my station," he said.

I began running, with Sheriff a few paces behind me. We had to get to the hospital soon. My only prayer was that Emmie drove fast enough. The county police would be up at the highway, looking over the mess of August and the truck that hit him. They'd see Rook more than half dead in Emmie's truck. If they stopped her to ask questions . . . Rook didn't have that kind of time. *Get him there. Get him well.*

"You think he'll make it?" I asked over my shoulder.

"I pray he does," Sheriff answered. "Not sure about you, though."

I stumbled and turned around. "Wh—"

The question hadn't left my tongue before Sheriff threw me to the ground. I yelled, but the noise cut off as the air was suddenly choked from me. My fingers tore at the dirt. Sheriff's weight bore down on my back. I reached behind my head, scratched down his cheek with my bloody fingernail.

"Stop!" I wheezed.

"I can't let you live," Sheriff said. "You know too damn much."

His hands wrung my neck, and no matter the breath I tried to draw in, it never found my lungs. My limbs turned heavy and fell to the earth.

I never expected the ground to be so cold before I felt nothing.

My eyelids flickered. I lay face-down with my limbs sprawled around me on a wood floor. My throat ached, and I tried to cry; the pain was so great nothing but dry air came out.

"Jay, what the hell are you doin'?"

"Cleanin' up your mess. Same as before."

Footsteps passed close by. I didn't dare move, no opening my eyes, no breathing. I had no idea how long I'd been unconscious. Milo and Emmie would notice if Sheriff and I didn't arrive at the hospital soon, but would they return?

"Twenty-five years is too long to keep secrets, Marsh," Sheriff said. He'd brought me to the station. "When you told me what you'd done to Terra, who helped you? Who got that Markle boy out of his cellar and let him loose? You were so drunk you couldn't think straight, but I took care of it. You know she still had a pulse? She didn't after I was done, though, and I made sure that bastard was found by the body and everybody listened to the story I told."

My eyelid cracked to spy Marsh Freeman in the Glen's only jail cell. He leaned against the metal bars, his arm wrapped in a sling, and snorted. "Don't forget I know what you did to Birch Markle, Jay. I helped you track him through the woods, helped you put his body in a tree after you shot him. I never told."

Sheriff nudged me with his boot. "This one ain't telling, either. I'll get her buried in the woods before sunrise. No one'll find her. The Donaghy boy is dead. Guess he went and killed all those animals and poor Heather. Just a shame Ivy dug around. Scaring her off with the Birch Markle costume didn't work. She was running with Laurel Markle's kids, just like your stepdaughter. It wouldn't have been long before she figured out what went down years ago. My family needs a good life, and I've given it to them. I ain't lettin' anyone take away everything I've built. They'll say it was a bad year in Rowan's Glen."

A bad year and nothing more.

"What's that blood on you?" Marsh asked.

Sheriff let out a roar and picked up a chair, throwing it across the room. "My boy's dyin', Marsh! All 'cause of this shit! He's cut up and lost so much blood that I don't know if those townie doctors can save him."

"So go! Be with him. I'll still be here, and we can have it out then."

"No." Sheriff picked up Marsh's belt from a box on his desk, crossed the floor to meet him, and unlocked the cell. "I have things to finish up here, and when I get to the hospital, I'll tell those county police that the killing spree you and the Donaghy kid went on is all over with. Guess I forgot to take your belt when I caught you and put you in your cell, Marsh. Sorry 'bout that."

The cell door clanged as Sheriff closed it. Scuffling noises and shouts came from within, and I made out the shapes of the men shoving each other, the belt tightening around Marsh's neck as Sheriff held the ends. My own neck ached, but I pushed myself up to sitting. Sheriff shoved down Marsh, and in a few movements, he hoisted Marsh off the ground and secured the belt where a horizontal bar met the vertical ones. Marsh's feet banged on the metal as he kicked.

Leave. Go now.

Inch by inch, I backed away on my bottom. My hand groped the doorknob. With a swivel of my wrist, the door fell open, and I clambered to my feet to rush out of Sheriff's station.

"Ivy!" Sheriff shouted behind me.

I didn't look back.

My lungs burned, but I couldn't care. I couldn't think about the cramping in my thighs, muscles so overworked I no longer felt them. All I felt was fire. The cold in me was gone. Rook's acorn swung from side to side, smacking my jaw as I crossed the distance to my home. The fence and back steps were in sight. A light glimmered through the window.

"Mama!" My voice was a rasp. "Papa!"

I tried screaming for them, but the hoarseness was stronger than my voice, too much damage from Sheriff's hands. Wednesday leaped onto the windowsill. Her paw came up to the glass. I stretched out my fingers while I charged up the steps.

A hand clamped across my mouth, an arm snaking around my waist. Sheriff dragged me back from the door. My knees scraped against the front ledge of the bottom step. Suddenly, I was off the ground. Sheriff pulled me into the road. That strong hand silencing my mouth wormed down to my throat, but I tucked in my chin and set my teeth on his fingers before biting. Hard. I bit until my teeth came together and the taste of dirt and pennies spilled into my mouth.

Sheriff screamed.

A quiver of hope shivered through my belly as a black crack formed around the door frame. The back door opened, and Mama appeared in the doorway. "*Bonita?*"

The point of my elbow dug into Sheriff's side, and again my voiceless throat tried to shout, "Mama!"

She saw me and barreled down the steps, shrieking for my father.

Yet Sheriff swung me back around. Gut first, I smashed into the horse fence. My legs sailed over my head as I toppled across the fence and crashed to the ground. His grip lost on me, Sheriff reached through the fence and wound his fingers into my hair. I dug my heels into the earth and clawed at his hand. Yet he refused to let go.

The awful shredding sound of each hair ripping filled my ears. The locks gave up, and I rolled away, gawking at the dark rope in Sheriff's hand. He bared his teeth and leveled his boot on the fence, ready to propel himself over. I ran again. If I found somewhere to hide until my parents caught up, I might live. My scalp where the hair had torn away was raw and slippery, but my only care was escape.

I charged across the fields and ducked under a leaning scarecrow's arms. Voices behind me shouted my name, shouted for Sheriff. I ignored the insects bouncing off my face as I tore through their hovering clouds. The empty stable where Whimsy used to live was close, and I could burrow into the shadows there.

My feet carried me through the field, and when I reached the barn, I threw myself over the threshold. Much of the stable was filled with hay, feed buckets, and some stall rakes that had yet to migrate to the newer home for the horses. I staggered to Whimsy's old stall, turning the corner to hide before slumping on the ground with my head against the wall. My knee bumped a pail with abandoned grooming tools — brushes with grooves to comb the horses' coats, a metal hoof pick, a sweat scraper. I grabbed the wobbling bucket to keep it from falling over.

It wasn't so long ago I had spied Heather dancing by lantern light in this barn. I supposed that was the moment when I knew for certain things between us were different.

That first fracture.

It'd never heal. It wasn't meant to. Heather was why I was here. I'd learned everything she kept, everything there was to know. And if Sheriff found me, then I'd die for uncovering things that were much deeper than just two girls, one with a secret, one with a promise that she'd uncover it.

I saw Sheriff's shadow before I heard him. Moonlight framed the outline of his body in the doorway. His boots stepped onto the floor. I brought my knees to my chest, balling myself. My parents had to be close. They had to come soon. If they didn't, I was dead.

Sheriff rounded the corner of the stall and looked down at me. "This was the best place you could hide?"

"Y-you can't k-keep killing." I pressed my back into the wood. "My papa'll know. My mama—"

"I can make y'all disappear. Like I told your daddy, woods are wide. Nobody knows what all lives there. It wouldn't be the first time some family left the Glen when the name's been disgraced, and I do believe having a murderer in your family's enough to drive you out."

I clambered for the pail of grooming tools, dumping out the brushes and picks before I flung the bucket at Sheriff. It bounced off his shoulder and into the aisle outside the stall. His hand shot out to grab me. "No more fightin', Ivy."

The hoof pick coiled in my fist, I brought down the curved edge in the web between his finger and thumb and felt the pop of flesh as I ripped it straight through. Sheriff yowled and cradled his wrist with his other hand. New blood speckled the floor and hay. I forced myself to stand, and with an airless scream from my damaged throat, I ran at him, arm back to plunge the pick's curved hook in the side of his neck. Sheriff fell onto my shoulder, but I pushed him off. His body smacked the ground. His breath gurgled. I lurched into the aisle and stumbled outside.

"Where is he?" Papa yelled, running toward me. He caught me around my arms and pulled me against him.

"He's inside," I forced myself to speak even if every word scraped my vocal cords raw. "He killed Marsh. He killed Terra. He's been lyin' to you for years!"

Papa's nostrils flared, and he ushered me over to Mama, who had come with him. She and I tumbled to the ground, murmurs of Spanish soft in my ears. Papa placed his hand on Mama's shoulder.

"I'm goin' in."

Mama stroked the back of my head. I rested against her as she slowly rocked in place. My fingernail ached where the root protruded and bled. All the fight was out of me, my body so sore I couldn't move again.

Rook's acorn necklace hung over my heart.

I lived. I lived when Heather hadn't. I lived, and I'd keep living.

After a while, my father exited the barn. Wordlessly, he walked across the field in the direction of our home. Papa brought two pails of kerosene when he returned and poured them inside the stable. He soaked the doors. He watered the land with fuel. The fumes stung my nose and eyes, but I didn't know if the tears streaming down my cheeks were a reaction to the vapor or crying. Clouds in the sky roiled thick and impenetrable. A storm that'd bring soaking rain was on its way. Thank God.

"Ivy, stay back," Papa said.

Mama helped me to stand, and we staggered, hand in hand, her warm skin against mine.

"Don't worry. This must be done."

I wasn't worried.

She reached into her purse and offered a pack of matches to my father. "Timothy."

Papa's hand squeezed mine. Then he lit the match.

The fire devoured the stable, the stalls, the hay inside sparking up. Flames spread into the dried grass. Mama held me against her while the ghost of Heather dancing in front of her lover turned to ash. The bloodstains left from Journey's death became char and flecks rose against the dark sky as orange embers.

"Mama?" I asked.

"It's only fair," she said.

My parents led me away from the barn with the body burning inside. Behind us, fire scoured Rowan's Glen. Plumes of black smoke roiled over the fields, and the wind carried pieces of hot ash, dropped them farther away until more fields caught flame.

Ragged and torn, I was only vaguely aware of the sirens wailing closer.

The land burned. Burned out the lies. Burned out the rot. Burned out the secrets so buried they blackened and poisoned the roots.

Chapter Twenty-Three

And sometimes, Ivy girl, you know wrong's been done to you, wrong done on your behalf, and you best pray it's enough to be forgiven.

What do you do when the person who taught you how to fall in love dies?

That question lingered from my dreams each morning. The only answer I settled on was that you go on. Everything Heather had taught me — to be joyful, to have dreams, to share yourself with someone else — I took it and lived.

I reached out with my little finger. Rook's looped around mine.

Mamie and Dahlia waited inside the old house, but the weather was too nice, especially for mid-June with the sun gilding Rowan's Glen. Black earth and lush green crops on every field. Rook's movements were wearied, and I wrapped my arm around his back as much for balance as endearment. The bandage over his missing ear did little to hold his glasses straight. Briar had sewed a band to fit his head, but he couldn't wear it until he healed. Time yet for that.

Inside Mamie's home, Dahlia set out the mortar and pestle, dried comfrey root, and a kettle of boiled water with steam coming out the spout. Here she didn't wear the scarf. Her scars were a testament to the potency of the herbs. There was another bowl of wet, fat leeches, drenched with river water.

"Which do you choose?" she asked Rook.

He wavered from the herbs to the leeches. "Does bloodsuckin' actually work?"

Dahlia caressed her film-thin cheek so we could see it.

"Dahlia," I said, "we know you'd have nothing but a hole big enough for a peach pit if it weren't for leeching, but Rook's lost too much blood. Can't you tell by his color?"

Her mouth managed some kind of ripple of a grin. "Your granny's recipe is on the table. You write it down yet in that sketchbook of yours?"

"Indeed." I withdrew the book from the bag over my arm.

My sketchbook wasn't only a study of faces and scenery anymore. There were words mixed in, everything from the hushed talks by candlelight Dahlia and I had as we tried to reconcile the damage done — my pencil capturing the story and our hands knotted together in half-dark — all in the book. Dahlia and I spent time together, more than her teaching what she'd learned from Mamie and Rose Connelly, the way of charms and tinctures. She craved an understanding of her sister's secrets.

I understood that craving.

Mamie's recipe dictated to bloom comfrey root in hot water, then to grind it up with the mortar and pestle. No specific amounts other than a feel for it. Drops of plant essence. Drops of venom. Sometimes mixed at midnight or dawn, depending what hurt needed healing.

"You got too much water," Mamie said behind me. "You need to paste the boy, not bathe him."

On the first of June, Mamie had come out of her attic and asked for coffee. Mama, who'd been at my aunt's house tidying up, dropped the coffee mug so it shattered into pieces. After so many years of silence, I hadn't thought Mamie would talk again. Losing Gramps had thrust her into a quiet solitude, and maybe it took losing Heather to bring her voice back, to remind her that silence meant no more stories. I needed her stories, her secrets, her superstitions. I needed them because they were *my* way.

"Yes, ma'am," I replied, and sprinkled more root into the mortar.

Mamie knotted an oiled red thread around Rook's wrist. "Keep this on, and when it frays, don't you cut it with a blade, you hear? No metal must meet this string. Bad luck on you, and you've had more than your due share."

A baby cried from the other room. Mama's voice singing a Spanish lullaby to Sage traveled through the house. She and Papa kept him in a crib in their room most of the time. Aunt Rue took ill and wouldn't see him, spending the past week since his birth in her room. She needed help but wouldn't take the teas Mamie brought her, wouldn't listen to the urges for help. Baby blues, they first said. She refused to name the child, and for three nights, he had no name until I rocked him and mentioned to Mama how his eyes were wise.

It'd be nice to know what it was like having a brother.

"Your mama needs a rest," Mamie said. "Baby's looking yellow, and the sun'll take that outta him." As she left the kitchen, her hand stroked my cheek. "Dahlia, be a dear and come along."

She smiled as she left Rook and me in the kitchen. I set to peeling off the remains of the poultice from his back, withdrawing a pained hiss from him. The gouges were deep, the new skin thin. Angry pink trails carved across his skin. He'd complained about how tight they were, and Dahlia warned he'd be sensitive once the weather went cool.

Once the new bandages were in place, I pulled my chair around to his other side and moved for the one covering his ear, but he jerked away.

"Don't." He stared at the floor. "I don't want you to see it."

I tilted my head. "I n-need to look."

"I'll have Mamie change it later."

"You'll let me change it. Now."

My finger curled under his chin to lift his face. I leaned in close and touched my lips to his. He kissed me back, soft. He kissed me with all his breath, all that was warm inside, and I kissed him with all the shadows of grief burned out by daylight.

Papa had driven me to the hospital and made me wait while he broke the news to Rook that Sheriff was gone, that he had perished in the fire. The terrible howl that followed, the way Papa held him as he bawled, some scars weren't on the skin.

His ear didn't look as bad as he thought.

"I don't hear real well on that side," he admitted as I changed the bandage. "The doctors said there's nothin' to catch sound."

"You'll be okay," I promised.

"Everybody looks when I walk by." He tried adjusting his glasses, but they fell crooked until he gave up with a huff. "I won't ever be sheriff."

"I know." I tied off the bandage and repeated the same thing I told him every time he got into a slump. "You have your greenhouse and fields. You have your horse. You have me. That's all you need, Rook."

His lips formed a smile. "Maybe so."

I helped him stand. He put his arm around my shoulder; mine went to his waist. The cuts from the sickle had left nerve damage numbing his leg; other times it burned like brimstone. The night before had been a bad one, with Briar banging on the door after midnight, begging me to come with my medicine bag and Mamie's recipes.

Rook and I took the steps out of Mamie's house slow. For a while, we wandered the razed fields. The burned areas were bad. Fire had ravaged acres before the town's firemen contained the blaze. The stable was a loss. The ground still stank of char and ash, but rain fell after the fire that destroyed too many fields, and new green found ways to sprout.

"Hey," Milo called when he spotted us and wiped sweat from his brow.

He had a water pail. Fire could still be hot well below the soil, but he and Emmie had taken it upon themselves to tear away the stable's remains. Work moved faster now that Milo's cast had been switched to a soft one. Pieces of wood too damaged to reuse went into the forest to return to earth, while smaller things like doorknobs and hinges that had survived lived in a box in the bed of his truck for salvage.

Rook kicked at a green vine in the ground. "Get rid of it. Pull it out and kill the root."

Emmie knelt and tugged at the plant. "It's a persistent little shit, ain't it?"

"Burn it if you gotta. I don't wanna see it poisonin' this ground again," he said. "It's belladonna."

Something in the way Emmie dug at the plant changed. She grabbed at it harder, more determined. Funny how so much memory attached itself to the mere mention of one little plant.

Milo took Rook's other arm and helped me guide him to the open door of the truck on the road so he could rest. Their brother hadn't made it out of the last half of May, and without knowing what to do with themselves and nothing else to care for, Milo offered to help muck stalls and plant crops to repay Papa for healing his broken wrist. Hillfolk cared for hillfolk, Papa said. Still, I knew why the Entwhistles had demanded this field for working. The plan was to call it Heather's Garden.

I walked alongside Emmie, watching as she raked new soil into old. If drowning led to that silver place of dreams, then golden days right before the summer solstice were the grounding of life. Clouds like raw cotton spun overhead, and the blue sky was sharp. This was here. This was now. This was how life had changed.

Milo came away from the truck where Rook rested. He motioned me aside, speaking so hushed not even his sister heard. "You tell him yet?"

"Soon."

"He's got a right to know what his daddy did. The longer you let it go, Ivy, the harder it's gonna be to forgive."

I eyed Milo, didn't flinch, not even when I knew he disapproved. "Rook knows I love him. He'll forgive me."

"I wasn't talkin' about him needin' to do the forgiving."

Milo patted my shoulder before returning to work on the field. It wasn't that I needed to forgive Rook. He'd done nothing but love me. For all Sheriff's talk of wanting to keep me safe, all he'd wanted was to find out how much I knew. Keep himself safe. Self-preservation made us do the most damnable things. Our secrets, our lies, there were choices made to protect Rook's family and mine. Milo knew a thing or two about holding on to other folks' secrets, and he knew when it was time to give them up.

I approached the truck's open door. "You ready to go?"

"Already?" Rook asked.

I helped him stand. "We gotta talk."

Throughout the paths of Rowan's Glen, I spoke and Rook listened. He held my hand tighter, and when I was finished, he embraced me.

He knew.

He knew what his father did, the years of secrets, the damage wrought. My father had told him. He still didn't want to talk about it. Which meant that lost look about him would stay a while, the one he'd worn since the night he almost died, and I knew it well. It haunted my own eyes. Whenever I looked in the mirror, my ghost looked back.

Sometimes when I thought I was alone, I sensed someone watching. Of course, no one was there when I turned around. Maybe someday, though, I'd catch a glimpse of a skirt with red ruffles, a curl of red hair. Some things you can't ever let go.

ACKNOWLEDGMENTS

I wish I could say writing *The May Queen Murders* was easy. It wasn't. Delving into subjects you've cut off from memory and having them come rushing back is a trial. To have the faith of Julie Tibbott at Houghton Mifflin Harcourt — I couldn't be more heartened. Thank you so much for "getting" this book, homing in on how to make it better, and challenging me all the way.

Miriam Kriss, my literary agent and confidant. The believer in my word gremlins and the one who read the first pages and said, "Keep going. This is it." You were right, as always.

The SS Family: Zac Brewer, Cole Gibsen, Emily Hall, Jamie Krakover, Shawntelle Madison, Marie Meyer, L. S. Murphy, and Heather Reid. I can't do this without you.

The YA Scream Queens: Catherine Scully, Courtney Alameda, Dawn Kurtagich, Hillary Monahan, Jenn "J.R." Johansson, Lauren Roy, Lindsay Currie, and Trisha Leaver. The spooky girls and a bond I treasure.

Amanda Bonilla, warrior, cheerleader, mama bear, and warm blanket on cold nights.

Windy Aphayrath, Gypsi and Wolf Ballard, Lisa Basso, the Bromley and Freeburg clans, Sandra Fenton, Maria Fernandez, Meghan

Harker, Jenny McCormick-Friehs, Krista Winters-Irrea, Antony John, Beth Jones, Courtney Koschel, Andrew Lovitt, Gretchen Mc-Neil, Angela Mitchell-Phillips, Bebe Nickolai, Marcie Olsen, Kelly Rose Oswald, Mary Beth Pilcher, Rachel Rieckenberg, Timon Skees, Paula Stokes, April Terviel, Dawn Thompson, April Genevieve Tucholke (for the owl), Karen Utsmann, Alexandra Villasante, Dana Waganer, Judy Rhodes Williams (whom I miss so much), Melissa Williams, Cat Winters, the Handsome Family, JabberJaws, Wally, David, Annika. Thank you all.

Thank you to Dorothy Rush. Little girls who are forever friends. In memory of Jocelyn Stanley.

To Erich and Ericka Zwettler. Thank you for your faith, your love, your prayers. It took the unthinkable to become so close you, sister, and now I will never let you go.

To Jack and Lucille Powell. I watched your friendship with my mother from the time I was born until she died, and I learned how to be friends from you. Then you taught me how to be a mother.

Gwendolyn, Adrian, and Brendan, I pray I've given you the steel to be resilient, because you've given it to me.

Timothy, the boy next door. The one with his nose always buried in a book. The one who turns my head with a smile. I have you, and you have me.

My parents, Richard and Sharon, and my brother, Michael. I love you. I miss you. I'll see you on the other side.

SARAH JUDE lives by the woods and has an owl. She grew up believing you had to hold your breath when passing a graveyard. Now she writes about cemeteries, murder, and folklore. She resides in Missouri with her husband, three children, and three dogs. When she's not writing, she can be found volunteering at a stable for disabled riders. Visit her website at **www.sarahjude.com**.